# RAVEN'S CRY

# RAVEN'S CRY

## THE EMILY ETCITTY SERIES

## SANDRA BOLTON

## DESERT DOG PRESS

Text Copyright © 2018 by Sandra Bolton
All rights reserved.

Published by Desert Dog Press
www.sandrabolton.com

ISBN-13: 978-0692179529
ISBN-10: 0692179526


Cover Design by Carita Tanner

Printed in the United States of America

Dedicated to my grandchildren, Aaron Gillman, Alisa Gillman, Alex Bolton, Helen Bolton, Ben Bolton, and to my namesake, Sandra Bolton.

*Hozho Baa'na'sha'doo.*
May you walk in beauty and harmony.

# 1

The smell of rotting flesh permeated the air surrounding the watering-hole. Bloated bodies of a half-dozen sheep lined the banks, while fat, blue-bellied bot flies buzzed over the carcasses, and a wake of vultures perched on a nearby cottonwood tree, patiently waiting. A coyote approached, cautiously sniffed at the corpse of a dead lamb and began to howl, alerting his pack to the newly-found food source. Then, his ears perked and he backed away at the sound of a groan. The man lay under the cottonwood tree, holding his shoulder to stop the flow of blood from a gunshot wound.

The little girl sat astride her sorrel pony as confident and comfortable as if she had been born there. Although only six, she had a natural affinity with horses innate with many Navajo—an ease which her father, Abe Freeman, lacked. He was more comfortable navigating the bustling streets of New Jersey than riding a four-legged animal, but he had promised her a horse for her birthday and that he would go riding with her during their weekend time together. The girl talked to the horse and pulled gently on the reins, and the sorrel responded to her every move. Abe's horse, a spirited Appaloosa, had a mind of its own, but it did not object to Patch perched on his withers. Abe's three-legged dog was showing his years and lacked the boundless energy he had often demonstrated in the past.

It was mid-October, the time of year Abe loved best. Cottonwood and willow trees situated near water sources were dressed for autumn, their brilliant yellow leaves rattling in the crisp air. Bright patches of golden chamisa and lavender asters dotted the sage-blanketed flatlands while the surrounding mountains contrasted yellow aspen with dark green pines. The riders followed the dry creek bed aiming for a watering hole and a stand of cottonwood trees—an ideal spot to share a picnic lunch before heading home. Emily had been called away on police business and couldn't ride with them today, but she had promised to be back in time for dinner.

Navajo Police Sergeant, Emily Etcitty, still preferred to live with her mother and spend the weekends with Abe. It was an arrangement that suited both parties. Abe had established a reputation at the college and was in demand for concerts and accompaniments. This involved long hours of practice at the piano. And Emily often had to work erratic hours. Bertha had retired from teaching and was more than willing to provide full-time care for her only grandchild, Rose Sharon Etcitty Freeman. The girl also had a Navajo name which could not be said aloud, but her nickname was Raven and being a bit of a tomboy, that was the name she preferred. Rose Sharon had

2

come by the name Raven because, since a toddler, she had been heard on numerous occasions talking to the big black birds that often followed her from place to place. She could imitate their clicking sounds, and the birds would cock their heads and respond in kind, or with another utterance from their extensive repertoire of bird mimicry. To the bemused observer, the birds and girl appeared to be engaged in lengthy conversations.

Raven had acquired the most appealing features of her Navajo mother and Jewish father. Her long black hair did not hang straight, as she often wished, but bounced freely with untamed curls—her flashing eyes ranged from blue-black to lavender, depending on her mood. She had her mother's athletic body and headstrong attitude plus her father's gentleness and love for animals. Bertha made sure the young girl learned the Navajo language and the stories and legends of *Diné* history. Raven worshiped her mother's brother, Uncle Will, and could already sing some of the songs he performed at ceremonies as a respected *hataali*. All in all, she was a happy, well-rounded child, and Abe Freeman would do everything in his power to make sure nothing disturbed that happiness.

Patch barked as they neared the cottonwood grove, and Abe pulled on the reins. "Whoa, Jessie." He held up his hand. "Wait a minute, Raven."

"What's wrong, daddy?" She wrinkled her nose. "What stinks?"

"I don't know, honey. You and Red stay back here. I'll check it out." When he spotted the vultures, he thought there must be a dead animal, and he didn't want Raven to see it. They would find another place to eat lunch—possibly on the top of the nearby bluff. "I'll be right back."

The girl frowned but did as she was told. Abe put Patch on the ground, and the dog began barking again in earnest while he ran toward the cottonwoods. Abe did not carry a gun and was often chided for this. He covered his nose with a kerchief and cautiously approached the pond, shaking his head at the sight of dead sheep. A lamb's body lay ripped open by predators. "Damn," he muttered. "What the hell happened here?" After dismounting, he checked the animals. There were no apparent wounds on the others, but all were dead.

Patch continued to bark, but not at the sheep. When Abe looked at his dog, he saw the source. The wounded man's head lolled against the trunk of a tree. He reached out with a shaking arm.

"Help me, please. I've been shot."

"Jesus," Abe said. He ran over, kneeled down, and placed a handkerchief over the man's wound. "Who did this?"

"Don't know. I was just out here testing the water holes for uranium contamination . . . Saw the dead sheep—someone from behind . . ."

"Okay. Do you have a vehicle?"

"It's a long way off." The man took several heavy breaths. "I hiked in here."

"Can you mount a horse?" Abe said. "It's about five miles to my truck. If you can hang on, I'll get help or drive you to a hospital."

"I'll try," the man said. "I need my backpack."

Abe picked up the man's belongings and helped him onto the saddle. As they headed back, he heard Raven's plaintiff voice. "Daddy. What's taking you so long?"

"I'm coming, sweetheart. Stay right where you are. I'm afraid we have to go back home."

"But why? We haven't even had lunch yet." Her eyes formed round circles when she saw Abe leading Jessie with a doubled-over man sitting astride the saddle. "Oh."

A little over an hour later they reached the pull-over where Abe had left the truck and trailer.

Abe assisted the man off the horse and onto the front seat. He made a bandage from his shirt and placed it over the man's wound then quickly loaded the horses into the trailer. He told Raven it might be best for her and Patch to ride in the bed of the pickup—at least until he could reach a telephone and call an ambulance. Her eyes sparkled at the idea. Raven was always ready for an adventure. Abe knew he shouldn't let her ride back there, but this was an emergency.

"Make sure you sit down the whole time and keep your back against the cab. There's a blanket you can sit on."

"Okay, I promise. Daddy, is that man going to die?"

"Not if we can help it. Now hurry, get up there and hold on."

Abe drove as fast as road conditions would allow while pulling a horse trailer. They were on reservation land, and the prospect of finding a telephone amidst the scattered hogans and trailers was dim. When he finally reached the outskirts of Shiprock, he spotted a convenience store and pulled in. One look at the man slumped over in his seat with a blood-soaked shirt made his heart skip a beat. What if he did die?

"Mister."

The man lifted his head, and his eyes fluttered open. "Huh?"

"I'm going to call an ambulance. The paramedics will be better equipped to treat your wound and get you to the hospital faster. You got a name?"

The man nodded and answered in a raspy voice, "Steve Sanford." His head dropped forward as he lost consciousness once again.


After Abe called 911 and reported the incident, it took less than ten minutes for the EMT's to arrive and load the wounded man into an ambulance for transport to Northern Navajo Medical Center in Shiprock. Abe was told to stick around for questioning by investigating officers and to take them to the spot he found Sanford. He sighed and decided he'd better call Emily to explain what happened and to pick up Raven and the horses, but she had already heard the report on the scanner and was on her way.

When Emily arrived, Raven sat perched on a stool licking chocolate ice cream from a cone and watching with wide, curious eyes as the Navajo Police Officers questioned her father.

"Mom, daddy found a hurt man and saved his life. And I got to ride in the back of the truck with Patch."

Emily shot Abe a look that clearly said she didn't approve, and he shrugged. What was he to do? He had a gunshot victim in the front seat.

"Are you okay, Raven?" Emily said, putting her arm around her daughter. "I'm sorry your birthday ride was ruined."

"It wasn't ruined, mom. It was exciting, and the man's not dead, we saved him."

"Well, your Uncle Will is coming to take you and the horses home. Mommy has to stay here with Daddy for a while. We'll be back in time for birthday cake and presents, okay?"

A few minutes behind his sister, Will Etcitty showed up in his older model Ford F-150 4X4 pickup with dual rear wheels. He still owned his old Indian Chief motorcycle, but now that he was in demand in the community as a respected *hataalii*, he needed a vehicle that could safely transport him and his gear to remote locations on the sprawling Navajo Reservation.

"*Yá'át'ééh shik'is*," he said to Abe. "You sure have a knack for finding trouble, my friend."

"Hey, buddy. Thanks for coming."

"No need to thank me. I get some one-on-one time with my favorite niece. Come on, Raven. Let's get those horses home and unsaddled. Grandma's making your birthday cake, and if we hurry, you can lick the bowl."

"Will's right, Abe," Emily said as she watched her brother's truck pull onto the highway. "You do have a knack for finding trouble."

"I don't go looking for it, Em."

"Okay, I know. Guess this guy is lucky you found him in time, or he might have bled to death and ended up as buzzard brunch."

A young Navajo officer cleared his throat. "Excuse me, Sergeant Etcitty. How do you want us to proceed?"

Emily turned her attention to the rookie and his partner. "I'll handle the questioning of Mr. Freeman, Officer Martinez. Radio headquarters and let them know we need a crime scene investigating team. Mention a shooting victim and tell them to meet us here at the Red Mesa Trading Post ASAP and they can follow us in."

"Emily, there's something more they should know," Abe said. "What first got my attention was the smell. The watering hole was surrounded by dead sheep."

Emily wrinkled her brow. "Were they shot—attacked by a predator?"

"One lamb showed predator marks, but I think they were poisoned."

"Hmm." She turned back to Martinez. "Let the dispatcher know we need a truck to haul dead animals. Forensics will have to do an autopsy on these sheep, and notify the tribal environmental department that they need to get some water samples and test them. Then, you and Clee go to the hospital. See what you can learn about the victim."

"Right, Sergeant."

After the two police officers had left, Emily returned her attention to Abe while they waited in front of the store for the crime scene investigators. "I can't believe this happened on my baby's birthday ride with her dad."

"She handled it well." Abe leaned against the hood of his truck. The old Toyota had seen better days. He opened the door to let Patch in, and the dog circled twice before settling in the passenger seat. Both Patch and the truck had been through a lot with him, and now his daughter. "I told her to stay behind and wait for me. She didn't see the scene—the dead animals or the man on the ground."

"Well, that's good. How far from the dead sheep was the victim?"

"About twenty yards away, propped against a cottonwood, but I don't think that was where he was shot. I believe he dragged himself over there for protection."

"Was he able to tell you anything?"

"Not about the shooter. Said his name was Steve Sanford and he worked for the EPA. He was gathering water samples, and he left his vehicle to hike to the watering hole."

"You'd make a damn good cop, Abe. Want to think about changing professions?"

"Hell no." He knew he'd make a lousy cop. He hated guns, violence, and confrontations of any kind. "I want you to know I disturbed the crime scene as little as possible, though."

"I knew that. Ah, here comes our team. Lead the way, sweetie. We'll be right behind you."

* * *

As soon as Abe brought the officers to the crime scene, they secured the inner perimeter, sat up their equipment, and began a walkthrough search for physical evidence. The forensic photographer, Amy Goldtooth, snapped pictures of the dead sheep, the surrounding area, and the spot where the wounded man was found while her partners, Jimmy Atsa and Bob Haske, scoured the scene for footwear imprints, gunshot residue, fabric fibers, and blood or other body fluids. They hoped to establish where Steve Sanford was when he had been shot and the direction in which the projectile came. The preliminary report on the victim said that a bullet had entered the back left side and exited the front at a thirty-degree angle lower than the entrance wound. No internal organs were damaged, and Sanford was expected to recover, despite the massive loss of blood.

Abe showed Emily the tree Sanford had propped himself against, and from there it was easy to follow the trail of blood to the edge of the watering hole where a broken sample bottle had evidently fallen from his hand.

Emily stood in the spot she imagined Sanford had been standing, then turned around to appraise the lay of the land behind her. The ground made a gradual climb to a boulder-covered bluff about one hundred yards away.

"That's a good place for someone to hide and about the right angle to make the penetration wound. Let's take a walk up to that bluff," she said to Abe. "I think the shooter was probably positioned up there. If forensics can't find the bullet, maybe we can locate the empty shell casing and determine the caliber."

Abe had opened his mouth to speak when a shot rang out, glancing off a nearby rock "Emily, get down!"

Emily pulled out her Glock as she and Abe ducked and scrambled behind a large boulder. "Take cover," she yelled to the team, but they had already reacted to the gunshot and had crouched down behind their vehicle, their weapons out and pointed in the direction of the shooter.

Abe surveyed the rocky hillside. The terrain offered many places to hide. "Talk to him, Emily. Keep his attention."

"What are you up to, Abe? Oh no, you don't." Before she could stop him, Abe had sprinted for another clump of rocks shrouded in juniper. "You crazy damn idiot."

Circling left, he had taken off toward the shooter. Emily blew out a heavy breath of air in frustration and fired a shot towards the shooter's position.

"Put your weapon down and come out with your hands up. You're outnumbered and don't have a chance . . ." Another blast resounded from the shooter, and Emily fired back. "Don't be stupid. The man you shot is going to be okay. Lay down your weapon and come out with your hands in the air."

"I didn't shoot anybody yet, but I'm gonna. You poisoned my sheep, goddammit." The man fired again, the shot kicking up a cloud of dust six feet to the left of Emily's position.

"We didn't kill your sheep. We're Navajo Nation Police Officers, investigating a crime. Your sheep were dead when we arrived."

"You're government people. You killed them, just like in the old days. Slaughtered our livestock to starve us out."

The next bullet ricocheted off a rock several yards to Emily's right, and she realized she was dealing either with an intoxicated individual or the worst shot in the Navajo Nation. She signaled to Haske and Jimmy Atsa to close in, and the two men sprinted to the right, making their way up the slope while Amy Goldtooth fired shots from her position behind the forensic van to distract the shooter.

Abe slipped behind a boulder and studied the man thirty feet below. Bright sunlight glinted off the barrel tip of a Remington hunting rifle. He held the gun up to his shoulder and tried to steady shaking hands, cursed, wiped the sweat from his brow and fired wildly. He didn't have a chance to react when Abe crept up behind, knocked him down, and snatched the rifle from his hands. Holding the gun, looking down at the scrawny, white-haired old guy with a face etched in crevices like the land he stood on, Abe felt a wash of pity.

"Don't fire," Abe yelled. "It's under control. I've got his gun." Abe shook his head at the man. "Why the hell are you shooting at the Navajo Police, mister?"

The old Navajo hung his head and refused to look up or speak. Emily arrived on the scene seconds later. She talked to the shooter in Navajo, but Abe had a pretty good idea what she said. The man stumbled to his feet and put his hands behind his head, still not making eye contact.

"You're under arrest for assault on police officers and obstructing a criminal investigation." She finished reading him his rights and ordered him down the bluff where they encountered Atsa and Haske coming up.

Abe knew he'd catch hell for pulling that stunt. Emily flashed him a look that said, "You're in deep shit, Freeman." That was twice today he'd been on the receiving end of that look. He put his hands up in surrender, and gave her a wry grin, hoping his charm would work.

# 2

With Raven tucked in for the night, Abe and Emily were finally able to sit down, put their feet up, and share the remainder of a bottle of Cabernet Sauvignon. Their little girl had been running on full adrenaline all afternoon, overly excited about her birthday and presents and too full of chocolate cake to slow down. Finally, she dropped from complete exhaustion and now lay sleeping in Abe's spare bedroom with Patch curled at her side. A beautifully illustrated book of Navajo myths and legends, a gift from her Uncle Will, was still clutched in her hand.

"Are you still mad at me?" Abe said over the rim of his glass, a grin playing at the corners of his mouth.

Emily sighed. "I guess I'll forgive you, but that was a stupid stunt, and you better not ever do it again."

"Right. Does that mean we can kiss and make up?"

"Hmm. Let me think about it over another glass of wine."

Abe refilled their glasses and settled on the couch beside her. "Did your shooter confess?"

"No. Old Nakai denied ever seeing anyone and said he only shot at us because he thought we killed his sheep. Haske found an empty cartridge from a .300 Winchester Mag. Our shooter, Eddie Nakai, was carrying a Remington. He's seventy-eight years old and more than a little senile."

"Probably half-blind as well. The old man couldn't hit an elephant if it walked in front of him."

"I know. Nakai's not the shooter, but we're still holding him for assault. I located his grandson, and he's agreed to take care of the remaining flock until we release his grandfather. The dead sheep are undergoing autopsies and toxicology tests. The Navajo Nation EPA is also testing the water for contaminants."

"What kind of contaminants could kill sheep that fast?"

"I'm not sure. The EPA is checking for the usual suspects—uranium and/or bacterial. Other heavy metals have been found in tested wells and streams as well. Still, sheep would not have died that quickly from uranium. It builds slowly, often causing cancer or kidney failure after several years, the way it did the miners and their families. Safe drinking water is a priority health concern for the Diné.

Abe rubbed his chin, a pensive look on his face. "So, you think someone purposely poisoned that water hole."

"Yeah. But I don't understand why." Emily raised her arms over her head and stretched. "Sanford is being transferred to the San Juan Regional Medical Center in Farmington tomorrow. If he's up for it, I'm going to pay him a visit and find out what he was looking for and why he happened to be testing that isolated watering hole. And, if he knows of any reason someone would try to stop him. Personally, I've never seen the Feds this diligent about testing reservation water." She placed a hand over her mouth trying to stifle a yawn.

"Come on, sweetie. It's been a long day. How about a back rub?"

"And a foot rub?"

Abe began a gentle massage on the back of Emily's neck, slowly working his way to her shoulders. "Whatever needs rubbing, I'm your man."

"Ahh. You have good hands, Abe Freeman." Emily smiled and closed her eyes.

He tilted her head back and kissed her, softly at first, then exploring her tongue with his, with increased desire. "There's more to me than hands, Em. Want to see?"


Even though it was Sunday morning and her day off, Emily didn't want to wait any longer before questioning Steve Sanford. She arrived at the medical center just as the doctor was finishing his rounds. Emily rapped her knuckles on the open door of Sanford's room.

"Mind if I talk to your patient, doc?"

"Oh hello, Officer. I suppose a few minutes won't hurt but go easy with your

interrogation," the surgeon said, sliding a chart into a slot on the door. "Mr. Sanford needs to rest."

The wounded man, propped up with two pillows, his shoulder swathed in white bandages, looked up at Emily as she closed the door behind her.

"Who are you?" he said.

Emily had not put on her uniform this morning. She pulled out her plastic enclosed ID and introduced herself.

"Sergeant Emily Etcitty, Navajo Nation Police. Since the shooting occurred on the reservation, I have been assigned to investigate the attempt on your life, Mr. Sanford. Are you up to answering a few questions?"

Sanford's face showed skepticism as if he were wondering why the cops hadn't sent someone besides this petite woman, someone more capable. Emily had grown accustomed to that look and brushed it off.

He shifted his position and grimaced. "I guess so."

"What were you doing at the waterhole yesterday?"

"I was testing the water for contaminants."

"And who is your employer, Mr. Sanford?"

Sanford's pause before answering got Emily's attention. He averted his eyes and shifted once again. "I work for the federal government, the EPA."

"Were you on assignment from the EPA at the time you were shot?"

"Uh. Sometimes I do a little freelancing on the side."

"Yesterday?"

"Yeah. Look, Miss, I'm really in a lot of pain. If you don't mind . . ."

"Sure, sorry." Emily scribbled some notes on her pad. "Just a couple more things and I'll be out of here."

Steve Sanford closed his eyes, his mouth forming a tight thin line, and waited in silence

"Who were you working for that day? Did you poison the water hole?"


The jangle of the telephone interrupted Abe's pancake making. "Here, Raven," he said, handing his daughter the spatula. "Remember, when you see bubbles on top, flip it over, but be careful. Can you handle that?"

"Of course, I can, Dad. You showed me before. Can I make a mouth and eyes with chocolate chips?"

"Okay, but don't overdo it." Emily had accused him of spoiling their daughter and bribing her with chocolate, but he didn't care. He reached for the phone on the third ring, thinking it was probably Em letting him know when she would be back, and did they need anything at the store.

"Hello."

The male voice on the other end sounded far away and carried a distinct New Jersey accent. Abe listened while the caller identified himself as his cousin, Marty Jakovich.

"Abe, I had a hell of a time tracking you down. Why don't you keep in touch with your family?"

Raven gave her father a questioning look, and he cupped his hand over the receiver. "Turn off the stove, Raven. You go ahead and start eating without me. I'll just be a minute." He heaved a heavy sigh, moved his hand away, and spoke to the caller. "How'd you know where I was, Marty?" Abe had his reasons for distancing himself from family. His mother had tormented him all his young life, reiterating daily that he would never be good enough or smart enough to do anything worthwhile. In the end, she disowned him with the admonition never to set foot in her home again—all because she didn't approve of his relationship with Sharon, his beautiful dark-skinned girlfriend who had tragically died of cancer. After Sharon died, Abe packed up and left the East Coast, vowing never to return.

"It wasn't easy,  so I enlisted some help." Abe's cousin practiced law in New Jersey. He was rumored to have connections with a few unsavory characters as well. "I'm afraid I've got bad news. You're mother's dying. It's the big C, pal, stage four. She's asking for you."

Abe and Emily sat on a bench watching their daughter explore the many interactive science activities at the Children's Museum in Farmington. While the electromagnetic lab held her attention, Abe asked Emily about her interview with Steve Sanford.

"Well, he was quick to inform me that he did not poison the waterhole—that the sheep were dead when he arrived," Emily said.

"What did he say he was doing there?"

"Testing the water, but not for the EPA or the Navajo nation—he was moonlighting for a mining company.

Strathmore Minerals out of Canada wants to set up a new uranium mining operation in that area."

Abe raised his eyebrows. "Uranium? I thought that was banned on the reservation after all the health problems caused in the past. People are still suffering the consequences of those tailings. Surely the Tribal Council isn't considering opening that can of worms again."

"I can't imagine them doing that either. Uranium poisoning killed my father, uncles, and countless other people. Sanford said the company wanted proof that the land where they want to mine isn't suitable for grazing or agriculture, that the water is contaminated with high levels of lead and unfit for both livestock and human consumption." Emily scanned the displays for Raven and saw her at a specimen table examining slides under a microscope.

"Mom, come and look at this water bug," the child said.

Emily rose to her feet. "I'm coming."

"It sounds like a good motive to poison the water, for a company that wants to conduct mining or pays someone else to do it," Abe said, following Emily.

"Could be. That's something I plan on checking into. Meanwhile, let's see what new and exciting discovery our daughter has found. And, by the way, you still haven't told me about the phone call you received this morning."

The truth was, Abe didn't know what to do. Part of him said to forget it—his mother had made it clear she didn't want him in her life. Another nagging part of his brain kept repeating *she's your mom—blood is blood. How could I live with myself if I don't swallow my pride and forgive her?*

"It was a cousin of mine in New Jersey. He called to say my mom is dying. She doesn't have much time—and wants to see me."

"You'll go, of course."

Abe furrowed his brow, staring silently at a display of dinosaur bones. After a moment, he sighed and said, "Yes. But I'd like to take Raven with me. School will be out next week for parent/teacher conferences, both hers and the college. After the exams, I'll book us a flight if it's okay with you."

Abe made reservations for the following week and bought two round-trip airline tickets from Albuquerque to Atlantic City.. When he explained to his daughter that she had another grandmother in a faraway state and that they were going on an airplane to visit her, the child's eyes grew round.

"Do you think she'll like me?" said Raven.

"How could she not like you? She will love you," Abe answered, hugging his daughter, hoping he spoke the truth.

# 3

The dual excitement of flying on a plane for the first time and meeting a distant grandmother was almost too much excitement for Raven. She had packed and repacked her purple carry-on bag a half-dozen times, trying to make sure she wouldn't be leaving her most valuable possessions behind. Finally, Abe explained she could only bring three treasured items. Reluctantly, she settled on the horse figurine, her book of Navajo legends, and a stuffed toy raven. No doubt, she would repack the bag several more times during the two days before the flight was scheduled.

The following Monday morning, Chief Todechine summoned Emily, rookie Officer Martinez, and the three forensic members to an eight o'clock debriefing. Todechine sat at the head of a scarred wooden table cupping a mug of coffee while the others seated themselves along the sides. Emily pulled her notebook out and waited for her boss to speak first.

"Fill me in on what you've learned so far about the shooting at the poisoned waterhole, Sergeant," he said.

Emily opened her notebook and glanced at her entry for Sunday. "Steve Sanford, the victim, is an employee of the EPA. He also moonlights, without the EPA's knowledge, for Strathmore Minerals out of Canada. This company is petitioning the tribal council to allow them to begin mining uranium in the area of the shooting. Sanford states he was testing water for the mining operation at the time, and that the sheep were dead when he arrived. He stated he has no idea who shot him or why."

"Why was he testing the water?" the chief growled.

"From what I gather, he was hoping to prove the water was not potable, and therefore unfit for agriculture, livestock, or drinking."

Todechine frowned. "I guess that point was established by the presence of dead sheep. But, that doesn't make any sense. That sheepherder who took some pot shots at you—old Eddie Nakai—he's been running sheep in that area for years without a problem. Now the watering hole turns up poisoned. Forensics, what have you found out?"

Jimmy Atsa answered for the group. "We won't have any results back for a couple of weeks, Chief. All we know now is they died from something ingested." When he saw the disgruntled look on his boss's face, he said, "Sorry. I'll get the report to you as soon as it comes in."

"Eddie Nakai lives in a trailer out in the Round Rock area." Running a hand through his burr-cut gray hair, Todechine frowned. "Emily, I'm assigning Martinez to ride with you for the next month as part of his training, and I want you to involve him in this investigation."

Distracted by other thoughts, Emily bit her lip, nodded, but said nothing. She didn't like the idea of training a newbie, especially at this particular time. Even though they had agreed their daughter should accompany Abe on the trip to New Jersey, concerns about Raven and how she would be received by Abe's mother and other family members worried her. Prejudice was a reality she had learned to deal with, but Raven had so far been spared the cruelty and demeaning attitudes of ignorant people."

"You and Martinez go out there and have a talk with his son and grandson," Todechine continued. "To my knowledge, the three men live alone. The son has an arrest record for drug abuse and drunkenness, but we have nothing on the grandson. We'll hold onto old Nakai for a while until we're sure he's told us everything he knows, then I'm cutting him loose. I know the family can't pay bail, but keeping him locked up accomplishes nothing." He cast a stern look at the rookie. "Are you prepared for this assignment, Martinez?"

The young officer straightened up. "Yes, sir. I'll do my best sir."

"All right, then one more thing. I'll have Officers Gomez and Talltree check out Strathmore Minerals. Find out who they have been negotiating with and why they think they can mine for uranium on the reservation."

Emily looked askance at the young man sitting beside her in the Chevrolet Blazer. Clean-shaven, uniform pressed and creased, serious, intense eyes—he looked as green as new grass. "You graduated from the Academy three months ago if memory serves me right," she said. "Have you participated in many assignments?'

"No, ma'am. I've mostly been observing the other officers and familiarizing myself with paperwork and procedures. Sunday was my first opportunity to view a crime scene."

A silent groan died before becoming audible. *No experience at all in the field.* "Do you have family here, Officer Martinez?"

"Yes, ma'am. My mother is *Tséikeeheé*, Two Rocks-Sit Clan. My father is Hispanic from Cuba. Uh, that's Cuba, New Mexico."

"Okay, I figured that much. So, you are familiar with the area, I assume. Do you speak Navajo? And cut out the "Ma'am, please. Makes me feel old."

Martinez reddened. "Yes, Sergeant—to both, I mean. I speak Navajo and Spanish, and you can call me Raymond or Ray."

*Well, at least speaking the language is in our favor,* Emily thought as she steered the Blazer onto Indian Route 36, past Morgan Lake and the old Hendrickson Mine. She turned onto Routes 12 and 13 in Arizona, through red rock citadels and flat plains pock-marked with yucca and sage. Because of the natural beauty and open land, this was the area Abe had chosen to take Raven horseback riding.

The drive of an hour and a half brought them to the Round Rock Trading Post where Emily sent Martinez in for further directions. Fifteen minutes later, she parked the vehicle in front of a faded trailer house with squares of cardboard covering broken windows. A sheep corral sat behind the trailer beside a rusted-out truck with four flat tires, but there was no sign of sheep or goats. She honked and waited for someone to appear at the door. When no one responded, she told Martinez, "Okay, Martinez, let's go see if anyone is home."

Raymond Martinez stood with his back against the siding and his hand on the butt of his gun while Emily rapped on the door. "Mr. Nakai. If you're in there, open up. This is the Navajo Police. We'd like a few words with you concerning your father." The sound of a television blared from inside, but Emily could not detect movement. "Raymond, go around to the back and see if you can find a window to look in or a back entrance. Maybe he's sleeping, but I'll keep knocking to divert his attention in case he wakes up."

Emily continued to pound on the door until she heard footsteps. She pressed her back against the trailer and waited for the door to open. When it did, she was greeted by Raymond Martinez.

"The back door was wide-open. I peeked inside and saw Nakai slumped over in a chair—thought he might be hurt, so I went in and checked."

"Is he all right?" Emily said.

"Not dead, just dead drunk. There are about a dozen beer cans scattered around Nakai's chair—the tv blasting away.

Everything I saw looked pretty old and worn out, except for a new television, and it's an expensive model. I sure couldn't afford it."

Emily was about to step into the trailer when she heard the tinkle of a bell and a chorus of sheep. A slender young man of sixteen or seventeen walked beside the flock—a dog brought up stragglers in the rear.

"Go on back the way you came in and meet me here in front," Emily hissed to Martinez. "We've got company, and it's just as well you're not caught inside without a search warrant."

"*Ya'at'eeh,*" she said as the herder approached. "Are you Leonard Nakai's son? We were hoping to ask him a few questions."

The young man put out his hand. "*Ya'at'eeh.* I'm Mike Nakai. You won't get anything out of my old man. He's on a drunk." He turned his head away, looking embarrassed, and watched the dog herd the sheep into the corral.

Emily knew what the kid meant. Her brother, Will, was a reformed alcoholic who would disappear for days on a bender. Will no longer touched the stuff, but she hadn't forgotten the worry and shame her mother suffered through when she had to go out searching the bar scene for her son.

Raymond appeared around the corner of the trailer and stood beside Emily. He greeted the young man and introduced himself.

"Maybe you can help us," Emily said to Mike Nakai. "Tell us about your grandfather's sheep."

Nakai drew in a deep breath and blew a stream of air between his lips. "Grandpa loves his sheep. Saturday morning the dog brought the herd home. She was barking like crazy, and six sheep were missing. That never happens—sheep stay together, and our dog, Dolly makes sure there are none left behind. So grandpa and I went out looking. Dad was already in the bag, and he doesn't help out much anyway."

Officer Martinez had remained quiet but pulled a pad out of his shirt pocket and began scribbling.

"Did he find the sheep, or did you?" Emily said.

"He did. I guess he returned to the house to get his gun— an old Remington 81 he hasn't shot in years, and that's when he saw people around the waterhole messing with his sheep. I shouldn't say saw—grandpa has macular degeneration—he's legally blind and easily confused."

"Where were you at this time?" Emily asked.

"I came over the ridge just when you were cuffing my grandad and putting him in the police vehicle. I stayed hidden until everyone left, then I ran back home to try and wake dad."

Emily nodded and made a mental note to ask old Eddie Nakai if he had noticed the wounded man when he discovered his sheep. "Did you happen to hear any gunfire that Friday morning, before your grandfather found his sheep?"

Nakai nodded solemnly. "Yeah. A single shot. Thought someone was hunting rabbit."

Martinez looked up from his notepad. "Do you own a gun, Mike?"

He shook his head. "Sometimes I go hunting with my father's."

"What's the make and model?" Martinez said.

"A Winchester .300 Mag, unless he's pawned it to buy liquor."

Emily and Martinez exchanged a quick look "Do you mind showing it to us?" Emily said.

Mike Nakai shrugged. "Sure, why not. Wait out here—I'll get it."

"Think the father might be the shooter?" Raymond Martinez said when the kid stepped inside.

"It's a possibility," Emily said. "But young Nakai said his father was already drunk that morning."

They waited for what seemed like a long time. When Mike Nakai appeared at the door, he had a troubled look on his face. "I can't find the Winchester. I've looked in the truck and everywhere I can think of. It must be at the pawn shop."

"Hmm," said Emily. "Mike, we're going to have to bring your father in so he can sober up, and we can ask him some questions. Your grandfather will remain in custody until tomorrow, then he will probably be released, considering his condition. Do you have a vehicle you can drive to pick him up?"

"Yeah. What about my dad?"

"If we're satisfied with the answers he provides, he would be released at the same time."

Mike Nakai chewed his lower lip. "Okay. Can you help me get him in your SUV?"

Martinez and young Nakai entered the trailer and got on either side of the comatose father slumped over in the recliner. Each man draped one of Leonard's arms over a shoulder and walked him to the vehicle where Emily stood beside the opened the door. Once they had him settled behind the barrier, Martinez faced Mike Nakai.

"There's one other thing I'm curious about. When we went inside, I noticed a big-screen TV that looks new and must have cost close to a grand. Did your father buy that?"

Shaking his head, Nakai said, "No. Some men I didn't recognize drove up in a truck and dropped it off four days ago, along with a case of beer. I don't know what that's about, but no one has ever given my old man anything for nothing."

# 4

Once Leonard Nakai was ensconced in the Huerfano holding tank, Emily updated the chief on their meeting with Mike Nakai.

"Check the pawnshops. See if you can come up with the missing gun," said Todechine. "When Nakai sobers up, you two can interview him."

Raymond's eyes sparked with eagerness. He looked proud as a peacock to be Sergeant Emily Etcitty's partner on his first case. "Right, Chief," he said, and almost saluted.

Martinez settled in the passenger seat of the Blazer and waited for Emily to switch on the ignition. "Where do you want to start, Sergeant? All the pawnshops in Farmington?"

"Uh-uh. I'm going to pawn that job off on Gomez and Talltree. We're going to pay a visit to Strathmore Minerals. I like to get an impression of a place firsthand, and I want to meet the man in charge."

Strathmore Mineral's headquarters was located on the western outskirts of Farmington. Emily called the company ahead of time and asked if the owner or manager was in. The receptionist transferred her call to Ernest Whittington, director of local operations, and they agreed on a one o'clock meeting. Since they had over an hour to kill, Emily decided they'd eat lunch, and she would try to learn more about her new young partner. While waiting for the daily special, "meatloaf with green chile," Emily struck up a conversation.

"Are you married, Raymond?" she said after sipping on her glass of iced tea.

"Yes, ma'am. My wife and I have a two-year-old boy, and another is on the way."

A wash of sorrow swept over her as she thought once again of her lost son—her firstborn. *He was only two years old when he drowned in the flooded ravine along with his drug-crazed father. How old would he be now? A young man, almost the same age as this rookie.* Emily shook her head to erase the painful memory. "That's great. Congratulations. Where do you and your family live?"

"We're staying with my wife's folks," said Raymond. "It's okay, but I'm trying to save enough so we can start building our own place near her mother's people, the Many Goats Clan. Once the baby comes, we'll need more room. How about you, Sergeant? Do you have any kids?"

Emily smiled. "I have a little girl. She just turned six—a real pistol." Emily considered what it would be like for her and Abe to have their own place amid her clan members. She knew it wouldn't work. He couldn't live in an isolated area so far from his work, and neither could she.

Small talk stopped when the food arrived, and the conversation turned to the complexities of the case they were on. Raymond Martinez dug into his meatloaf and mashed potatoes. He ate with the ravenous appetite of a teenage football player while Emily paced herself. "You don't have to rush, we have lots of time," she said.

Raymond put his fork down and gulped some tea. "Sorry. This is so good. I didn't have time for breakfast this morning." He patted his mouth with a napkin. "I guess we should go over some of the key questions we'll be asking Whittington."

"Primarily," said Emily, looking intently at Raymond, "we want to find out by what authority he thinks he has the right to mine uranium on the reservation. That would have needed a majority vote by the tribal council and a comprehensive study by the Navajo Nation Division of Natural Resources. I haven't heard anything about this."

Raymond slowly chewed a bite of dinner roll, as if he were contemplating his next words. "That section of the reservation with the poisoned waterhole borders BLM land, doesn't it?"

"Hmm. Yes, I'm pretty sure it does. I'd have to verify the boundaries with a map, though. That's another possible angle. Maybe the Bureau of Land Management is trying to cut a deal with the mining operation." *The kid is sharp*, she thought.

"But why poison the water and shoot the EPA guy testing it?"

"Finish your lunch, and we'll try to get some answers."

Emily drove to a barren patch of land between Farmington and Fruitland. She parked the Blazer in a dirt lot beside an assortment of Jeeps and other four-wheel-drive vehicles and looked around for a sign that indicated the office. Numerous metal-sided warehouses and outbuildings dotted the patch of dirt surrounded by a high chain-length fence.

"That two-story over there," said Raymond, pointing his lips at a structure with the lettering "Strathmore Minerals" emblazoned across the front. The two officers were met by a receptionist inside the door.

"Go right in," she said, directing them to a door with a nameplate reading *MANAGER*. "Mr. Whittington is expecting you."

Whittington stood up from his desk, white shirt sleeves rolled up to his elbows, and shook hands with Emily and Raymond. He was tall and paunchy with thin blond hair and a sunburnt face, steel-blue eyes, and a fleeting smile that passed over his lips like it wasn't accustomed to being there.

"Thanks for taking the time to talk to us, Mr. Whittington," Emily said. "I'm sure you're a busy man, so we won't take long."

"What can I help you with, Officer?" He remained standing and didn't offer a chair to his visitors.

"We're interested in learning more about your plans to begin uranium mining in this area. Can you provide a little information to clarify some details?"

"We have several operations in the Four Corners—gas, oil, coal, and Strathmore Minerals has provided jobs and opportunities that you people wouldn't ordinarily have."

*You people*, Emily silently seethed. *You are the ones who brought disease, poverty, and death to the Dinétah, you arrogant asshole.* She held her tongue.

"We're asking specifically about uranium," Raymond said, hands resting on his hips.

"Specifically?" said the manager.

"Who have you contacted concerning uranium mining on the reservation, Mr. Whittington?"

"Our company is in the negotiating stage, and the terms of an agreement are private. I'm afraid I can't provide you with that information."

"Have you had a public hearing regarding your plans?" Emily let her eyes wander around the office. The opulence was in stark contrast to the utilitarian surroundings. Expensive leather furniture, oak desk, Native American artifacts and paintings covering one wall; certificates and photos lining the other. One picture showed Whittington with the past tribal chairman. The two men were smiling as Whittington cut a ribbon on some sort of ground-breaking ceremony.

"We have not reached the stage where a public hearing is relevant."

Emily blew out air from between her lips. "It would make it a lot easier for everyone concerned if I didn't have to serve a subpoena. This involves a criminal case, Mr. Whittington, and you are obstructing the investigation."

"I will consult my lawyer regarding my company's rights to contractual secrecy. Now, if you don't mind, I am very busy."

"One more question," Raymond said, thumbing through his notepad. "Is Steve Sanford an employee of Strathmore Minerals?"

"We're a big company—we hire a lot of people," said Whittington. The telephone on his desk buzzed, and he turned his back to Emily and Raymond. "If you'll excuse me."

The two officers exchanged looks and left the office.

"He wasn't much help," Raymond said. "Why so secretive about the deal?"

"Competition, bidding, secret meetings with council members, bribes, or maybe he's just a jerk. He's stalling for time, and until we get a subpoena for the paperwork, there's nothing we can do about it."

"Where are we going now, Sergeant?"

"Window Rock, to try and get some answers from tribal leaders."

# 5

Emily and Raven were staying at Abe's house so they could have more time together, and she could drive them to the Albuquerque Airport early Tuesday morning for their nine o'clock flight to Atlantic City. After their daughter dropped off to sleep that night, she and Abe had time to talk. It had been a frustrating work day, and Emily felt conflicted about Raven's trip to meet a woman she had only heard horror stories about. What Abe had shared concerning his mother made her wonder how anyone could treat their child with such disdain and cruelty. She snuggled with Abe on the porch swing under a blanket of stars and a waning gibbous moon while he traced the outline of her face with his long, sensitive fingers.

"Nothing compares with New Mexico skies, except your beautiful face. You look worried, sweetheart. How'd your day go with the rookie?"

"Raymond's fine—sharp as a tack, but we've been chasing rumors and shadows all day and didn't learn anything. The manager at Strathmore Minerals clammed up, and the council members were out of town for meetings, or so the secretary said. The case doesn't make any sense."

"And, you're concerned about Raven going on this trip."

"Yes. I don't want my child hurt, scarred in any way."

"I won't let that happen. From what my cousin said, my mother doesn't remember or say much of anything. But if you're really upset, we can change plans."

"No. I think it's important that you go—that Raven goes. She needs to know your roots as well as mine." Emily took Abe's face in her hands and kissed him. "I will miss you both. Be sure to call every night."

Abe promised. They would be gone only two days, but for Emily to be away from her daughter, those two days would feel like an eternity.


After the hugs, reminders to brush teeth, speak politely, be careful of traffic, strangers, and numerous other unknowns, Raven pulled away from her mother, waved goodbye and boarded the plane. She found her seat in the mid-section and plopped down, her nose pressed against the round porthole. That is where she remained for the duration of the four-hour flight, mesmerized by the patchwork quilt of cultivated land and the ever-changing scenery.

"Dad, look at those mountains—why is everything so green? What is that big river's name? Oh, there are clouds down there below us. Dad, we're higher than the clouds."

When they flew over a city, her eyes widened in wonder, and Abe felt pleased that he was sharing this big adventure with her. At one point during the flight, they ran into some turbulence, and Raven tightened her grip on the armrests, taking her eyes away from the window for the first time.

"It's only a little wind," Abe said. "Make sure your seatbelt is fastened."

Raven pulled on the strap and leaned back, looking more relaxed. "Uncle Will told me the story about One Who Grew on the Earth. She's an ancient goddess who travels from one sacred mountain to the other. When she holds out her feather, she creates the wind to tell the holy ones to fertilize the earth. I didn't know her power would work this far from *Dinétah*."

Abe smiled. "Then she must be a mighty goddess and a good-hearted one. Look, Raven. We're getting close. See all the buildings."

"They're so tall they reach the clouds."

"That's why they call them skyscrapers, sweetie."

Raven nodded, her face solemn. "Dad, do all the people here live stacked on top of each other like the Pueblo people?"

"Not all, but some do. We're going to stay in the house I grew up in. It just has two stories."

Returning to his childhood home evoked a rush of memories, both bitter and sweet. There had been good times when his father was around—time spent together building model airplanes in the basement, hiking in the nearby woods while his father described the names of plants and insects and their importance to the balance of nature. Abe had loved this man, but he knew the relationship between his mother and father was strained. One day when he came home from school, his father was gone. After that, everything changed. His mother channeled her anger and bitterness toward her only child. Abe had tried to please her through learning the piano by merely listening to his mother's skillful playing. He had an ear for music, and after much secret practice, he had mastered a problematic Bach piece and wanted to surprise her. But as his fingers ran over the keys, her face went white, and she slapped him, screaming to never to touch her piano again. After that, Abe avoided her as much as possible, but he became more determined than ever to master the keyboard by playing when she left the house and while he was at school. He wondered if she were afraid he might surpass her. She had never stopped reminding him that he was not any good and would never become a success at anything. Abe cleared his head. The plane touched down, and his cousin Marty would be waiting for them.

Marty wore his lawyer garb, a gray sharkskin suit, pale blue shirt, navy tie. His latest trophy wife, bleached-blond Millie in a low-cut floral dress and high heels stood at his side. They waved when Abe and Raven emerged from the crowd.

Marty patted him on the back while Millie cooed over Raven.

"You're looking good, Abe. This your little girl? She's a beauty—sure doesn't take after you, does she? What's your name, young lady? Where's your luggage, Abe?" Marty rattled on, not waiting for an answer.

"This is it," Abe said, indicating his backpack and Raven's roll-on. *Fast-talking Marty hasn't changed a bit,* he thought. "Thanks for picking us up."

"You hungry?" Marty said. He eyed Abe's jeans, tee shirt, and loafers. "I know a decent place you can get in dressed like that, and then I'll drop you off at the hospital. Not sure they'll let your girl into the room, though, you know, your mom is on the short list."

*All the more reason to let Raven in*, Abe thought. "Okay. I bet my daughter's hungry. All we had to eat was peanuts and juice on the plane. We'll just stop at a bathroom and freshen up first, all right, Raven?"

"Oh, I'll go with her. Is your name really Raven? Isn't that some kind of bird?" Millie said, taking Raven's hand.

Abe's little girl turned around to give her dad a questioning look.

"It's okay. I'll be right out here. Everything is so new," Abe said to Marty. "She's gotta be feeling a little overwhelmed."

They got in Marty's Lincoln and drove to a delicatessen not far from the hospital. Raven couldn't stop staring at the tall skyscrapers, the bustling crowds, the colorful shop windows. Abe already missed the openness of New Mexico where you could see as far as the next horizon without witnessing another person or building. He felt closed in and as if he couldn't get enough oxygen. He felt his senses being affronted. The noise level was too high, the colors too bright—nothing like the subtle earth tones and solitude in New Mexico. Raven had been quiet as well. He wondered what she was thinking.

"I'll pick you up in an hour," Marty said when he dropped them at the entrance to Atlanticare Cancer Center. "You won't need

41

any more time than that. Your mother never says anything, and she probably won't even know you're there."

Abe sighed, wondering for the moment why he had come back in the first place, but he took Raven's hand and walked toward the receptionist.

"Could you tell me the room number of Jana Freeman?"

The receptionist pulled up a list on her computer and began scanning. Freeman, Freeman, Freeman. "It appears we don't have anyone by that name. There is a Jana Jakovich in Room 321."

So, his mother had changed back to her maiden name. There were so very few of Abe's Jakovich relatives left, only Marty. Everyone except for his grandmother and an uncle had died in the Holocaust.

"Are you a relative?" The round-faced woman asked.

"Yes. I'm Jana's son, and this is her granddaughter."

"You will have to check with the head nurse on duty to see if the little girl can go in. Generally, children under twelve are not allowed to visit patients, but they may make an exception, considering Mrs. Jakovich's, uh, condition."

Abe pushed the button for **Intensive Care – 3** and smiled down at his daughter as the look of wonder grew on her face. He thought that Raven must be a little frightened, even for one as adventuresome and daring as she had always been. When they reached the third floor, he told her to sit in a chair while he asked the nurse a few questions. The hallway was ghostly quiet, smelling of antiseptic and something else. Imminent death?

The nurse spoke in a hushed voice. "I'm so very sorry, Mr. Jakovich. Doctor Fish decided to take your mother off life support this morning. It is just a matter of time now. Cancer has spread throughout her organs, and there is nothing more we can do."

Abe inhaled a deep breath. "Could my daughter and I go in and say our goodbyes?"

"Well, I don't see what harm that could do, but please, no loud noise and buzz the nurse if you notice a change in your mother's condition."

The shriveled woman lying on the bed with gaping mouth and parchment skin bore no resemblance to the towering fearsome mother of Abe's childhood. Occasionally her lips would move, and she would mumble disconnected phrases in Yiddish.

"Mother, it's me, Abe. I've come to say goodbye and that I forgive you. I've brought your granddaughter," Abe said, also in Yiddish.

She blinked, sunken rheumy-blue pinpoints darting around the room, and lifted a hand that fluttered over her chest like an injured bird. Raven stepped closer and grasped the hand in her own. "Hello grandmother," she said in her high-pitched child voice, and Abe saw a transformation. His mother's lips trembled, then formed a faint smile and tears rolled down her cheeks. His heart filled with love for his beautiful girl but felt broken for the love he had never experienced from this woman. He and Raven sat by the bed and talked quietly about their life in New Mexico. After an hour, they said goodbye and left to wait for Marty.

"I couldn't understand what you and Grandmother were talking about," Raven said. "What tribe do you belong to, Dad?"

"Me? Some call it The Lost Tribe, sweetie."

"Millie brought our cleaning lady over to your mom's place to spiff it up, and they left some food in the fridge—some kind of sandwiches and stuff for the kid," Marty said as he exited onto the interstate and headed for the suburbs.

"Thanks, I appreciate it. Look, Marty, you don't have to chauffeur us around. I know you're a busy man, and you and Millie have already done enough. Public transportation works for Raven and me."

"Yeah? Well, I would have had the two of you over tonight, but there's this important dinner meeting I can't skip, and tomorrow I'm tied up all day with a bunch of *shtunks*. You know how it is."

"Sure," Abe said as they pulled into his childhood driveway.

"Well, here we are. Home sweet home, huh." Marty Jakovich handed Abe a key and business card. "Your mother made me her legal custodian and gave me power of attorney, so if you've got any questions, call me."

Marty sped away, and Abe turned around to gaze at the familiar brownstone structure that held so many painful memories. He shrugged off his reluctance and turned the key in the door. "Okay, let's check things out, see where dad grew up."

Chemical freshener had done a poor job of concealing the musty air that greeted Abe as he stepped into the entryway. Raven followed him into the living room, pulling her small rolling suitcase behind her. While Abe scanned the room, Raven darted around, investigating everything. *Nothing has changed*, Abe thought, staring at the baby grand in the corner.

"Where's your room, Dad?" Raven said, breaking into his melancholy.

"Upstairs. Here, let me carry your suitcase," thinking his daughter had to be exhausted.

"I can do it," she said, bounding up ahead of him.

The twin beds were covered with fresh linens, and a stack of towels sat on his bookcase. The room had been stripped of his models and books, his posters, and collection of insects. In their place was an older model TV and a mini-fridge. *Just like a motel.* Abe had eliminated television from his life years ago, but maybe he could convince Raven to take a nap if he found a children's show. He dropped his backpack on a chair and opened the mini-fridge smiling at the six-pack of premier beer that perched on the shelf beside a quart of milk, a stack of sandwiches, salad, and a bowl of fruit. Millie had done well. Everything was kosher.

Raven chose one of the beds and opened her carry-on, pulling out her stuffed bird, her horse, and the book of Navajo legends. She placed the prized items on the bedside table, and the bird on the pillow then bounced on the mattress. "It's nice and soft," she said leaning back against the pillow.

"Do you want to rest a while and watch cartoons?"

"Would you read me a story instead? You know which one."

"Sure." Abe sat on the bed and began reading:

*Raven belongs to the inner world, that place where we protect the part of us that's often injured by the sting of rejection. He is the keeper of secrets, the messenger who flew out from the cosmos and brought the light of the sun. Raven becomes a powerful friend who encourages us to embrace the shadows because they're also part of who we are. His magic brings the power needed to take your dreams, give them time to form, then make them real.*

Before he could finish, his daughter was sound asleep. Abe slipped off the bed and popped the cap on a bottle of beer. He opened the window, allowing a fresh breeze into the room and went downstairs, opening more. Abe turned the knob on the basement door. It was not locked, but he was not sure he wanted to return to the place that had been his refuge and dredge up more memories. The telephone rang, negating the necessity to make a decision.

"Marty here. Afraid I've got bad news. The hospital called—your mother passed. She died shortly after you left. Sorry, Abe."

Abe held his breath for a moment, then let out a slow stream of air. He had expected it and even welcomed the news. It meant his mother's suffering was over. "It's okay, thanks for letting me know."

"You sticking around for the funeral? She had me make the arrangements a while back—wanted to be buried in Rodof Sholom next to my dad, Bubbe. That's the only family she had here after grandma died ."

"No, I can't stay. My flight leaves the day after tomorrow, and I need to take my little girl home. I've paid my respects— no reason to stick around."

"I hate to break the news to you Abe, but I'm the one handling your mother's estate. She cut you out of the will. Sorry."

"It's okay. I understand." He hadn't expected anything different.

# 6

That evening, after they had eaten, Abe called Emily. She was staying at his house while he was away, but before he could get anything more than a greeting, Raven begged for the phone. He handed it to his daughter, knowing Emily wanted to hear her voice as well.

Satisfied that her mother had remembered to feed and curry her horse, Red, feed Patch, and put out corn for the birds, she let Emily talk, and responded to her questions.

"Yes, I met my other grandmother, and I used my best manners with all the grownups, and Grandmother held my hand. She was very sick, but Dad said now she has gone to a better place. Did you know everything is tiny when you look down at it from an airplane, and the buildings here scrape the sky?"

"I have noticed that. Maybe you could draw me a picture of what it looked like. I love you, and I am very proud of you. I want to hear all about your trip when you get home. Let your dad have the phone now, okay."

"Okay. I love you too." She handed the phone to Abe. "Mom wants to talk to you, Dad."

"Hi, sweetheart. I miss you."

"Patch and I miss you too. From what Raven said, I understand your mother died. I'm sorry, Abe. Will you be staying longer?"

"No, I'm not waiting for the funeral. We'll be home on schedule. Tomorrow I'm taking Raven to the Boardwalk and beach. We'll spend the day sightseeing. I can't wait to get back. Tell me about you. Are you managing to hold down the fort with your two right hands missing? How's the investigation going?"

"Abe, this case gets more and more complicated the deeper I dig into it. We found out what happened to Nakai's gun, but have no idea who took it."

The following morning, Chief Todechine summoned Emily and Raymond Martinez into his office for an update. Emily tapped Raymond on the shoulder and grabbed her coffee mug.

"Chief wants us in there, pronto."

Raymond, who had been pouring over a police procedural manual, sprang to his feet and followed Emily.

"Pull up a couple of chairs and fill me in." The unsmiling division chief's eyes burned under bushy brows.

Emily consulted her notes. "I talked to David Whittington personally, Chief. You know how I need to get a feel for a case. The manager of Strathmore Minerals is stonewalling us. He shut us down, wouldn't talk about a uranium deal, but I think he's hiding something."

"I thought Gomez and Talltree were doing that interview," the chief growled. "What about tribal council members?"

"No one available," said Emily. "We spent the day trying to track someone down without any luck."

"Contact the local chapter houses and the Natural Resources Committee. The Navajo Minerals Department should know something about this."

"Right, Chief." Emily made some scribbles in her notebook. "Did Leonard Nakai tell you what happened to the gun?"

The chief leaned back in his swivel desk chair and clasped his hands behind his head. "Just finished talking to him a few minutes ago. Said he always carried his gun in the rack of his truck. He was short on cash, so he sold it to a guy he met in the parking lot of a bar—didn't know the person and was too drunk to provide much of a description. If he did sell it for booze money, he drank it all up, and the rest of the family was unaware of his actions."

"What could he tell you?" said Raymond.

"Only that there were two men in a white pickup. One was short and fat, the other tall with a scar running down the side of his face, and both wore red bandanas tied around their heads."

Raymond jotted the information down. "Sounds like they could possibly be members of a group of militants I've heard rumors about. They're an off-shoot of Red Power— extremists—call themselves the *Diné* Freedom Fighters. They're trying to recruit people from the rez."

Todechine raised his eyebrows and Emily stared at Raymond. "I haven't heard anything about this group."

"Neither have I," said Emily.

"The leadership is a secret, and so is the location of their headquarters. My cousin told me they had enlisted a kid to pass out flyers at the college. They only want young people." When he saw the frown on Emily's face, he said, "Sorry, Sergeant. I wasn't implying . . ."

"Right," Emily said. "Go on. What else do you know about this organization."

"I've heard they're armed and advocating for the elimination of federal government intervention in tribal affairs."

"It might give a believer of this group's policies reason enough to shoot at an EPA employee," Emily said, "but doesn't explain the poisoned waterhole."

"Or Leonard Nakai recently receiving a new TV from strangers, unless it was payment for a job," Raymond said.

"Okay," Todechine cut in. "Martinez, I want you to go undercover. Tomorrow morning dress like a regular student and hang out at the college until you get your hands on one of those flyers. Find out everything you can about this group, the *Diné* Freedom Fighters, or whatever the hell they call themselves. Get invited to a meeting if you can, but don't go anyplace with them. I know you're a little green, but you'll be in touch with Sergeant Etcitty at all times, and there shouldn't be any danger. Emily, have another whack at Leonard before I cut him and his father loose. Find out where that television came from."

The small room with a one-way mirror was sparsely furnished with two chairs on one side of the bolted-down metal table and a single chair on the other.

"Your first formal interrogation, Raymond?" Emily asked as she set up the recorder and waited for the guard to bring Leonard Nakai into the small sparsely furnished room.

"Yes, ma'am."

"You're getting quite an initiation, undercover assignment and all. Take this chair beside me so Nakai can face us."

"Yes, ma'am."

"Are you up for this? And drop the ma'am."

"You bet, Sergeant. I want to move up the ranks someday."

"Observe the procedure first. If you think of a relevant question, jot it down and ask later, after the preliminaries are taken care of."

"Right."

The door opened, and Raymond looked up as the guard escorted a gaunt, disheveled Navajo man into the room. The whites of Nakai's eyes had a yellow tint; his nose and cheeks appeared flushed and webbed with tiny broken capillaries. Beads of sweat dotted his forehead—indications of chronic alcoholism. Emily flipped on the recorder.

"Sit down, Mr. Nakai," Emily said, indicating the empty chair. I'm Sergeant Emily Etcitty, and this is Officer Raymond Martinez. How are you feeling?"

"Not so good," Nakai mumbled as he slumped in the chair, trying to steady his shaking hands under the table.

"Would you like a soda or a glass of water?"

"Water."

"I'll get it," Raymond said.

Emily switched on the recorder. "Wednesday, October 14, 1998. For the record—is your name, Leonard Nakai?"

"Yeah."

"Mr. Nakai, you have the right to remain silent, the right to know anything you say can and will be used in a court of law, the right to consult an attorney before answering any questions, and the right to have an attorney present during an interrogation. If you cannot afford an attorney, the court will appoint one. Do you understand your rights, sir?"

"Yeah. I don't need no attorney. I didn't do nothin'."

"We're not accusing you of a crime at this time. There are just a few questions that you may be able to clear up, then you'll be free to go."

"All right. Shoot."

"Well, that is one of the questions, sir. Did you or your father fire a shot at a man near the waterhole on Saturday, May 12?"

"Hell, no. I was in town Saturday, and my old man can't see good enough to shoot anything."

"Do you own a .300 Winchester Mag?"

Nakai put an elbow on the table and propped his head. His left foot tapped the floor. "Not no more. I sold it."

"When did you sell your Winchester?"

"Uh, Thursday night. I needed some cash to pay bills."

"Who did you sell it to?"

"I already told the other cop—two guys I met in the parking lot of Bruno's, both wearing red kerchiefs. I never seen them before that night."

Raymond jotted some notes on his pad. "Bruno's? Isn't that out on the west side of Farmington? How much did these two men give you for the gun?"

"I don't remember." Nakai wiped the sweat from his forehead. "What's it to you anyway?"

"Was it enough to buy a new TV?" Raymond said.

"I earned that television. It was payment for a job I did."

"Who were you working for?" said Emily. "Take your time."

"I don't remember." He took a drink from the paper cup. "I can't talk anymore right now. I feel sick."

"I understand. We're just about finished here—a couple more questions. Do you want something to snack on? No? Well, about that new TV, how long have you had it?"

"Umm." Leonard wiped the perspiration from his forehead with his shirt sleeve."A week—maybe two. I forget."

"And, you forgot who you were working for as well as what sort of work you were doing? That sounds very odd, Mr. Nakai."

"Two men—said they were with the tribal council—that I'd be helping my people and all I had to do was keep an eye on the waterholes—report back if anyone came around. Promised me a new TV if I did what I was told and kept my mouth shut. So, I told them about that white guy, but I didn't shoot him."

"Leonard. I need a name."

"They didn't give me a name, but one guy, the fat one, I heard the other one call him Chupa."

Raymond looked up from his note-taking and caught Emily's eye. "Charley Redhorse, nickname, Chupa. He's new on the tribal council."

Emily nodded, impressed with Raymond's knowledge of board members and made a note to track down Charley Redhorse. "Is there anything else you can tell us about these men, Mr. Nakai?"

"That's all I know. Can I go now?" The prisoner's face looked ashen. "I think I'm going to get sick."

Emily nodded. "For now, you're free to go, but I'll be checking back with you later, so make yourself available. We'll be releasing your father as well. Your son is out front waiting in the truck. Leonard, my brother, Will Etcitty, is a *hataali*. I'm going to ask him to pay you a visit. He can help you if you want."

Leonard Nakai nodded and stood, steadying himself by holding onto the table and stumbled out to be met by the guard waiting outside the door.

"What do you think, Raymond,?"

"He was telling the truth about the gun, but he's withholding information concerning the council members and the work he did. He's scared of something. We did learn one thing we didn't know before—the place where he connected with the *Diné* Freedom Fighters."

"Right. So, our next move is to pay another visit to Steve Sanford, then to Bruno's. If there's any more time in the day, I'd like to get a lead on Charley Redhorse."

Sanford had been released from the hospital the day before, and they located him at his home in Farmington. The tan stucco ranch sat at the end of a cul de sac in a tract at the edge of town. A yellow patch of grass lined the sidewalk leading to the door. Sanford, his arm in a sling and a swath of bandages encircling his left shoulder opened the door after the third knock. Dressed in green shorts and shirtless, his scowl showed no pleasure at seeing the two officers.

"Officer Etcitty, I thought we had our talk. I told you I don't know anything."

"I hate having to disturb you again, Mr. Sanford, but there are a couple of things that my partner, Officer Martinez, and I would like to clear up. Mind if we come in?"

Sanford sighed audibly and held the door open, stepping to the side. "I was trying to get some rest, so can you make it quick?"

"Sure, I understand," Emily said.

Raymond Martinez nodded his head in agreement and pulled out his notebook.

"You mentioned you do contract work in addition to your employment with the EPA. Is that correct?"

"Yes," said Sanford, his mouth twitching at the corner.

"Have you recently done any work for Strathmore Minerals?" Raymond asked, his pen poised, eyebrows raised in question marks.

"Okay. Strathmore contracted me to test some water holes and springs. It's all on the up and up. What's the big deal?"

"Were you working for the EPA or Strathmore when you were shot?" Emily asked.

Steve Sanford's mouth made a tight line, the corners turned down. "I was on assignment for Strathmore to test the water. He wanted results that showed the wells, springs, and watering holes registered contaminants that were above the federal drinking water limit so that he could justify his mining operation and remove the occupants from that area. I didn't have any trouble verifying the contamination. Nearly one-hundred percent of these damn water sources in this area of the rez are unfit for consumption—some have readings of uranium as high as seven hundred micrograms, and the federal limit specifies anything above thirty micrograms is unsafe."

Emily met Sanford's eyes. "Did you add anything to the water to make sure it wouldn't be safe to drink?"

"Hell, no. I wouldn't do that. I told you. Those sheep were dead when I arrived. Thought that was going to make my job easy. Instead of a shooting victim, I'm a suspect. Shit. Why aren't you out looking for the shooter instead of harassing me?"

"What are the contaminants you are finding in your tests?" Sanford paused. "It varies from place to place."

"Mr. Sanford. I want copies of the results of all the water sources you've sampled sent to the Navajo Nation Department of Water Resources. We will have our people double check your readings. If there are any discrepancies, you'll be hearing from us." Emily took a business card from her front pocket and handed it to Sanford. "If you think of anything else you want to share, here's the number where I can be reached."

"Whatever," Sanford said, taking the card and tossing it on the coffee table. He looked away, not bothering to stand while Emily and Raymond let themselves out.

Back in the patrol vehicle, Raymond Martinez turned a thoughtful gaze toward Emily. "Do you think he added something to the water to raise the uranium readings, Sergeant?"

"Wouldn't surprise me. If that's what Sanford did, he increased the chance of our people dying a slow death from kidney failure or cancer." Emily gunned the engine. "These mining companies don't care about the health risks to the Navajo. All they're interested in is profits."

"I guess we better track down those so-called Freedom Fighters, Sarge."

Emily made a U-turn and pointed the vehicle toward Shiprock. "Call in our 10-20, and tell dispatch we're headed for Bruno's."

# 7

Bruno's was the closest thing to a neighborhood bar the Fruitland area had to offer. The low-slung building sat unobtrusively on a corner lot and lacked the attention-getting flash of neon beer signs. When Raymond and Emily left the blazing outdoor sunshine and stepped through the door, it took a few minutes for their eyes to adjust to the dimness. It was early afternoon, and only a few patrons, mostly old men nursing their beer or whiskey, occupied the barstools. Bruno stood behind the bar, conversing with a white-haired man. A country-western singer crooned mournfully about betrayal in the background.

"My credit's good," the man said, pushing his empty glass forward. "One more, Bruno."

The bartender picked up the glass and began wiping down the table. "Sorry, Shank. You've reached your limit." His voice rumbled like distant thunder." The owner of the bar crinkled his eyes and cracked a grin when he spotted Emily. He had discovered long ago it was good business to get along with law enforcement. Putting his dishcloth and glass in a sink, he walked toward the officers.

Bruno Tapia moved with surprising alacrity for a man of his girth. Muscular arms hung loosely from broad shoulders. His bald head, encircled with a black headband, gleamed in the overhead lights as he approached Emily and Raymond.

"We ain't got no trouble here, Officer Etcitty. What's up? Can I buy you a drink or something?"

The day had been hot, and Emily's throat was dry. A cold beer would have hit the spot, but she smiled and shook her head. "Hey, Bruno. Thanks, but we're on duty. Meet my partner, Raymond Martinez."

"How's it going?" said Raymond, and felt the grip of Bruno's massive bone-crushing paw.

Emily suppressed a grin as she observed the wide-eyed expression on Raymond's face. "We're looking for someone, Bruno. Have you ever heard anything about a group called the *Diné* Freedom Fighters?"

Bruno scratched his head. "No, can't say that I have. Who are they—a new breed of Navajo superheroes?"

At the mention of the Freedom Fighters, a young Navajo sitting alone at the other end of the bar lifted his head and looked their way. While Emily continued her conversation with Bruno, Raymond sauntered over.

Emily watched out of the corner of her eye as he began speaking in Navajo to the man. At first, Raymond did all the talking, but after a while, the man appeared to loosen up and join in the conversation. They talked quietly—their heads bent close together, and Emily could not hear anything they said.

Back on the road, Emily appraised her new partner. He appeared to be in deep thought.

"What was that about on the other end of the bar?"

A sheepish grin flashed across the young man's face. "Might have picked up some new information. Did you learn anything about the Freedom Fighters from the bartender, Sergeant Etcitty?"

"Bruno had never heard of them, and he couldn't recall seeing any strangers in the bar, especially wearing red kerchiefs around their head. He did remember when Leonard Nakai came in with a twenty because it was unusual for Leonard to have cash in hand. Nakai was already so drunk Bruno refused to serve him. Now tell me who you were talking to and why you look so smug."

"The name of the man who is in charge of the *Diné* Freedom Fighters is Malcolm Keetso, or as he likes to be called, 'Thunder Eagle.'"

"Hmm. Very original. Now how did you find this out?"

"I told that guy in there my wife's clan name. It's the same as his. Turns out my wife and he are cousins. This Thunder Eagle was recently released from prison. He was doing state time for robbery and assault—has a long criminal record and a big grudge against the 'white man.' He and his followers have built a bunker somewhere in the Shonto area, but the guy says no one has discovered exactly where it is."

Emily considered this new bit of information with surprise "You should have called me over. We need to question your wife's cousin. He might be able to provide more information. What's his name?"

"No, Sergeant. Let's leave him out of this. I think he told me everything he knows. He said they tried to recruit him, but he turned them down. They threatened to get revenge if he talked, and he's from Shonto. This is the first time he mentioned it to anyone, and he's scared. Keetso has a reputation for being vicious."

Emily didn't bother to hide her annoyance. "You're going to impede an investigation, Martinez?"

"I don't know his name. I didn't ask. His family lives out there. They could be in danger."

Emily scowled and stopped the Blazer on the side of the road. She sat there a few minutes, watching the sun drop behind the silver rim of a mesa, and told herself to calm down.

"What are you doing, Sergeant?"

"We're going back, and you and I are going to interview your friend again, this time, we'll follow procedure. I don't like the fact you didn't inform me right away, Martinez."

The young officer slumped in his seat and stared out the window. "Sorry, Sergeant Etcitty."


They reentered Bruno's and looked around. Someone else sat on the stool where Martinez's wife's cousin had been sitting five minutes ago. Emily looked around, then approached Bruno.

"That young man that my partner was talking to—do you know where he went?"

Bruno shrugged. "Home, I guess. He left right after you."

"Do you know his name or where he lives?"

"Bobby is all I know. He doesn't come in very often—just drops by after his shift at the mining company and has one beer. Afraid I can't help you much Emily."

"Shit. Martinez, get on the phone and talk to your wife. I want that information now."

Bruno pointed his chin toward a pay phone against the wall near the bathrooms and Martinez, looking grim-faced moved in that direction. A few minutes later he returned and handed Emily a scrap of paper.

"Bobby Grayfeather, Shonto, Arizona," Emily read.

"You're not taking me off the case, are you, Sergeant Etcitty?"

"This day is shot, but first thing tomorrow morning, I'm headed to Arizona alone, Martinez. Do you think you can handle that undercover assignment without screwing up? Keep your eyes and ears open and report back to me anything you learn?"

The stricken look on his face vanished, and Martinez grinned. "Yes, ma'am."

Emily had to smile as well. He was so young and earnest. She could still remember when she joined the force right out of the Police Academy and how the fear of messing up felt. Being a woman in the male-dominated police force had made it even tougher.

# 8

Abe had managed to save enough money to put a downpayment on a small house located on a knoll between Star Ditch and a branch of the Animas River. The bungalow needed a lot of work, but he was close enough to the college to ride his bike when weather permitted, and from his deck, he enjoyed the view of surrounding mesas and the twisting Animas. That evening, Emily, Raven, and Will joined him as he grilled hamburgers and sipped a cool one. Raven sprawled on the floor beside Patch, sharing with him her book about corvids.

"Patch, did you know that ravens are one of the smartest animals in the world and that they can even imitate human voices?"

The little dog cocked his head and perked up his ears at the sound of his name, but even if he had understood what Raven was saying he wouldn't have been impressed by the big black bird known to steal his food while another lured him away.

Abe chuckled at the memory then turned his attention back to Emily. "So, it was Todechine's idea that Raymond goes undercover. He's a brand new cop. How do you feel about it?"

Emily crunched a potato chip between her teeth and chewed slowly. "I was reluctant at first. Then I figured all Martinez has to do is dress the part, carry a backpack with books, and hang out at the student union and act like he's studying. If he spots anyone he thinks could be a member of Keetso's bunch, he's to observe, take notes, but not confront. I made sure he understood the 'do not confront' part."

Abe flipped the burgers and placed a slice of Pepperjack Cheese on top of each. "Is he going to wear a wire?"

"Yeah—pen style micro recorder with audio. Should fit right in with the student image. Looks like a pocket protector."

"Maybe Martinez won't be in any danger, but what about you—going out to find that guy alone? I could go with you," Abe said.

Will turned his gaze from the waning crescent moon barely visible over the mesa top. "It would be better if I went with you, sis. I can change the sweat session and healing ceremony for Leonard Nakai to the day after tomorrow."

"Neither of you are coming along. If I do find out where Keetso's holed up, I won't be going in there without backup, so quit worrying. When are those burgers going to be ready, Abe? I'm starving."

"Wow," their daughter said. "Patch, did you know ravens can live up to forty years in the wild?"

Raymond Martinez arrived at work dressed in jeans, Aerosmith tee-shirt, plaid flannel with the sleeves rolled up, and tennis shoes. The backpack slung over his shoulder bulged from the weight of textbooks he had borrowed from his sister. "What do you think, Sergeant Etcitty? Do I pass inspection?"

Emily rubbed her chin while she silently appraised her partner. Out of uniform, he looked younger than ever. She decided he would definitely pass as a student. "Turn that ballcap around and let me see how it looks." Smiling at the effect, she drilled him once more on the importance of following procedure and made sure he knew how to use the pocket recorder. "You've got your radio?"

"Yes, ma'am. The two-way's in my old Jeep. I'll check in every couple of hours."

"Okay, Martinez. I guess you're set. I may be out of range, but keep in touch with the dispatcher, got it."

"Yes, I do. Don't worry, Sergeant." Then, he was off.

Emily watched until the faded red Jeep Wrangler pulled out of the parking lot and headed toward Farmington. She couldn't help it—she was worried, but she had her own assignment and a trip of over two hours one way ahead of her. There wasn't time to second-guess the wisdom of sending Martinez on a reconnaissance mission alone.

The tiny community of Shonto was located forty-three miles southwest of Kayenta on the Arizona side of the Navajo Nation. A natural spring flowed through the bottom of Shonto Canyon, which is connected by a labyrinth of canyons that stretch all the way to Navajo Mountain just north of the Utah-Arizona border. Emily pulled over to the side of the road and gazed at the mountain. She pulled out the small pouch she carried in her pocket and made an offering of white corn pollen to the looming laccolithic dome the *Diné* called *Naatsis'áán,* "Head of the Earth Woman." She vowed to bring Raven here soon and share the creation myth of how the *Diné* traveled far in their quest for their homeland and carried with them five animals—a bear, a snake, a deer, a porcupine, and a mountain lion. Having no use for the snake and porcupine, they set them free on the mountain. Some say that is why there are so many snakes and porcupines in that area. Yes, she would show Abe and Raven this beautiful canyon land with its sandstone spires and natural arches. Will would come and perform a Blessing Way Ceremony. They would stay on the lower elevation of *Naatsis'áán,* however. Traditionalists believed the spirits of the dead *Desha* and *Anasazi* people roamed the peak.

Emily shook her head, told herself to stop daydreaming and to focus on her purpose for coming to Shonto—she needed to find Bobby Grayfeather and ascertain if he has any information about Malcolm Keetso and the *Diné* Freedom Fighters. She drove into Shonto, the birthplace of Navajo Codetalker, Alfred Peaches, and found the trading post. A wizened old gentleman, his eyes narrow and downcast, told her the Grayfeathers lived in Navajo Housing on the corner of Sagebrush and Cedar. After thanking him for his help, Emily bought an orange soda and a pack of gum. Before heading for the address, she radioed headquarters to see if there were any messages from Raymond Martinez.

"1-6-5 to dispatch. Do you read?"

The unit crackled with static, but she managed some weak reception.

"What's your 10-20, 1-6-5?"

"I'm in Shonto—will be at Bobby Grayfeather's house, 106 Sagebrush Drive in ten minutes. Any word from Martinez?"

"10-4. The kid's bored from reading his sister's chemistry book, but he's learned how to balance chemical equations. No incidents to report."

"He should have brought a mystery novel."

Emily signed off, feeling somewhat relieved, and drove to the Grayfeather's residence in the Navajo Housing Complex. All the houses were identical one-story ranch-style units with tan vinyl siding and hard-packed dirt yards. A stray mongrel, wary as a coyote, roamed the street. The differences lay in the overall neatness of the residences, or the lack thereof. The exterior of the Grayfeather's home was immaculate with a pot of geraniums adding color to the porch. Numerous vehicles were parked in the driveway and others in front of the house. Emily wondered if they were having a celebration of some sort as she knocked on the door and waited for a response. When the door opened a crack, she heard the sounds of crying and caught a glimpse of a teary-faced woman. Several older females attempted to comfort her.

"I'm sorry to disturb you. Have I come at an inconvenient time?" said Emily.

"You've come about the accident, haven't you?" the young woman said in a strained voice. "Please come in. Do you have any information about Bobby? Can you tell us what happened to him after the accident?"

Feeling confused, Emily stepped into the hallway. "I've come here to talk to Bobby. Are you his wife?"

"Yes, she nodded emphatically. "I'm Nina Grayfeather. Did you find Bobby?"

"What accident are you referring to?"

"Why, Bobby's, of course—about the car crash last night when he was coming home from work in Farmington. My uncle's truck was found abandoned early this morning. Bobby stays with Uncle Jim in Farmington during the week and only comes home on weekends because it's such a long trip. But he called yesterday sounding upset and said he got laid off from work and was on his way home. He never showed up. Did you find him? Why else would you be here?"

Emily tried to hide the shock she felt. Why hadn't Arviso told her Bobby Grayfeather was missing? "When did you learn about the accident, ma'am?"

"Just now—about half an hour ago. My uncle called me. The police thought Uncle Jim had been driving the truck because it's registered in his name, so they weren't looking for Bobby at all. But when my uncle returned from sheep herding a while ago, he found a policeman at his door."

"Did you report Bobby missing when he didn't come home last night?"

"I waited until this morning because . . ." The young woman cast her eyes to the floor and began to cry softly. "I thought he might have got drunk because he lost his job and was ashamed to come home. But, that's not like Bobby, so this morning I reported him missing."

Emily still could not understand why no one had contacted her about the accident. "Do you remember who you spoke with, Mrs. Grayfeather?"

Hesitating before answering, the young woman said, "I'm not sure. I was so upset."

"Was the name Arviso? Sergeant Arviso?"

"No, I don't think so. It might have been a Mexican name, I just don't know," the wife said, wringing her hands.

"Emily spoke briefly with other family members then turned her attention to Bobby's wife. "I assure you, we'll do everything we can to find your husband." She asked for a recent picture and description of what Bobby was wearing when he last left home, then handed Nina Grayfeather her card. "Please call me if you receive any new information."

# 9

Abe usually packed a lunch and ate in his office, but today he decided to go to the Student Union to eat his chicken sandwich and satisfy his curiosity. He wanted to watch Raymond Martinez. Though having seen Emily's new partner on only one occasion, he thought he could spot the rookie and unobtrusively observe who he might be talking to. The dining area was packed with students chatting in groups or hunched over a book with a paper cup of coffee in front of them. When a couple got up and left a corner table, he quickly claimed it, ignoring the glares from a group that had the same idea. Abe opened his brown paper sack, extracted an apple and his sandwich and took stock of the students. He knew the young man was tall, but so were many of the others. The task of finding Martinez in a crowded dining room with so many dark-haired students dressed similarly presented a challenge.

A young man seated alone at a table near the door glanced up from the textbook he listlessly perused when two men sat down and began talking to him. One was blocky with a broad chest, the other had long, rangy arms, a thin face; both wore red headbands. Abe took a bite of his apple, slowly chewed, and waited. He had found his man and the *Diné* Freedom Fighters had found Raymond Martinez. Abe didn't have another class that afternoon and had planned on practicing a piece of music he and a violinist were performing next week but decided Beethoven's *Midnight Sonata* could wait a little longer. The two men huddled near Raymond, their heads bent in conversation, occasionally using hand gestures for emphasis, but they were too far away for Abe to hear what they were saying. After about a half-hour Raymond nodded, and the three left the student union together. Abe waited a minute then followed a discreet distance behind as they headed for the parking lot. *What the hell is the kid doing? Emily explicitly told him not to engage or confront.*

The news of Bobby Grayfeather's accident came as a shock to Emily. She had heard a brief report of a one-car rollover on the highway leading to Shonto, but the driver was reported missing, and it was assumed he had walked away or hitched a ride with someone. Vehicle accidents were frequent on the reservation, and if the driver had been drinking, it was not uncommon to leave the scene. A feeling in the pit of her stomach told her that this was not the case with Bobby Grayfeather. Bruno had said he drank one beer. The truck was registered to Bobby's wife's uncle, and after questioning family members, she discovered no one believed Bobby was drunk or would leave on his own volition without finding a way to contact his wife.

Emily radioed headquarters and asked Arviso why he hadn't told her Bobby Grayfeather had been reported missing and waited while Arviso seemed to be shuffling papers or searching reports on the internet website.

"Because there's no report of him being missing. I tried calling you the minute I heard about it, but no reception. We located Grayfeather's uncle a short time ago and informed him that his vehicle had been involved in an accident, and that's when we learned Bobby was the driver," Arviso said.

"Where did the wreck occur, Sergeant Arviso?"

"Uh, let's see. U.S. 160-E northwest of Marsh Pass—6.9 miles southwest of the Anasazi Inn at Tsegi. The guy was almost home."

"I didn't notice anything when I drove right by there at about ten-thirty this morning."

"The truck rolled and landed in an arroyo. Talltree and Gomez were sent to the scene, but they didn't find anything suspicious other than a missing driver. They called in a tow truck."

"Thanks, Arviso. I think I'll stop by and have a look-see myself. Keep me updated."

Now that she knew what she was looking for and approximately where the accident occurred, it wasn't hard to spot the broken shrubbery where the tow truck had pulled out the wrecked vehicle. Grayfeather's pickup must have slammed on the brakes and veered sharply to the right. He probably overcorrected, and the truck flipped and rolled down the embankment into the arroyo. Emily tried to imagine what would cause such a sudden reaction in the driver—an animal, an oncoming vehicle on his side? Or, did someone intentionally force him off the road? She knew Gomez and Talltree would have taken photos and measurements, and canvassed the area. The wrecked vehicle was in the impoundment lot, and she would need a closer look at it, but Emily wanted to get a feel for the accident scene herself. And, maybe that hollow feeling in the pit of her stomach was guilt. Someone might have seen the young man talking to the cops at Bruno's or observed them when they returned to ask more questions.

She grabbed the camera from her vehicle and followed the trajectory of the pickup down the arroyo to the area where it must have landed upright. Most of the prints had been obscured by the tracks of the tow truck driver and the investigating officers. Emily hoped they had taken decent photos before walking all over the scene. She snapped stills and made measurements of the tracks that were clear, then jotted down the information in her notepad. As Emily started back up to the road, a rust-colored stain on a juniper branch caught her eye. Careful inspection revealed several more drops of what appeared to be blood on the ground. *It had to be Grayfeather's. But, where did he go? Is there a chance the blood came from someone else?* Emily pulled a zip-lock baggie out of her shirt pocket and, using a pen-knife, carefully scooped up some of the blood-soaked soil. After sealing it, she extracted another bag and scraped off some of the juniper bark. When she had documented everything, Emily followed the drops of blood up the embankment to the highway, then for about two-hundred meters further where the trail abruptly stopped. It was nearly seven miles west to the nearest structure, the Anasazi Inn, with nothing but marshland and rugged canyons to the east. She decided to stop at the Inn and ask if anyone knew anything about a wounded man on foot.

"Reasonable Prices and Very Clean," said the sign announcing the Anasazi Inn. A single line of six blue and white units perched against a backdrop of picturesque rock formations. Two plastic lawn chairs and a pot of petunias sat in front of each room. Flat-topped mesas alternated with sandstone spires behind the buildings, and a grove of cottonwoods hugged the bank of a small stream. The parking lot was nearly empty. Before entering the office, Emily checked back in with Arviso and advised him of her location.

"I'm at the Anasazi Inn near Tsegi. Any word from Martinez?"

"Negative. Looks like the fish aren't biting the bait today."

"Let me know as soon as you hear from him or receive new information on Bobby Grayfeather, Arviso. And, I have a favor. See if you can get a trace on Tribal Council member, Charley Redhorse."

"Roger that, Sergeant Etcitty. Any particular reason?"

"I want him brought in for questioning regarding some work Leonard Nakai did."

"Roger."

It didn't make sense to head back to the office before interviewing possible witnesses, but worry nagged her like a dog with fleas as she entered the motel and approached the smiling East Indian behind the desk. A nametag attached to the pocket of his immaculate white shirt read Anuj Sharma, Manager. She handed him the photo of Bobby Grayfeather and said, "Mr. Sharma, I'm Sergeant Emily Etcitty with Navajo Tribal Police. We're looking for a missing man. He was involved in a vehicle accident near here last night and has turned up missing. Did you happen to see anyone resembling this individual? He may have been injured."

The manager scrutinized the picture and slowly shook his head. "No, no one looking like this man and no one with an injury. But my wife was on duty last night. Maybe she can tell you more."

"Where can I find Mrs. Sharma?"

"She is in the café serving customers. It's the offseason, so I had to lay off some of my regular help. There's only one unit rented out to a couple from Ohio. I believe they are in there as well."

The café, sitting perpendicular to the manager's office, had two pickup trucks and a black sedan parked in front. When Emily opened the door, she was greeted by the enticing aroma of fresh fry bread and felt a rumbling in her stomach. Two Navajo men sat on stools at the end of the counter, a family of four in a booth, and a middle-aged couple in the corner. A blackboard read "Today's Special – Navajo Tacos - $3.99." It was a deal she couldn't refuse. Emily sat on a stool at the counter and questioned the attractive East Indian woman. Mrs. Sharma assured her she had not noticed anything unusual last night, but she might want to talk to the motel's guests, nodding her head in the direction of the two people in a corner booth. Emily placed her order for a Navajo taco with everything to go and wandered over to the Ohioans.

The man, a dribble of ketchup on his double chin, looked up and stopped the forward progress of the hamburger heading toward his wide-open mouth.

"Yes, Officer," the woman said after patting her mouth with a napkin. "How can we help you?" Black-pencil-drawn eyebrows formed question marks over blinking round eyes. Sleek black hair pulled into a tight bun framed a narrow hawk-nosed face. *She must have been a crow in an earlier life,* Emily thought before introducing herself and telling them she was seeking information from anyone who might have witnessed a vehicular accident or seen an injured man the previous night.

"Elmer Anders, my wife, Agnes," said the man as he returned the hamburger to his plate and extended a pudgy hand. Agnes made furtive gestures, brushing at her chin with her hand until he got the hint and wiped off the ketchup. "You bet we saw something funny last night when we were coming back from Farmington, didn't we Agnes?"

Emily had pulled out her pocket notebook and was prepared to take down the pair's names when her pencil froze. She looked first at the man, then his wife, her eyebrows raised. "Yes? What did you see that seemed strange?"

Agnes blinked and pursed her lips before speaking. "We didn't want to get involved. It appeared someone was already there helping the young man into an SUV."

"Were you aware there had been an accident and did you stop and offer assistance?"

"Didn't see any wreck and it looked like Navajo business to me. Like my wife said, we didn't want to get involved. We need to be on the road in the morning. Got a reservation at Mesa Verde."

Emily bit her lip and cursed under her breath, thinking that if they had bothered to call 911, Grayfeather might have been found. Her voice was terse when she spoke again. "Can you give me a description of the injured man, the person or persons you say were helping him, and the SUV."

"Well, I'm not sure," the man said. "We didn't stick around long enough to get a good look. There were two of them, one on each side of this here injured guy, kinda holding him up."

"Please try," Emily said. "A man's life may depend on it."

Agnes jumped in with, "They were Indians, all of them. I could tell that much. The two doing the helping wore red headbands. They were supporting this other fella. He looked like he could hardly stand and he had blood running down his face. We figured they had it under control, so we went right on by."

"Tell me about the SUV. What direction was it headed?"

"It was in front of us, going the same way we were headed—southwest. They were driving one of those Ford

Explorers I think," said Elmer. It was pretty dark by then, hard to tell for sure.

"It was a navy blue Toyota," argued Agnes. "I know because it had that tire thingy on the back."

"Aggie has better night vision than I do," said Elmer. "I had cataract surgery back in ..."

Emily raised a hand in frustration. "Okay. Did either of you notice the license plate?"

The Ohio couple exchanged looks, then both shook their heads.

"We were in a hurry. These folks got a special going on here at the café on Tuesday nights—two for one steak dinner. It's quite a deal, but it shuts down at nine, and we didn't want to miss that," said the man.

Emily pursed her lips. "So you just drove on and didn't think any more about the accident."

"Didn't know there was an accident till now. I heard tell there's always some kind of accident out here though with all the drinking going on with these Indians. You know what I mean?" The man looked sheepish as if he suddenly realized he was speaking to a Native American police officer, and his gaze dropped down to the half-eaten hamburger on his plate.

Emily stared at the man and took a deep breath before speaking. "Please call this number if you think of anything else, and thank you for your concern. Sorry for interrupting your meal." She turned around and walked out of the restaurant biting her tongue before her temper caused her to say something regrettable. She had spent a lifetime listening to white people talk about drunk Indians. Seconds later, feeling chagrined, she went back inside for her Navajo taco.

# 10

*Damn. By the time I get to my truck, they'll be gone.* Abe watched Martinez climb into the front seat of a deep olive-green Jeep Liberty. One of the men sat behind the young police officer, and the other in the driver's seat. Abe couldn't see the license until they pulled out and turned onto the street leading away from the campus. Then, he was only able to catch the last three digits—4-9-7 before the Jeep was too far down the road. He wanted to know which way they were headed before he called it in, and thought he'd be able to find them if he hurried. Sprinting to his pickup, he dismissed the thought that Emily would be furious if she knew what he was doing.

Once on the highway, Abe knew if the vehicle had turned east it would be heading away from the reservation and toward Aztec, so he gambled and turned west. Traffic was heavy with students returning to the college after the lunch break and housewives set on finding bargains at the Farmington Mall. He drove fast, skirting in and out of traffic, keeping alert for the forest-green Jeep. Once, he thought he had lost them but then caught a glimpse of a dark SUV four cars ahead. Abe stayed back until the vehicle turned onto U.S. Highway 160, the direction he knew Emily had traveled this morning. That's when he pulled over to place a quick call to the Huerfano Substation.

"This is Abe Freeman. Radio Emily that Martinez is in a dark green Jeep Liberty with two men, and I don't think he went voluntarily. They turned onto 160 about three minutes ago and are headed in her direction. I could only make out the last three digits of the license plate: New Mexico, 4-9-7."

"We'll handle it, Mr. Freeman. I'll notify Emily and send another unit. Thanks for your assistance."

"I'm following them."

Abe let the pay phone dangle with the dispatcher's words falling unheeded in the desert air and raced back to his truck. Throwing up a cloud of dust and gravel on his way out, he reentered the highway. He wanted to make sure the Jeep didn't disappear down an unknown side road.

Emily heard her radio crackle as she reached her Chevy Blazer and received the message that her boyfriend was in pursuit of a vehicle containing rookie Officer Martinez and two other men and was headed in her direction.

"Shit. How long ago, Arviso?"

"Not more than three minutes—called from a convenience store outside Shiprock," said the irate dispatcher. "Vehicle described as a dark-green Jeep Liberty, New Mexico plates with the last three digits reading '4-9-7.' I have a backup unit on its way."

Cursing under her breath, Emily tossed the styrofoam box containing her uneaten lunch onto the passenger seat, made another U-turn, and peeled out of the parking lot.

"10-4. I'm headed that way." *First Martinez screws up, now Abe sticks his nose in. Doesn't he realize he's a father now, he's got responsibilities? Damn pig-headed men.* She switched on the emergency vehicle light to warn oncoming cars of the urgency of her speeding.

Abe drove faster than the law allowed, passing slower cars and swerving in an out of traffic. He left the outskirts of Shiprock and turned on more speed, intent on finding the Jeep with Martinez.

He hadn't stopped to think why he was doing it. He knew he would catch hell from Emily, but his adrenalin was pumped. It had been several years since he'd been involved in a chase. Maybe there was some darkness in his character that needed an outlet.

Away from the outlying businesses and scattered houses, the highway stretched straight and open. Few vehicles impeded progress, and it wasn't long before the back end of a green SUV came into view. Abe slowed to keep his distance but remained close enough to notice any turns or stops the Jeep might make. He had followed the car for nearly an hour and thought Emily would surely be along soon when the Jeep turned down a barely perceptible dirt track bounded on both sides by clumps of juniper and piñon. He gave the vehicle a few minutes head start, then pulled onto the shoulder. Abe had no sooner stepped out of his truck to stretch his legs and wait for Emily when a rustling of branches got his attention. A heavyset man wielding a shotgun, a red headband tied around scraggly black hair, emerged from the woods.

"Why are you following us, mister?" said the man, pointing the gun at Abe's mid-section.

Abe tried to think fast and stall for time. *Where the hell is Emily?* "I don't know what you're talking about. I'm just passing through and pulled over to take a leak."

"Like hell you did. I didn't see you pull your weiner out, and we spotted you tailing us back in Shiprock." He nudged Abe with the barrel of his gun. "Let's take a walk."

*Well, hell.* The knowledge that he had made a big mistake and possibly jeopardized his Both Emily and Martinez hit him and filled Abe with remorse. Fifty yards up the narrow track they reached the Jeep hidden behind thick brush. Raymond Martinez sat in the back seat, a lanky Native American sporting a sparse goatee sat beside him holding a pistol aimed at Martinez's head. The young police officer's eyes mirrored Abe's feelings. If the *Diné* Freedom Fighters didn't kill them, Emily would. Abe tried to protest again but was told not to talk and was shoved into the front passenger seat. Moments later, the Jeep bounced down a rocky trail and into a labyrinth of brush, ravines, and hidden canyons.

They seemed to be going in circles, backtracking over terrain they had already covered. The landscape looked the same no matter where they went—a dense forest of juniper, piñon, and clusters of scrubby oak interrupted by massive boulders and towering rock walls of sandstone. He thought they were lost when a sudden clearing came into view. An armed guard standing at the entrance of the open space gave them the once-over then waved them ahead. The compound contained a horse pen with several mustangs, a large plastic water storage tank perched on the bed of a pickup, and a fleet of trucks, trailers, and pickups. Two over-sized dome-type tents and a dozen or so smaller army tents encircled a covered outdoor cooking area. Several men and a clutch of women standing under the canopy of the cooking area stared at Abe with wary eyes.

A tall, muscular Native American, his hair tied into a gray-streaked club held in place with a blood-red bandana, stood in front of one of the larger tents. His arms were crossed across his chest, his eyes narrowed, his mouth a tight thin line. To Abe, his dark features resembled a Hollywood version of a Native American rather than an authentic Navajo—Johnny Cash dressed in a buckskin vest. His heavy-lidded eyes framed by wire-rimmed glasses looked like they carried the weight of a thousand sorrows. A half-moon scar rested under his right eye, another, long and jagged, on his left cheek.

The Jeep came to a stop, and the man slowly surveyed the occupants of the SUV then tilted his chin toward the tent flap. Abe and Martinez were ushered inside and ordered to sit down on a mat against the wall. Kerosene lanterns illuminated the space with flickering shadows. The flag of the American Indian Movement hung on one side—against another was a large gun cabinet containing an assortment of pistols and rifles, and a shotgun set ready on a rack by the door. In the back, Abe saw a battered school teacher's desk with an ancient Underwood typewriter. A stack of papers cluttered the desk. Books with titles like *Custer Died for Your Sins: An Indian Manifesto, The Indian Movement from Alcatraz to Wounded Knee,* and *Black Elk Speaks* filled a makeshift shelf against a third wall. A man's face, mustachioed with wavy black hair, stared back at him from a poster that read "Free Leonard Peltier." Another spelled "Warrior" in blood red. Most incongruent, though, was the old spinet piano mounted on four large wheels and parked near the center of the room.

Emily checked her speedometer—75 mph. There had been no sign of anything resembling a forest-green Jeep, and she wondered if they had turned off somewhere. She whizzed past an older model Toyota pickup parked on the shoulder to her right, then slowed down. Her heart skipped a beat when she realized it was Abe's truck. Emily put on the brakes and whipped a U-turn stopping beside the abandoned pickup.

*Abe, what have you done?* Her heart sank even further after discovering the door unlocked with the key still in the ignition. Emily pulled out her Glock and scanned the surroundings, noting the narrow track leading through the underbrush, her senses alert for any sounds or signs of movement. The harsh cry of a blue jay caused her to jump. *They have Abe and Martinez. Who knows how many there are?* She switched on her handheld and called headquarters.

"I've got a unit headed your way," Arviso said. "Should be there any time. Don't go in alone, Etcitty."

No, she couldn't do that—it would be crazy, but waiting became unbearable. Emily followed the trail a short distance into the woods, heard a vehicle approach, the crunch of tires on the graveled shoulder, a car door slam, and she crouched behind a cluster of chamisa. Barely breathing, she gripped her Glock in both hands.

"Sergeant Etcitty," said a male voice.

With a sigh of relief, she stepped out into the open. "Over here. What took you so long? I think the *Diné* Freedom Fighters have Officer Martinez and Abe Freeman—most likely Bobby Grayfeather as well. We're going in there and bringing them out."

The two officers glanced at one another. "What the fuck is your boyfriend doing out here?" said the one called Gordie Gomez. His belly protruded over a silver belt buckle, and Emily knew he'd have a tough time meeting the physical standards when put to the test.

"Don't ask me. I just know that's Abe's truck out there, and he's not in it."

Gomez's partner was younger and more fit. Harold Talltree had been with the Navajo Police fifteen years but had failed to make sergeant because of several infractions staining his record. He had been written up more than once for using excessive force. "Should never have let that greenhorn rookie work alone. I knew he'd get his ass in a sling. He hasn't got the balls to be a cop."

Emily bit her tongue. Now was not the time to address the surly officer's complaints. "We have to hike in, don't want the vehicles to alert anyone. You guys up for that?"

"Let's do it," said Talltree.

"Gomez, get the canteen and flashlight out of my vehicle. We don't know how far in they are. Both of you, silence your radios and no talking. I don't want any unnecessary noise.

Gomez hitched up his pants headed for the SUV then fell in line behind Emily and Harold Talltree. Sweat dripped from his unhappy face.

# 11

The picture of Leonard Peltier was replaced by the unsmiling face of the man who had been standing in front of the tent. He towered above the two men sitting on the floor then looked directly at the rookie cop. In his hand, he held Raymond's wallet and the pocket microphone. He extracted the identification card, and as he read, his voice was soft and cultured, devoid of any accent or inflection that could otherwise identify him with a particular culture.

"Officer Raymond Martinez, Navajo Tribal Police," he read. "Would you like to explain why you were recording your conversation with my men? Are the *Diné* Warriors under investigation?"

Abe and the young cop exchanged a quick look and Martinez shook his head.

"No. I was assigned to learn as much as I could about your organization is all. Just doing my job. I couldn't come out here and ask you. No one knew where you were, so I pretended I was interested in joining."

"Hmm. Why the sudden interest?"

"You or someone in your group bought a rifle from Leonard Nakai. Someone shot a man on the rez near Nakai's house using a gun of that caliber. It's part of the investigation, Mr. Keetso."

Malcolm Keetso raised his eyebrows then settled on a mat across from Martinez. "You know my name. Interesting. Well, we might have bought a gun from this individual, we're in the market for weapons, but we haven't shot anyone—yet. The guns are purely for self-protection. His lip curled into a frown of distaste. "Who's this white man with you?"

"Name's Abe Freeman. I teach music at the college. My girlfriend is Martinez's partner and superior. He's a rookie. This was his first assignment on his own, and I thought he might be in trouble, so I followed him. That's my only interest."

Martinez hung his head and looked as if he couldn't believe what Abe was saying. "I don't know this man. I saw him once, but I've never even spoken to him."

Malcolm Keetso smiled. "Your girlfriend, hmm. You tell her what you were up to?"

"No," Abe lied. "She doesn't know anything about this. She went to Shonto to talk to Bobby Grayfeather."

"Well, I guess she missed him. Bobby's here."

"What?" said Raymond. "What did you do to him?"

"Calm down kid. We're not out to harm our own people. We are rising up against the white man's intrusion, his abuse of the *Dinéah,* and poisoning of our land."

"Then why is Grayfeather here?"

"A couple of my boys saw this kid staggering along the highway. Young Grayfeather had a head wound, was covered in blood, scratched and bruised all over—said he couldn't remember anything—not what happened—not even his name. They picked him up and brought him here. I found his driver's license, and we checked it out, but the rural address listed is abandoned and currently property of Strathmore Minerals. So, my Lakota wife, Akicita, is taking care of him. Don't worry, she knows what she's doing."

At the mention of her name a tall, stately woman entered the tent. She appeared to be about the same age as Keetso but without the wear and tear of a hard life. Silver gray hair was held in place with turquoise barrettes and hung in a single long braid down her back. High cheekbones, a long straight nose, and a regal carriage provided both dignity and authority. Her face, rather than being etched in crevices like Keetso's, was smooth and unlined. She had dressed casually in blue jeans and a denim shirt with the sleeves turned up.

"Shall I make tea for the guests?" she said, the hint of a smile turning up the corners of her mouth."

"Yes, but first, how is our patient?"

"He is coming around. Resting peacefully."

"We need to take him to a hospital, notify his family," said Abe.

"Yes," said Martinez. "His wife must be crazy with worry. Drive us back so we can let his family know where is and send an ambulance."

At these words, Akicita nailed him with a piercing glare. "He is getting the best care possible right here, and he is not ready to be moved."

"I learned a long time ago that you cannot win an argument with my wife," said Keetso. "Her name means 'warrior' in the Lakota language, and believe me, she lives up to it."

Abe didn't know what to think. According to the description Emily had given him, Keetso was a cruel con man who would rob his own mother and hurt another person just for the fun of it. This soft-spoken individual seemed thoughtful and intelligent. He even planned on serving them tea. "What do you want from us, Mr. Keetso?" Abe said.

Keetso sighed, his eyes turning mournful. "I want nothing from you, but you shouldn't have tried to follow my men. It may mean trouble for us and our mission, as there are enemies within the tribe who wish to do us harm."

"I didn't follow you in. I was brought here by your men."

Keetso shook his head. "A mistake in judgment on their part, but now that you're here, I am going to have to decide what to do with you."

Abe glanced nervously around the area, briefly meeting Martinez's eyes before looking at Keetso. "What mission are you talking about?"

"To put a permanent halt to uranium mining on Navajo land and demand that all earlier sites be cleaned and our people compensated for the harm that has been caused them. I intend to expose the insidious relationship individual greedy council members have made with Strathmore Minerals. Is that too much?"

Abe silently agreed that was not too much. He felt burgeoning respect for this puzzling man. "I don't understand. I've heard you were a man to be feared, did time in prison for assault and theft. My girlfriend checked your arrest record—goes all the way back to junior high."

"This girl you speak of—she is a Navajo woman I presume. She is very inquisitive."

"That's her job. She's a sergeant with the Navajo Nation Police—Emily Etcitty, my partner and the mother of my child."

Akicita returned carrying a tray with three mugs of fragrant herbal tea. After giving one to each man, she said she was going back to tend to the young man and left as quietly as she had entered.

Abe breathed in the aroma and took a sip. He couldn't identify the herb, but it tasted fruity, both sweet and pungent.

"Chokecherry and amaranth," said Keetso, seemingly reading Abe's mind. "Going back to your statement regarding my delinquent youth—yes, I did some tough time in different prisons. I consider myself lucky to be alive, but it may have been the best thing that ever happened to me. I was sent to Marion, Illinois, the same pen as Leonard Peltier, the man who turned my life around. I learned about fighting for a just cause. I read everything I could get my hands on. Leonard was transferred to Florida, and I never saw him again, but I'll never forget what he taught me. That's why I'm back here fighting for native rights."

"But why so secretive about recruiting college students?" Martinez said.

"Persons in power would shut us down if they knew what we're doing," said Keetso. "College students are young and idealistic, and they have access to computers and printers. They are able to make copies of our flyers, and since they come from all over the reservation, they have a broad range of distribution."

Abe ran his fingers through his hair. "Are you going to let us go?"

"Of course, but I would like a promise from you that you will not disclose our location to anyone, especially not to that police officer girlfriend of yours. Do I have your word?"

"What about Bobby Grayfeather?" asked Abe.

"He stays until he is well enough to be moved. When that time comes, one of my men will drop him off at the Shiprock Hospital."

Abe's mind was churning. *How am I going to explain this to Emily without telling her the location of Keetso's camp?* More urgently, what if she stumbles in here now. *Keetso will know I lied.* Raymond Martinez must have been thinking along similar lines.

"I can't keep this information about Bobby Grayfeather from Sergeant Etcitty. I think you should tell her your version—that your men found him and brought him here for medical attention."

"Let's speak of politics and power structures for a moment. I am sure you are aware that there are significant divisions within the tribe's council members, and the different sides have their alliances. My sources have informed me that there are some on the Navajo Nation Police Force who have pledged their allegiance to my enemies as well. Some would even prefer to shoot me on sight rather than listen to any kind of explanation about . . ."

When Emily spotted smoke from the camp, she ordered the two male officers to spread out and stay hidden until she gave further instructions. "We're going to remain quiet and keep watch until we can ascertain how many men are in the encampment and rather or not they are armed. One of our officers and a civilian may be inside, and I don't want anyone's safety endangered." She had noticed the armed guard standing at the entrance of the road.

"We should storm the place—take them by surprise," said Talltree. "I can pick off that guard. They won't know what hit them."

Emily gave an adamant shake of her head. "Stay down until I give the word," she said.

Gomez mumbled something under his breath but dropped behind a dense juniper and knelt down, his shotgun held at the ready. Talltree crouched under cover of a cluster of boulders but within sight of Emily hiding behind a stand of oak brush between the two men. They had been waiting several tense minutes when a man appeared outside one of the structures. He took a cigarette from a pack in his shirt pocket, lit it, and exhaled a cloud of smoke. Emily watched him intensely, then glanced at Gomez, noticing his sudden movement. The overweight cop had raised his rifle to his shoulder and sighted in a target. Anticipating Gomez's next move, Emily made a run for him, knocking his gun in the air just as he pulled the trigger.

"You damn idiot. What the hell are you doing?" Talltree turned to look at her, confusion on his face. "Do not fire unless ordered to do so," Emily said. She heard barking dogs and felt her stomach roil. Then she heard Abe's voice cry out, "Don't shoot."

Malcolm Keetso stopped in midsentence at the sound of a gunshot. Abe and Martinez passed a look of panic and jumped to their feet.

Abe raced to the door and began waving his arms. "Stop!" he yelled. "Hold your fire! Emily, If you're out there, listen to me. We are not being held against our will. No one is hurt."

"Everyone is safe. Put down your guns," yelled Martinez.

At the sound of gunfire, several *Diné* Freedom Fighters came running toward the tent. They hustled Keetso, Martinez, and Abe back inside; took up their weapons and hunkered down in protective positions.

# 12

"Let me talk to them," Abe said. "That's my girlfriend. I can tell her you mean no harm—convince them to put their guns down."

Contempt was written all over Keetso's face as he glowered at Abe. "You said you didn't tell anyone where you were going. Why should I believe you now? You're just another lying white man."

"I admit I was wrong. I'm sorry. I didn't know how you would react if I told the truth, but I'm not lying now. I'll convince Emily that you saved Grayfeather's life—that they should put down their weapons and come in peacefully."

"I'll go," said Martinez. "Those are police officers. They'll listen to me."

"No," said Keetso. He narrowed his eyes, clenched his jaws, his voice decisive. "You're both screw-ups, but the white man goes." He kept his attention directed at Abe. "Find out how many there are and tell them to step out in the open—all of them—to throw their weapons on the ground and put their hands on their heads. My men will be armed and watching to make sure no one tries anything. I'll send a few of my boys out to pick up the guns and bring the woman inside. The young cop stays here as a guarantee you don't try to get away."

"All right," said Abe.

"I've treated you fairly up till now," said Keetso. "But I won't hesitate to shoot this young man if I have to. Do you understand?"

Abe swallowed hard and nodded. He thought of the child he loved so much. He had vowed he would never do anything to hurt her. Abe had to do whatever this man asked for if it would enable Emily and him to return to Raven.

His hands in the air, his heart thumping, throat constricted, Abe stepped out of the tent and started walking toward the edge of the woods where Emily and the two officers hunkered down behind trees. "Let me explain, Em."

"Keep your hands where I can see them and proceed slowly." Emily shook her head; her eyes narrowed in anger and lowered her Glock.

"Emily, listen," Abe pleaded. "It's not what you think. I had no intention of coming here. I was waiting for you at the side of the road when some of Keetso's men found me."

"Want me to cuff him, Sergeant?" said the taller of the two officers as he approached Abe.

"Back off Talltree. That won't be necessary. Let me handle this."

"No offense, Sergeant, but you've kind of got a personal conflict of interest here," added Gomez. "What with this clown being your boyfriend and all."

"Shut up, Gomez." Emily returned her gaze to Abe, her eyes still burning with anger. "Where's Martinez, Abe?"

"He's inside the tent with Keetso. He's not hurt."

"Bobby Grayfeather?"

"They found him wandering down the road after he had been in an accident. They brought him here and are treating his wounds."

"Bullshit!" said Talltree.

Emily ignored the officer's outburst and kept her focus on Abe. "Why did Keetso send you out here? What does he want?"

"To talk to you, Emily, alone. He wants you and your officers to surrender your weapons and do as he says."

"Or what?"

Abe put his palms up and shrugged. "I don't know, but I don't want to find out."

"The hell," said Gomez. "Let us cuff this asshole and go in there. If we pick off Keetso, his band of pussies will surrender."

"No they won't," said Abe. "You're outnumbered and surrounded right now. If anyone pulls another dumb stunt like firing their weapon, there's going to be some bloodshed, and it won't likely be Keetso's. Don't forget, they've got Raymond Martinez."

As if on cue, a dozen men stepped out from hiding and encircled the Navajo Officers. Each man had either a rifle or a pistol aimed at the cops.

Gomez swung his rifle around and prepared to fire when a warning shot rang out, the bullet embedding itself in the tree beside his head.

A burly Navajo with a red headband shouted, "I wouldn't try any more stupid stunts, or someone's gonna get hurt. Throw your weapons down."

Emily chewed her lower lip. She glanced at the heavily armed Freedom Fighters.

"I don't think Keetso's out to hurt anyone, Emily," Abe said. "In fact, I'll bet my life on it. He wants to make some kind of deal." Abe took a deep breath. "Just hear him out."

Emily matched his sigh with one of her own and furrowed her brow. "Okay. What choice do we have? Do as he says," she said to her officers before tossing her weapon to the ground. "Take off your duty belt and drop it."

"I don't like this," Talltree grumbled. "I'm not throwing in my weapon."

"Do it," said Emily. "Now. That's an order, and that means everything you're carrying—including shoulder and ankle holsters."

Scowling, the two men unbuckled their belts and tossed them in the dirt. No sooner had they finished, when two dogs on leashes and the twelve armed Freedom Fighters approached the officers. Two men scooped up the weapons and accessory belts, while the others kept their guns trained on the cops.

"Your vehicle keys," one of the Freedom Fighters said. "Hand them over."

"This had better be good, Abe," Emily said as she gave her keys to the armed man. "If anything happens, it's on you. Now, take me to Keetso."

The two male cops, looking angry and distressed, were frisked, their keys confiscated, and were summarily marched into a tent.

Emily stepped from the bright sunlight into the interior of a dimly lit tent. She quickly surveyed her surroundings—posters of Leonard Peltier; more signs proclaiming Indian rights and unity; the bookshelf; the small piano; Raymond Martinez sitting on a rug and leaning against the tent wall. Her eyes stopped wandering when Keetso swiveled around from his desk and met her gaze. The thoughtful gray-haired man with a face as weathered and scarred as the land of the Diné was not what she expected. Though she was not sure what she expected—maybe a fiery devil spouting curses and threats, but not this calm individual who stood now and offered his hand.

"Allow me to introduce myself, Malcolm Keetso. You must be Emily Etcitty. I have heard much about from your colleague, Officer Martinez and your friend, Mr. Freeman. Won't you have a seat," he said, indicating a nearby stool.

"I'm not here on a social call, Keetso. I want those men you are holding released, including Bobby Grayfeather. What kind of deal are you offering?" She turned to look at Martinez. "Are you all right, Raymond?"

"Yes, ma'am." He blushed and cast his eyes down. "Sorry about this."

"You got yourself into this mess. I'm trying to get you out."

"Right, Sergeant."

"I just want to say one thing," Abe said. "Keetso and the *Diné* Freedom Fighters are protesting against uranium mining on the reservation. They're not involved in any illegal activity."

A poster claiming 'Water is Life' caught Emily's eye, then she stared at Abe. "How do you know?" Before Abe could reply, she turned her attention back to Keetso. "If that's your purpose in being here, why are you so secretive, and where is Bobby Grayfeather?"

"The young man is well cared for. You can see him after our talk. As to why we must remain covert—there are people in power who would gain financially if uranium mining were to commence again. They would do anything to stop us from spreading the truth, including murder, as evidenced by what happened to Grayfeather. I am truly sorry the young officer was brought here, and that your friend stumbled in as well. That was a mistake. And now, with your two colleagues, more spectators have discovered the location of our camp. How do I know I can trust you or your men, Officer Etcitty? One of you already tried to take a shot at us. We have to relocate our headquarters."

"What do you want from me," Emily said.

"Twenty-four hours. I've already given the order to start dismantling the camp and notified my men of the location for our next site. You know, I grew up here. These canyons and hills are as familiar to me as my mother's face. I know places no one can find."

Emily's mind was racing. She looked at Martinez, then into Abe's eyes—those unclouded blues that never lied. She saw chagrin, anxiety, but not fear. "How is this supposed to work?"

"Unfortunately, you will all have to stay here, as my prisoners. After twenty-four hours, we will have disappeared, and you will be free to go."

"We have a daughter," Abe said. "She'll be frightened if we aren't home when she returns from school. Emily's mother will call the authorities if we don't show up."

"Someone will get word to her," Keetso said. "It's the only way. Give me the phone number of the person you want to be notified. I can't let you go until we are gone. Do you understand?"

"What's to stop us from leaving sooner," Emily said.

Keetso stood, rubbed the back of his neck. The lines on his face appeared more profound, his eyes sadder. "A guard will remain with you. If necessary, you'll be tied. I hate to do this, but you could unravel all our work, Officer Etcitty. Do you agree to my terms?"

Abe gave a slight nod, then Martinez did the same. Emily felt trapped. "Do I have a choice?"

Keetso chuckled without humor. "Not really."

"Any harm comes to my men, I'll hunt you down myself, Keetso."

"Of course, officer. Now let's have some tea, and you can meet my wife. Akicita, dear," he called. "Will you heat some more water in the kettle, then take Miss Etcitty to Bobby?"

# 13

Emily followed the tall, dignified woman called Akicita across the campground to a small tent adjacent to the one where Keetso waited with Abe and Martinez. *She's native, but not Navajo,* Emily thought, observing the finely beaded geometric designs on the woman's mocassins and jewelry, and her long beaded braids. She remembered Native American women she had met in North Dakota several years back. They had worn similar beaded necklaces and bracelets. *Maybe Lakota Sioux.* As they walked to the nearby tent, the discordant sound of a tinkling piano drifted from Keetso's canvas, filling the camp with chords of a familiar Beethoven tune. *Moonlight Sonata? What is Abe up to now? Trying to charm Keetso with music?* Men stopped what they were doing to listen, a look of wonder on their faces. She had to grin and shake her head, in spite of the situation.

When the flap was pulled back, and she entered the small tent, she found herself once again having to alter her vision in the dark interior. A lone candle burned in the corner. Emily blinked, and as her eyes adjusted, she was able to make out the form of a man lying on a pallet. A Navajo blanket covered his body, white bandages swathed his head. Another woman knelt at the man's side offering him sips of water from an earthen cup.

"Bobby, Bobby Grayfeather," Emily said.

"He doesn't remember anything—the blow to his head . . ." Akicita said. "We found identification papers on him, but no address or phone numbers—only a picture of a young woman. I hope that with time and care, his memory will return. He has only regained consciousness today, and it comes and goes."

She could make out his face now in the flickering glow of candlelight. Despite the swelling and bruises, it was the same person as the man in the photograph Grayfeather's wife had given her. "Bobby," Emily repeated, more softly. "Can you hear me?"

He looked at her, blinking with uncomprehending eyes. At the same time, the woman kneeling beside the pallet ducked her head, stood, and hurried from the tent.

Something about the woman's profile and movements struck a familiar chord in Emily, but she shook her head and turned her attention back to Grayfeather.

"Bobby, I'm going to take you home to your wife. Nina is waiting for you."

"Wh-what? Who are you?" Grayfeather said, a puzzled and pained look on his battered face.

Akicita touched Emily's shoulder. "It's time to go. The young man needs to rest."

When Emily stepped outside, she encountered a scene of frenzied activity. The large tent was in the process of being dismantled and loaded onto a truck bed. People were filling wagons and pickup trucks with everything that could be moved. The tents were being taken down, the horses led into trailers. A man rolled the spinnet piano onto a ramp, loaded it on a truck bed, and strapped it down. Emily made a mental note of the types of trucks and trailers—a couple of heavy-duty Rams and a Ford 350 were connected to several cargo flatbeds. There were also some smaller older model pickups. Most of the vehicles bore  New Mexico or Arizona license plates, but some carried tags from South Dakota, Oklahoma, and Utah. She filed this information in the back of her mind and turned her attention to Akicita.

"Where's Abe and my officers?"

"They have been taken to a small tent we will leave intact. Before we go, Bobby and his medications will be brought to the place where you and the officers will wait. I'll leave a container of water and food. It should be enough to hold you over."

Emily pursed her mouth and thought of her daughter. Judging from the long shadows cast by the trees, it was late afternoon. Raven would be coming home from school. Of course, Emily's mom would be there, and she wouldn't expect Emily until later, but Abe was supposed to have dinner with them before they went to his house. What will her mother tell their child, so she won't be upset? How is Chief Todechine going to react to this mess? Was she still angry at Abe? *First things first. We've got to get out of here, then I'll figure out how to explain it all.* She turned her head when she caught a flash of color and a sudden movement out of the corner of her eye then drew in her breath. The woman who had been tending Bobby Grayfeather was loading a bundle of blankets onto a truck bed. This time, there was no doubt in her mind—it was Chipeta Longtooth, the fugitive Ute woman who had once saved her life.

The faces of the hostages looked grim, and no one spoke. Abe was silent as well, lost in contemplation as he sat on the floor of the small tent, sharing space with Emily, Martinez, the two police officers, and Bobby Grayfeather. Gomez and Talltree sat on the opposite side of the tent, glowering at Abe and Emily who were seated beside each other. Raymond Martinez stood and paced, undoubtedly concerned about what his wife would think when he didn't come home from work that evening. Grayfeather had been carried in on a stretcher and lay sleeping on the other side of Emily. Abe watched her as she applied a poultice left by Akicita to the young man's abrasions. A tea made from a concoction of herbs had also been left behind with instructions to offer him sips whenever he awoke. The wounded man groaned softly and tossed his head but didn't open his eyes. An armed guard stood at the entrance of the tent, checking on his prisoners every fifteen minutes or so.

From outside the tent came a clamor of noise as truck beds were loaded, engines revved up, and trucks and trailers rumbled down the dirt road—then a sudden quiet. An atmosphere of tension and apprehension filled the small space. Abe wanted to talk to Emil, to get a feel for what she was thinking. He wished he could hold her and tell her how much he loved her, and that he was sorry.

"You sure he can't remember anything?" Talltree said, breaking the silence.

"That's right," Emily answered in a quiet voice. "Amnesia. Whether it's temporary or long-term, only time will tell. He's had a bad concussion."

"Yeah. Thanks to those assholes you let go free," said Gomez.

The guard at the entrance poked his head and shotgun in the tent. "Keep it quiet in there. Any more smart remarks out of you," he said, staring at Gomez, "you're gonna be hog-tied and gagged."

This silenced the group once again. They ate tortillas with Vienna Sausages and shared water from the canteen. When Emily needed to relieve her bladder, she was allowed some privacy outside the tent. Not so the men, who remained in sight of the guard at all times. With dusk came purple shadows, then the horned moon in the western sky, accompanied by Venus, brighter than any visible star. Darkness soon descended filling the night sky with a broad brushstroke of the Milky Way. The wind rustled the juniper, bringing a sudden chill. A coyote howled. Grayfeather mumbled softly, and Abe tucked the blanket around the unconscious man. On the other side of the tent, snores sounding like a wounded hog erupted from Gomez's open mouth. Emily leaned her head on Abe's shoulder. He put his arm around her and felt her warmth, her steady breathing. Comforted by her closeness, he told himself, *We will get through this.*

The following morning, Abe stepped out of the tent, sauntered to a nearby bush, and opened his fly. The guard kept a watchful eye but didn't leave his post at the tent flap. The campground was eerily empty—the only indication of anyone having been there was the cold ash pile in the center of the clearing and their own tent with the guard's truck, a beat-up Ford with Arizona plates. It was a bright fall morning, a Saturday with a brisk breeze rattling the turning leaves of the scrub oak. Fall had always been Abe's favorite time of the year, and Raven would be home from school spending the weekend at Abe's place. On Saturdays they liked to ride the horses or hike a new trail, searching for hidden treasures in nature's bounty—a smooth stone, a brightly colored leaf, a turkey feather. The thought of his daughter brought on a feeling of urgency. He would not be able to go to her until this evening, and then, only if all went as planned.

The day passed slowly; Emily tended to Grayfeather; Gomez and Talltree, like caged cats, paced the confines of the tent. Martinez remained sitting off to himself, quietly brooding, no doubt concerned about his pregnant wife and the possibility of losing his job. Tempers became short, and no one had any appetite for more Vienna Sausages. The hours dragged by, and when four o'clock, the time of their freedom finally arrived, the guard told them to take off walking toward the road.

"Your vehicles are around the halfway point, behind some boulders," he said. "The keys are inside. Here's your flashlight—you're going to need it. And don't bother to come looking for me. I'll be long gone."

Abe nodded, then before they left, turned to the guard and said, "I told Keetso his piano needs tuning. He can reach me at the college."

Both the guard and Emily gave him a quizzical look.

Abe smiled, then he and Martinez picked up opposite ends of Grayfeather's stretcher and followed Emily. Talltree led the way, and Gomez brought up the rear. Their tent had already been broken down and loaded into the guard's truck bed before they made it around the first bend. A few minutes later, the guard drove around them, leaving a trail of dust. Bobby Grayfeather blinked into the fading sunlight, tossed his head, tried to sit up, and spoke for the first time.

"What's going on? Where are you taking me? Where's Nina?"

Abe and Martinez stopped and gently set the stretcher down as Emily rushed to the young man's side. "Bobby. Can you hear me?"

Bobby blinked. "Who are you?"

"I'm a police officer. You've been hurt. We're taking you to a hospital where you can see your wife. Can you remember what happened?"

Grayfeather looked confused as he studied the faces of the strangers staring down at him then slowly shook his head. "I don't know. I want to see my wife." He closed his eyes, drifting off, and his stretcher was lifted once again.

It was rough going. As darkness descended over the landscape, Emily switched on the flashlight and led the group to a cluster of three boulders where they found their vehicles as promised. Their duty belts with their firearms and accessories lay on the seat; their keys were left in the ignition.

Emily sighed with relief and activated her radio. It sputtered and crackled to life.

"Arviso, this is Sergeant Etcitty." She gave him their location and requested an ambulance for Bobby Grayfeather. "Yes, Martinez, Talltree, and Gomez are with me. So is Abe Freeman. We are unhurt."

After she had signed off, Emily looked at the three officers. "The chief wants to see us all in his office the second we get back."

# 14

Abe opened the front door of his truck and spotted his keys in the ignition as promised. On the seat next to his backpack lay a folded slip of paper. A phone number with the initials MK was scribbled in pencil. Abe put the note in his wallet. He had a pretty good idea what this was about, but it would have to wait. His daughter came first, then his dog and horses. Driving as fast as he could manage without alerting traffic cops or being a threat to society, Abe reached Bertha Etcitty's house in under two hours and rushed to sweep his little girl up in his arms.

After being assured that Will had gone to Abe's house and taken care of Patch and the other animals, Abe tried to answer the deluge of questions while he wolfed down the food Bertha kept piling on his plate. *Where were you, Dad? Where's Mom? Why didn't you come home yesterday?*

Not wanting to alarm Raven or Emily's mother, he tried to keep his answers simple. He ended up saying they had been looking for someone and got stuck in a place without any radio reception to call for help. Neither a complete lie nor the entire truth, he hoped it would hold Bertha off until Emily arrived.

113

He could tell by her skeptical look that she was not buying his story and wondered what Keetso's men had told her. When Emily walked in the door an hour later, and the hugs and assurances started all over again, Abe breathed a sigh of relief.

Later that night, Abe packed his daughter and her purple backpack into his truck cab. They would have at least one day together, and he would not think about the significance of finding Malcolm Keetso's contact number in his truck or the fact he had failed to mention it to Emily. She looked like she had been put through the wringer during her meeting with the chief, and Abe felt enough was enough for one night. Emily had decided to stay with her mother and fill her in on the truth concerning her absence. "I swore I'd never lie to Mom again," she had said. "And, I don't want anything upsetting Raven. Go on, and take her to your house tonight, and I'll come over tomorrow to bring her back. I'll fill you in on what the chief said then." Abe had agreed.

The following day, Emily joined Abe and Raven as they followed a deer trail that led through a wooded area down to a shallow pool on the Animas River's edge. A pair of ravens swooped overhead, gracefully riding the wind currents in a game of tag. As they cackled and cawed to one another, diving and soaring, Raven called back, mimicking their sounds and skipped ahead, spreading her arms as if in flight with the birds. Patch scampered on his three legs behind her, trying his best to keep up.

"She should have been born with wings," Emily said with a smile.

Abe draped his arm over Emily's shoulder and matched her grin with one of his own. "But then she might fly off and leave us. Best we keep her wings clipped for a while." He cocked his head and caught her eye. "Want to tell me about your meeting? You've been pretty quiet."

Emily paused before speaking. "Todechine wanted to put Martinez on probation. The kid caught the bulk of the chief's wrath. I managed to talk him into giving Martinez another chance—reminded him it was his idea to let the rookie work undercover and said I would be responsible for whatever he did from now on. He'll be riding with me tomorrow when we go back to Window Rock to track down some council delegates."

Abe nodded. "What about your two sidekicks?"

"They tried to make it look like I bungled the entire thing with Keetso and let him get away. I talked to Todechine alone after they left and told him what I thought."

"In my opinion, those two are a couple of assholes. What do you think, Em?"

"They've always been assholes, and I don't know what's up with Gomez firing his gun." Emily paused to examine some tracks on the trail. "Coyote," she said, "but they're old."

Abe knew from experience that if the coyote had crossed their trail recently, they would have to turn around. Navajo tradition deemed that if you did not turn back, something terrible would happen to you. Evidently, Emily felt it was safe enough to move on.

"I guess I think Keetso's intentions are good," Emily said, returning to Abe's question. "But I want to know more about what he's up to and why he thinks some people are out to get him. I'm curious about the tribal delegate he mentioned and where the different council members stand on the uranium mining proposition. I'll try to find out which members represent the chapters involved in the proposal."

This was the opening when Abe should have told Emily about the phone number. He didn't know why the hell he still hesitated. He started to speak, but before he could get the words out of his mouth, Raven let out a squeal and tumbled to the ground. Emily rushed to her side, and though it was no more than a scuffed knee, the opportunity to mention the piece of paper had come and gone. He lifted his daughter onto his shoulders, and they turned for home and a Snoopy Band-Aid.

Will was waiting in front of the house, seated on his vintage Indian Chief Black Hawk motorcycle. He had brought a container of grilled mutton and fresh tortillas to share as well as a lot of questions concerning their mysterious absence.

Abe lifted Raven from his shoulders and shooed her into the house to get a washcloth for her scratch.

While Raven was inside, Emily told Will as much as she was willing to, then asked how things were going with Leonard Nakai.

"Well, he showed up at the sweat lodge," said Will, "and I performed a healing ceremony. He's coming again the day after tomorrow, and we'll continue with the cleansings and songs to give him strength. He brought his son with him, young Mike. Or, rather, Mike drove him over. Leonard had been drinking. It will take some time for that man to remove the demons and walk in peace once again."

Abe nodded. He recalled that it had taken some time for Will to cleanse himself of his demons, and even then, the temptation of backsliding was ever-present. "How's his kid holding up?"

Will sighed heavily and cast his eyes down. "I didn't come here just to share some fresh mutton. I have something to tell you. Mike has been carrying a heavy load on his conscience— a secret he could no longer keep to himself."

Emily and Abe looked intently at Will, waiting for him to continue.

"Mike Nakai knows who shot the EPA guy," said Will.

"Who? And how does he know?" said Emily.

Will gazed toward the river then looked into his sister's eyes. "Because he's the one that fired the shot."

Raven's appearance in the doorway broke the stunned silence.

"Dad, I need a Band-Aid, she whimpered."

"Right, sweetheart. Let's look at that knee and see if we have any Scooby Doo or Snoopy Band-Aids. Will, come on in the house and bring that good-smelling grub with you. There's coffee in the pot. Pour yourself a cup, and I'll join you in a minute."

"Something for my princess, first," said Will, reaching into his saddle-bag. He extracted a beautiful tail feather and handed it to Raven. "See this red hawk feather? It has special powers. When you face the east and shake this feather as an offering to our creators, it will help you know and understand your dreams, and it will show you how to recognize those gifts that come as you grow. *Awéé*. Put it in a safe place."

Raven clasped the feather in her hand and gently ran her finger across its length. "Thank you, Uncle," she said and blew Will a kiss before Abe picked her up and carried her into the bathroom. When they returned, Raven smiled at her uncle and showed him her bandaged knee. Abe grabbed a mug for himself, poured a glass of milk for Raven, and the two of them joined Will and Emily at the table.

Emily preferred that her daughter not overhear this conversation, so she prepared Raven a plate and told her she could sit on the rug by the stove and read a book while she ate her dinner. Once she had settled the child, Emily rejoined the men.

"Now, what's this about Mike Nakai. He's old-man Nakai's grandson, right. Wasn't it his grandad's sheep that were poisoned?" said Abe.

Will blew on his coffee, took a sip. "Yeah, and everyone thought it might have been Leonard, Mike's dad, that shot that EPA agent. But Mike told me what happened."

"Well, out with it, Will," Emily said impatiently.

After helping himself to some tortillas and roasted lamb, Will made a sandwich and took a big bite. He kept his audience waiting while he chewed. "Man, that's good. A gift for a protection way ceremony I performed in Shiprock."

Abe and Emily gaped at him while he slowly chewed and savored his bite of lamb and tortilla.

"Will," Abe said.

Using the back of his hand, Will wiped grease from his mouth and swallowed a slug of coffee. "Mike saw that EPA man put something in the water. The next day, he discovered the dead sheep. When he was checking them out, he heard this guy coming up on the watering hole and hid behind some boulders. Mike had been hunting rabbits and had his dad's gun with him. As he watched, the man walked around the sheep, kicked a few, and smiled. Mike heard him say, 'success,' and rage consumed the kid, I guess. He knew how much his grandfather loved the sheep. He sighted the guy in and took a shot. He could have killed him if he was trying."

"You're sure he did it? I'll have to put a warrant out for his arrest," said Emily.

"He's gonna turn himself in tomorrow morning," Will said. "Let him do this."

Abe wondered aloud, "What about the gun? He pretended to look for it, didn't he?"

"Why don't you two get something to eat before it gets cold?" said Will. "Then I'll tell you the rest of the story."

When Will seemed satisfied he wasn't going to eat alone, he continued. "Mike's dad happened to be standing on the top of the hill when he heard the shot. He realized what Mike had done, so later that evening, he took the gun into town to get rid of it. That's why he sold it to Malcolm Keetso's boys. Leonard wanted to protect his kid, not just get drunk, though that is what he ended up doing."

"So, why are they coming clean now?" Emily said. "We're going to have to arrest both of them."

"Leonard knows that. Conscience, I guess. He wants to get clean, and feels like being in jail is the only way that's going to happen. Mike wants something out of this, too."

"He's trying to cut some deal?" said Emily.

"No, he wants to be my apprentice, to learn the prayers and songs of the holy ones. I told him, if he turns himself in, I would come to the jail every day and teach him. I think he has the makings of a *hataalii*." Will took another big bite of his tortilla sandwich. "Are you two gonna eat or stare at me with your mouths open."

# 15

The next morning while driving to headquarters, Emily mulled over the facts she had learned concerning her case. What had started out as a poisoned waterhole and a random shooting incident now had overtones of something far more sinister. Emily did not believe in coincidences, and this case had more than its share. Strathmore Minerals was intent on re-initiating uranium mining on the reservation. The EPA employee who had been shot by Mike Nakai was moonlighting for Strathmore. Bobby Grayfeather had recently been fired by Strathmore Minerals and had experienced a possible attempt on his life. Leonard Nakai had sold the gun used in shooting the EPA agent to members of the *Diné* Freedom Fighters, who in turn appeared to have rescued Bobby Grayfeather. Leonard had also recently received a gift from a tribal council member for some un-named work he had done for them. Malcolm Keetso and his men were opposed to uranium mining and were convinced people in power were out to get them.

Giving in to Will's request, she had not sought an arrest warrant for Mike Nakai. Now she wondered if she had made a mistake—if the kid would actually turn himself in or make a run for it. Leonard was an accomplice. He would be back behind bars as well. Emily blew out a whoosh of air. She would have to bring Steve Sanford, the EPA agent, in for further questioning, and if forensics had identified the cause of death in the sheep, possibly arrest him. She needed more information about the uncooperative Ernest Whittington, manager of Strathmore Minerals, and his involvement in the poisoning of the waterhole.

Emily wanted to question Bobby Grayfeather, if he was up to it, to learn why Strathmore Minerals had fired him. On top of all this, she and Martinez needed to make another trip to Window Rock to meet with the chairperson of the Resource and Development Committee, and in the process, learn which Navajo Nation Council members were for and which were against uranium mining. She knew that council members would not be in Window Rock unless they were in session, but if necessary, she would go to their homes. Emily also had more questions for Malcolm Keetso but had no knowledge of his whereabouts. First of all, everything had to be laid out to Chief Todechine. That in itself was challenging enough. She parked her unit and headed for the Chief's office, her jaw set in grim determination.

Monday workdays were slow for Abe. He left home early for his office in the College Music Department, checked his emails, and updated his correspondence. He had a voice-training class and one for beginning piano students in the morning. The afternoon was given over to office hours. The slip of paper Malcolm Keetso left in his truck was burning a hole in his shirt pocket. As soon as Abe finished his classes, he dialed the number.

"Who is this?" answered a young-sounding female voice.

"Abe Freeman. Someone left this number in my truck."

"Right. Can you tune pianos?"

Abe paused. If he agreed to do what he felt the woman was going to ask him, he would have to borrow a tuning kit from the music department. "Yes, if I have the proper tools."

"Can you get your hands on some?" said the woman.

"Possibly," said Abe. "When?"

"Today."

Abe hesitated. He would have to attend his morning classes, then put a sign on his office door asking students to reschedule their appointments. *That shouldn't be a problem*, he thought. *Keeping this from Emily is the problem.* Curiosity and his love for music won over. He sighed. "Okay. I'm free this afternoon. Where do I go?"

"Someone will pick you up. Be in front of the college library at 2 o'clock. Bring your tools with you."

"Okay, Miss. How will I identify you?"

"Don't worry about it. I know who you are."

The tuning kit was in the locked storeroom in a black case. It included a tuning hammer, all the mutes, a mute clamp, and a temperament strip. The kit would fit in his backpack. *Why do I feel so guilty?* He knew why. He had failed to mention Keetso's number to Emily, and he was going to take something that didn't belong to him without permission. Furthermore, he was going to help someone who had held him and three police officers at gunpoint and against their will. *I'm borrowing, and I'll return it before anyone even knows it's missing,* he told himself as he retrieved the key to the storeroom.

In his mind, Abe justified his actions. He held no fear for his safety and felt satisfied that Keetso and his men were not dangerous, though he knew Emily would disagree with his actions. *She'll be mad as hell if she finds out, but I'm not interfering in police business. It's about the music.*

*First things first,* Emily decided when she reached her desk. She nodded to Martinez then rapped on Chief Todechine's office door, letting herself inside before he had a chance to respond.

Todechine looked up from his desk, a telephone receiver held to his ear, and a scowl darkening his round face. "What's so important you had to interrupt me in the middle of a call, Etcitty?" he said as he placed his hand over the receiver.

"Sorry, Chief. I've got some new information concerning the case I'm working on, and it can't wait," Emily said, closing the door behind her. "Martinez and I have a lot to cover today, and I wanted to fill you in before we get started."

After Todechine had hung up, Emily explained that Mike Nakai and his father would be turning themselves in for the shooting of the EPA agent and that she needed to have Steve Sanford brought in for further questioning. She had the police chief's attention. He rubbed the back of his neck, then squinched his eyes and looked at Emily. "How do you know this about the Nakais?"

"They confessed."

"Why didn't you bring them in right away?"

That was one of the questions Emily was dreading. "They needed to make arrangements for old man Nakai, and they gave me their word."

"Their word?"

"Yes, sir."

The meeting was interrupted by another knock on the door.

"Whadda ya want?" Todechine bellowed.

"Sir," said Martinez, poking his head in the door. "Leonard and Mike Nakai are here. They say it's about the shooting of that EPA guy."

The chief looked at Emily. "I'll have Gomez and Talltree take their statement, and I'll send them out to pick up Sanford."

Emily shook her head. "Get someone else, Chief."

"What?"

"I've got a bad feeling about those two."

"Do you have something you want to tell me?"

"Nothing concrete, but they've both got their asses in a sling as far as working with me is concerned. I'm requesting you remove them from this case and assign someone else, like Begaye and Gillmore, to take the Nakai's statements. Or, Martinez and I will do the intake before we leave."

"Where are you headed, Sergeant?"

"To start with, I need to track down some council members and a Mining Company Manager, Chief. Like I said, Martinez and I have a lot on our plates."

Todechine scratched his ear. "Maybe you have too much. I can assign someone else to this case, give you a break."

"No, Chief. No way. I've invested too much time and effort. Why would you even suggest that?"

Drumming his fingers on the desk, Todechine said, "just looking out for your interest, being a mother, I thought you might want more time with your kid. This case has got you tied up."

"I can handle it."

The chief closed his eyes and rubbed his forehead as if he felt a migraine coming on. "Okay, Emily. I'll assign Begaye and Gillmore to do the intake interview on the Nakais. When you get back, I want you to fill me in on why you don't trust Gomez and Talltree."

"Yes, sir." On her way out of the office, Emily paused and turned back to Todechine. "One more thing, Chief. Do you think you can get Forensics to speed things up? If Steve Sanford did put something in that waterhole, I want to know what it was."

Highway 371 wasn't well maintained, and you had to keep an eye out for free-range animals, dogs, and pedestrians. But Emily preferred driving this isolated stretch of road over the busier 666. It eliminated having to deal with truck traffic, and it passed through the Bisti Badlands. Emily loved that incredible expanse of strange and colorful eroded rock formations and undulating mounds that ranged in color from vivid red, oranges, browns, and grays. The two-hour drive gave her time to feast her eyes and compose her questions for the Resource Committee, and she wanted to see if any Tribal Council members were currently in Window Rock.

Raymond Martinez had barely made a peep since they started off in Emily's Police-issued Blazer. She figured he still felt chagrined by blowing the undercover assignment, a deduction that he verified when he finally spoke up.

"Sergeant, I just want to say, it will never happen again."

Before she responded, Emily let her gaze linger on an assortment of weirdly formed hoodoos near a small slot canyon. "Let it go, Martinez. I think you learned your lesson; now we need to move on." During the young officer's long silence, Emily had briefed him concerning the recent developments. He had listened attentively, but only nodded in response. She turned off of 371 at the intersection of Indian Service Route 5 and followed it until they had reached the tiny community of Sheep Springs before he asked any questions.

"If we find him, how do we approach Charley Redhorse?"

"Straight to the point. We'll ask him why he hired Leonard Nakai and why he is campaigning for uranium mining on the reservation."

"Do you think that's what it's about, Sergeant?"

"Yes, and I think there's more to it. Someone is getting a pay-off."

In a little over an hour, Emily pulled into the parking lot of the Navajo Nation Council Chambers in Window Rock, Arizona.

A short, bespectacled receptionist with frizzy permed hair informed Emily that Councilman Redhorse was not in his office and that the twenty-four member Tribal Council would not be in session until Friday when they were scheduled to vote on the proposal for resuming uranium mining on the reservation.

Emily had expected this to be a working day for council members and had not called to make an appointment. She clenched her jaw, silently cursing her mistake, then drew in a breath before speaking. "Are any of the councilors around today?"

"Earl Chee came in to do some work. He's chairman of the Resources and Development Committee," the receptionist said.

"He'll do just fine," said Emily. "Please tell Councilman Chee that two Navajo Police Officers would like to speak to him."

Earl Chee, a slight, weathered man, was dressed in blue jeans and ribbon shirt, a bright turquoise color decorated with black and red silk ribbon trim. He stood and offered his hand when Emily and Martinez entered the office. Indicating a pair of worn leather chairs, he sat back down, and with elbows resting on the oak desk, fingers interlaced, said, "What can I do for you, officers?"

Emily took notice of the dark circles under Chee's eyes, the half-full tumbler of an amber-colored liquid, the sweet smell of whiskey, the scattering of papers on the desktop.

"It's not officially a workday for me," said Chee, taking a sip. "I'd offer you something, but I see you're in uniform, so you must be here on official business."

After introducing Martinez and herself, Emily got to the point. "My partner and I have a few questions concerning Strathmore Minerals bid to conduct uranium mining on the reservation. What is the status of their request?"

"The council will have the final vote on Friday," said Chee. "Initially, it ended in a tie with twelve men for and twelve against the proposal, but since that time there has been some heavy campaigning on the part of both sides of the argument. Three members have abstained, and I have the tie-breaking vote."

"How do you stand on this issue, sir?" Martinez asked.

"Naturally, I'm opposed. It would be a catastrophe for the *Diné*. We already have many people without potable drinking water and lingering diseases from drinking contaminated water." He leaned forward. "Water is life here on the reservation, and you know that."

"Yes, sir," said Martinez.

"Who is leading the fight for the mining company?" Emily asked.

Chee screwed his mouth up and spit the words out, "Charley Redhorse."

Martinez asked the councilman the location of the proposed mining operation.

"Charley's district, of course," said Chee. "Nenahnezad."

Emily's eyebrows raised. "One more question, and we won't take any more of your time, sir. Has anyone offered you money to sway your vote one way or the other?"

"Yeah, Whittington tried. I told him where to stuff it," said Chee then picked up the tumbler and downed his drink.

Before leaving the Council Chambers, Emily and Martinez got directions to the home of Charley Redhorse.

# 16

At precisely 2 p.m., a black Jeep Cherokee with tinted windows stopped at the curb in front of the library. A hand emerged from the passenger-side window and beckoned to Abe. As soon as he neared the vehicle, the back door swung open, and a male voice told him to get inside and crouch down on the seat so no one would see him. The door slammed shut, and they took off.

"Stay there until I say," said the male voice from the front seat. "Did you bring the tools?"

"Yeah," Abe mumbled to the back of a pony-tailed head. "Where are we going?" Tinted windows had made it nearly impossible for him to see either the driver or the passenger when he had approached the vehicle.

"It's best you don't know," said a female voice from the driver's side.

Abe recognized the voice as the same person he had spoken with on the phone, and now he was able to put a face with it. She was a student in one of his classes—a young Navajo woman who asked more questions than most and scored high on tests.

"I know you," said Abe. "You're in my music history class. Annie Lightfinger?"

His declaration elicited no response from the driver, but the man spoke up. "You can sit up when we get away from town, but you gotta put this over your head." He turned slightly in his seat and passed a black cloth sack to Abe. "I'll let you know when it's safe."

Abe could make out the profile of a young man with high cheekbones and a straight nose, but the face was no one he recognized. "Why all the secrecy? I'm not going with you so I can turn you in."

"It's for your protection and ours. What you don't know, you can't talk about." said the man. "You can sit up now," he added several minutes later. "Keep that sack pulled down over your head. And remember, when we bring you back, you never saw us before in your life."

Abe rode in silence and darkness for what seemed like well over two hours  The road changed from straight to a twisting route with undulating hills, then into something that didn't feel like a road at all as the truck bounced over rough terrain. When they eventually stopped and told him he could remove the sack, he found himself in another camp, nearly identical to Keetso's last outpost, but this time set in a steep-sided canyon. The bottom of the canyon was a grassy meadow with clumps of willow trees and a narrow meandering stream—an idyllic-appearing oasis in the arid semi-desert.

*How could this place exist?* Abe thought as the pair led him into Malcolm Keetso's spacious tent. It had been set up similarly as before with bookshelves, posters, and piano. The clickety-clack of an ancient typewriter came to a halt when Keetso looked up and saw Abe.

"Thanks for coming," said Keetso, shaking Abe's hand as if they were old friends. "My piano's in bad shape, and my wife has been complaining about the terrible noise I make when I try to play. Do you think you can fix it?"

"I can try," said Abe. "No guarantees. It depends on how much damage occurred with all the moving around. How'd you find a place like this?"

"I've known about it since I was a kid. It was a little rough getting in with all our gear, but we managed. Are you sure no one followed you?" he said to the pony-tailed man.

"Positive," the man said. "Let me know when you want Annie and me to take him back."

Keetso nodded, then turned to face Abe. "I know you need to get back as quickly as possible, so why don't you get started. I'll pay you for your time. I need to finish some work here, so don't let me disturb you."

"Sorry, but I need quiet while I'm tuning. I can't hear the octave if there's any other noise going on. And light—gotta have better light than that kerosene lantern." Abe retrieved the tuning kit from his backpack, then propped open the lid of the piano exposing the wires and pins. "Can your work wait?" Abe couldn't help thinking how ludicrous it felt to be in this secret place talking about piano-tuning with a man wanted by the police.

"Give me five minutes, I'll finish this paper, then, I'll get you a high-powered flashlight."

Abe nodded and craned his neck to gaze at the paper in the old Underwood carriage. From what he could read, it looked like a call for a protest march to the Navajo Nation Council Chamber to oppose uranium mining. There was a date, but he couldn't make it out. Trying not to look obvious, Abe leaned in closer and read that the demonstration was scheduled for Friday, October 30. *The day before Halloween.*

Keetso chuckled. "Curiosity got the best of you? I'm not trying to keep this movement a secret anymore. When Annie and George take you back to the college, they'll bring this paper and make enough copies to spread to every family on the reservation. All the politicians in Window Rock will hear the voice of the *Diné*, and they'll know that we will not tolerate another assault on our land and people with this fiasco of uranium mining."

"What about you?" Abe asked. "Aren't you afraid of being arrested?"

"Afraid? No. I've been called to lead my people in a just cause. They can throw me in jail, but on what grounds? I've harmed no one, and this will be a peaceful demonstration."

"You held three officers of the law at gunpoint and against their will. I think that's reason enough."

"And then I let them go, unharmed. Your girlfriend said there would be no charges filed. Part of the deal." He pulled the paper out of the typewriter and placed it on the desk. "I'll get that light."

Charley Redhorse represented and lived in the Nenahnezad Chapter of the Navajo Reservation, the area where Abe had stumbled into the Nakai's dead sheep. Emily made the two-and-a-half-hour drive back from Window Rock over the same highway she and Martinez had previously traveled, then on to Redhorse's home. The house perched at the end of a graded and graveled road in a rural area where all other roadways were dirt. A cottonwood-lined circular driveway brought Emily and Martinez to the front entrance of the sprawling adobe home.

"It's gotta take a lot of water to make all this green," Martinez said. As his eyes swept over the manicured lawn and flower beds, the automatic sprinklers turned on.

"Humph," Emily snorted. The site seemed ludicrous sitting in the midst of the barren and water-rationed Nenahnezad division of the rez."I wonder where all that water comes from." She knew that half the Reservation residents lacked even basic plumbing and that forty percent were without electricity. She leaned her hand on the doorbell, already disliking this council delegate.

A young Navajo woman—heavily made-up, tight jeans, shirt unbuttoned revealing ample cleavage, cigarette dangling from painted lips—opened the door. "Yeah," she said, blowing a cloud of smoke at the visitors.

"We're looking for Charley Redhorse." Emily thought the little floozy-looking thing must be his daughter.

"Charley," the woman yelled. "You got company." She took off toward a BMW parked in front of the four-car garage, leaving Emily and Martinez standing on the front porch.

A moment later a paunchy bandy-legged man, twice the age of the young woman, appeared in the doorway. He walked with a noticeable limp. "Denise," he yelled. "Where the hell do you think you're going?"

"To town, old man, to have a little fun." The BMW started up with a roar, threw up some gravel, and sped away.

Only then did Redhorse acknowledge his guests. "You'll have to excuse my wife. She gets restless being cooped up in the house all the time. What brings out here, officers?"

"We're looking for information concerning the uranium mining proposal," Emily said. "Do you mind if we come in for a few minutes? It might be more comfortable if we can sit down and talk."

Redhorse showed Emily and Martinez into a large living room. The interior of the house was decorated in tasteless opulence but hadn't seen a good cleaning for a long time. Overflowing ashtrays, dirty glasses, and magazines cluttered tabletops and spilled over onto the Persian carpet. Emily pushed a pile of newspapers to the side and sat down on the black leather couch while Martinez perched on the edge of an uncomfortable-looking Victorian chair.

Redhorse sighed heavily. Before either Emily or Martinez could ask a question, he said, "This mine will bring jobs to the reservation. That's what the people need."

"Councilman Redhorse," said Martinez. "Did you hire Leonard Nakai to do some work for you?"

Redhorse paused, then said, "Never heard of him."

\* \* \*

"This is going to take a while," Abe said as he placed mutes on the strings adjacent to the center wire. He pressed the corresponding key, listened, tightened the pin with the hammer, and tapped again. While Keetso held the light, Abe repeated the procedure, starting from the middle keys and working to the outside, tightening each wire until he was satisfied every note sounded right.

Three hours later, Abe stood up and rubbed the back of his neck. "I think that's it." When Keetso reached into his wallet and held out five twenties, Abe shook his head. "No, that's for not harming my girlfriend and me, and for taking care of that kid, Bobby. Just get me back to to the college."

Before he left, Keetso shook Abe's hand once again, then instructed Annie to make five-hundred copies of the flyer initially and more as needed. Other students he had recruited into the *Diné* Freedom Fighters would distribute them.

"Use different copy machines on the campus, so you don't arouse suspicion," he had told his volunteers.

Night had fallen while Abe worked on the piano, a moonless pitch-black night, so Annie and George saw no reason to place the sack over his head on the return trip. Besides, he couldn't make out anything through the tinted windows, so he closed his eyes and tried to rest, relieved that Emily wasn't coming to his house tonight so he wouldn't have to explain why he was so late. *I'll come clean tomorrow*, he told himself. *Once I figure out a way to explain things.*

Annie dropped Abe off in front of the music department, and he hurried inside to return the piano tuning kit before heading home. Once in the truck, he turned on the ignition and heaved a sigh of relief. The day had gone without a hitch and with no one the wiser. He was on the highway when he noticed the flashing blue lights behind him. Abe pulled over, thinking the cops wanted to pass and felt surprised when the Navajo Nation Police vehicle stopped behind him.

"Hey, I know you," Abe said when Officer Talltree peered in the window. "What's up?" His first fear was that something had happened to Emily.

"Your driver's license and registration," said Talltree.

"What's the matter? What'd I do?" He knew he hadn't been speeding. Abe reached in the glove department for his papers.

"Keep your hands in sight," the officer said.

"I was getting my registration. What the hell's going on?

"Step out of the truck," said Talltree.

"I want to know what I did wrong."

"Gomez," Talltree yelled. "I need some assistance here." To Abe, he said, "Are you going to cooperate, Freeman, or do we have to put you under arrest?"

Abe felt the heat rise in his face then heard the sound of shattering glass. "What the fuck?"

"Yep, broken taillight," said Gomez as he joined his partner. A police baton swung from his right hand. "Looks like two of them are busted."

"You broke them, goddamnit," Abe said.

"Did you see me break anything?" Gomez said to his partner.

"Nope."

Abe tried to keep his voice calm while white-hot anger burned his gut. He wondered if they might have been following him after all. "Why are you doing this? What do you want from me?"

Talltree sneered. "Where were you today? You weren't in your office all afternoon. We dropped by to pay a courtesy call."

"I bet he was out making music with that faggot, Keetso. You two hit it off, didn't you? Now you're old buddies," said Gomez. He stepped up close enough for Abe to smell his sour breath. "You know where he's hiding?"

*So, that's what this is about,* Abe thought. "I don't know anything about Keetso, or have any idea where he is, and where I go in the afternoon is my business."

"I bet that girlfriend of yours, Sergeant Etcitty, would be curious about where you were today," said Talltree.

No longer able to contain his anger, Abe narrowed his eyes and stared into Talltree's face. "Go to hell. Both of you."

Gomez hitched up his pants and chuckled. "What do you say, Talltree. Should we write up a citation or let it go with a warning this time?"

"Maybe we should go easy. We'll just let the sergeant know that she needs to keep a closer eye on her boyfriend."

The two turned and walked back to their vehicle. Before getting in, Gomez yelled, "Hey, Freeman, that little girl of yours—she sure is a pretty thing. I'd hate to leave a little girl like that alone. Something could happen."

Abe gripped the steering wheel with shaking hands as he drove home. His fury at Gomez for the disguised threat to his daughter had his blood pounding. When he got home, he rushed into the house and called Emily.

# 17

"Abe, it's past ten. Why are you calling so late?" It had been a long hard day at work, and Emily had gone to bed early. Having been awakened from a sound sleep, she was not in the best of moods. "What's wrong?"

"Where's Raven?" Abe said, his voice sounding solemn.

"She's in her bed, asleep, of course, as everyone should be at this time of night. What's the matter with you?"

"I have to talk to you about something important, Emily."

"Well, go ahead. I'm listening."

"No, not on the telephone. Come over here."

"Abe, I'm in my pajamas. I'm exhausted, and I was sound asleep. What's so important it can't wait until morning? And why can't you come over here?"

"Sorry, Em. I don't want your mom to hear what I have to say. It's best if you come to my place, and I'll explain everything."

The line went dead before she could offer any further resistance. The digital alarm clock by her bed flashed 10:15. *Shit. I'm going to have to wake mom.* She hastily pulled on a pair of jeans and a sweatshirt, peeked in at her sleeping daughter, and shook her mother's shoulder.

"Mom. I have to go out for a while. Business. I'll be back soon." Something in Abe's voice when he had asked about Raven, made her pause. She looked down at her sleepy-eyed mother. "Would you make sure the doors are locked when I leave and keep an eye on Raven?" Her daughter was curled in a fetal position still clutching her favorite stuffed toy, her raven. "In fact, I'd feel better if you stayed in her room until I come home."

Abe's face, when he met her at the door, was a road map of emotions—brow furrowed in worry lines, mouth pursed, and shaded blue eyes that avoided her penetrating black stare.

"What happened?" Emily said.

"Sit down. Want some coffee?"

"No, just tell me what's so urgent."

He related what had transpired between him and the two cops, how Gomez had broken his tail lights and the subtlety disguised threat concerning Raven. As Abe spoke, his voice sounded increasingly more agitated.

"Sons of bitches. I'll report this, write them up. But why are they harassing you?"

"There's more, I went out to see Keetso this afternoon."

"What?"

"He left his phone number in my truck—said he needed his piano tuned. I decided to go, and two students from the college took me to his camp."

Emily stared open-mouthed, her breathing becoming more rapid as she realized Abe had betrayed her. "You kept this from me. You know where he is, and you didn't tell me. Damn you, Abe."

"Emily, please, I have no idea where his camp is. They put a bag over my head on the way there. I couldn't tell anyone where it is, and I don't care about Keetso or his group. But he didn't harm us in any way. In fact, he probably saved Bobby Grayfeather's life. It was about the music. I tuned his piano; that's all. It took several hours, and I was away from my office all afternoon. Talltree and Gomez were checking up on me, saw that I was gone but my truck still there. They must have asked if anyone knew where I was then waited by my truck for a long time. When I still hadn't returned after a few hours, they decided I had gone to see Keetso, and they wanted me to tell them how to get to his camp. I wouldn't, even if I could."

Abe had talked fast, not giving Emily an opportunity to break in and vent her anger. When he saw her lip quiver, he took a deep breath. "I'm sorry, Em. I didn't do this to hurt you or betray you. But when Gomez mentioned our little girl, I knew I had to tell you what happened."

Still seething at Abe, but even more so at Gomez and Talltree, Emily said, "What exactly did Gomez say about Raven?"

After Abe had relayed the officer's exact words, Emily's face darkened. If Gomez had been around at that moment, she would have ripped his eyes out. "I'll take care of them," she hissed. "No one is going to threaten my little girl and get away with it."

"*Our* little girl, Emily. I don't know what I would have done if I'd had a gun on me."

This coming from a man who abhorred guns and violence gave Emily pause. She and Abe were in this together, and though still pissed about his secret meeting with Keetso, she felt some of that anger dissipate, or perhaps redirect itself. "Do you have anything stronger than coffee. I think I could use a drink."

A seldom-used bottle of Jack Daniels sat in the back of a high cabinet waiting for times like this. Abe fetched the bottle and two glasses, added a couple of ice cubes, and poured a generous shot into each. Emily noticed she was shaking when she took the glass. Holding her drink with both hands, she closed her eyes and swallowed a large quaff. Only an occasional drinker, Emily felt the burn of the whiskey as it went down her throat, warming her from the inside out, and calming her nerves. She settled on the couch, took a smaller sip, and patted the cushion beside her. "Sit down, Abe. Start from the beginning and give me the whole story again."

When he had finished talking, and Emily had emptied her glass, she found her anger at Abe overshadowed by rage at the two rogue cops. "I'm taking this to Chief Todechine and calling for an internal investigation. In the meantime, I'm requesting that he put them on unpaid leave. You will have to go in and file a formal complaint, Abe, and the Internal Affairs Unit will want to question you. Tell them everything."

"Everything?"

Her voice took on a sharp edge, and she glared at him. "Yes, even about going to see Keetso."

"Then I'd better tell you one more thing first."

"What? There's more?"

"You would have found this out on your own because it's going to spread all over the rez. Keetso's calling for a massive march on the Navajo Nation Chambers on Friday."

"That's the day of the vote on uranium mining. How do you know about this?"

"I saw the flyer. Keetso's student volunteers are making hundreds of copies and distributing them all over the reservation."

Emily remained quiet while she digested this new information. "I probably would have found out sooner or later, but damn it, Abe. Why is it I learn all this from you after the fact while I worked my butt off all day long and came up with nothing but detours and dead ends?" She pushed her glass toward him. "Pour me another drink. I've had a rough day."

"Okay. But I'll be the designated driver tonight. I'll take you home and stay the night with you and Raven if that's all right. Tomorrow, once Will arrives at your mom's, you can drop me off at home." After he had brought Emily a smaller second drink, Abe sat on the couch beside her and draped his arm over her shoulder. "You look exhausted, sweetheart. Now, tell me about your day."

Emily took a long drink, leaned back and closed her eyes. "If I weren't so worried about Raven, I would stay right here."

She stood and set her glass on the table. "Take me home, Abe, I'll tell you when we get there."

Propped up on pillows, with their daughter sleeping peacefully between them, Emily whispered her account of the day's events to Abe.

"Sanford had been brought in for further questioning, but he clammed up and demanded his lawyer. The attorney happens to be employed by Strathmore Minerals, and he arranged for bail. By the time I returned to headquarters, he had been released and had disappeared from the radar. Bobby Grayfeather still doesn't remember what happened the night of his accident."

"What about the guy from Strathmore Minerals, the manager?" Abe asked.

"'Not available,' the receptionist told me. I asked her if she meant he wasn't around or that he didn't want to talk to me. 'He had an emergency and cannot be reached at this time,'" she said. "And, we couldn't get anything out of Charley Redhorse."

"Well, shit. I see why you're so frustrated. I didn't help much either, did I?" Abe said.

"No, you didn't, Abe. It's a trust issue, and it hurts that you didn't trust me enough to tell me what was going on. This goes back to the moment you found that telephone number on your truck seat."

"I'm sorry, Em. I knew you wouldn't approve—things would get complicated. You don't understand, but it was never

146

about wanting to lie to you, or for that matter, a lack of trust. The man wanted his piano tuned. I couldn't turn him down. It's that simple. Abe chuckled. "You heard how awful it sounded out there at that camp."

A whoosh of air escaped from between Emily's lips. "Abe, you're an idiot."

Abe reached for Emily's hand and squeezed. "I know, but you love me anyway, don't you?"

"Ask me tomorrow," Emily said, between yawns. "That damn whiskey is about to knock me out. We're both idiots. Why didn't you stop me from drinking? Sometimes I think Raven is the only one in this family with any brains." Emily let go of Abe's hand and rolled over on her side. " I swear by all my holy ancestors that I won't let anything bad ever happen to our little girl." A moment later she was asleep, leaving Abe to stare at the ceiling.

# 18

"Do you want me to drop you off at your house and then follow you to the garage? That way no one will harass you about driving with no tail lights," Emily said the following morning as she and Abe climbed into the police SUV. They had just finished escorting Raven to her classroom where they had waited until Will showed up before saying goodbye. Will had promised he would keep a close eye on his niece. The child seemed confused by all the attention and the changes in her usual routine, but Emily, not wanting to worry her daughter, had assured her that everything was just fine.

"That would be great," Abe said. "Then, if you've got the time, maybe you could run me over to the college. I can hitch a ride with someone after work to pick up my truck." Abe tapped his fingers to an unconscious rhythm. Neither he nor Emily had mentioned the previous day's events, and he wanted to know where he stood but didn't know how to start. *Is she still angry? Will she trust him again?* "Or, if you have a little time, maybe you'd like to come in the house, have some coffee, talk things over, kiss and make up," he said with a wistful smile. His hopeful thought was that he could make love to her.

Emily's sideways glance told him that wasn't going to happen today, but he detected a slight curve in the corner of her lips, a softening of her features, and a twinkle in her eyes.

"Abe, I don't have time for commiserating with you right now—I've got work to do. I'll have to take a rain check."

When she smiled and squeezed his hand, he took it as a positive sign. "I know, sweetheart. Just a little wishful thinking."

After the repairs on Abe's truck had been arranged, Emily drove him to the Music Department of San Juan College. "Come over to the house after work," she said before pulling away. "You could take Raven and me out for pizza or something. And maybe we could spend a little time together afterward."

*Abe is about to find out that forgiveness comes with a price,* Emily thought. To get back on her right side, he would have to figure out a way to take her to Keetso's new headquarters. One of the reasons she had been so angry was that she wanted an opportunity to talk to Malcolm Keetso. It wasn't because she thought he was a threat, but rather that he had some knowledge that could help with the investigation. Curiosity concerning Chipeta Longtooth was another motive. *What had happened to the woman in the six years since she had doctored my broken leg then disappeared never to be seen again? How had she ended up with the Diné Freedom fighters?* Emily glanced at her watch. She'd have to hurry if she wanted to get to work on time to inform Chief Todechine about the actions of Gomez and Talltree. She needed to convince the chief that an internal investigation of those two was imperative, and the sooner, the better. Halfway to headquarters, her radio blared an emergency message.

Someone had made an attempt on Bobby Grayfeather's life. Emily switched on the siren, the flashing blue panel lights, and whipped a U-turn. Bobby was receiving care at the San Juan Regional Health Center in Farmington, a twenty-minute drive from her location.

"Code three, I'm en route," she responded to dispatch. "Is the suspect on the hospital premises?"

"Unknown," answered dispatch.

Farmington was not on reservation land and out of Tribal Police jurisdiction, but in select cases, law enforcement was shared. "Send backup and the CSI team," Emily said as she swerved around a vehicle that had not moved to the side to let her pass. "Dirtbag," she mumbled to the Anglo driving the luxury sedan. Her mind was full of questions. *How did the suspect get past the officer who was supposed to be guarding Bobby's room? Was he hurt in the incident? Who would benefit by killing and thereby silencing Bobby Grayfeather?* A short time later, she screeched to a halt in front of the hospital entrance and bounded through the automatic doors.

A crowd had assembled in the main lobby, and a Farmington Police Officer stood at the door, preventing anyone from leaving.

"Bobby Grayfeather's room number?" Emily said to the city cop.

"Two twenty-four," said the officer.

"Who's with him?"

"Lieutenant Murphy and Sergeant Hale. Oh, and Grayfeather's wife. She was there when the suspect tried to smother the kid."

"Thanks." Rather than wait for the elevator, Emily ran up the stairs and found room 224. She didn't know much about the Farmington Police Officer, Lieutenant Murphy. He was new on the force, but Emily had worked on a couple of cases with Hale. When she reached the doorway, she saw a nurse standing over Bobby, adjusting an oxygen face mask. The young man appeared to be unconscious. His wife, Nina, sat at the side of his bed, clasping his hand and crying softly. Emily tapped lightly on the door to get the policemen's attention.

When they saw her, both men sauntered over to greet her.

"Glad you're here, Etcitty," said Hale. "We can't get much out of the wife. She's pretty upset."

Emily motioned for the men to step outside of the room and spoke in a hushed voice. "What have you got so far?"

"The wife was evidently in the bathroom when someone wearing hospital scrubs and mask came into the room and placed a pillow over Grayfeather's face. When she came out and saw him, she screamed, and the suspect fled the scene," said the lieutenant.

"What's Grayfeather's condition now?"

"About the same, still in a semi-conscious state, in and out of it. It's a good thing his wife came out of that bathroom, or he'd be a goner," said Hale.

"Where's the officer who was supposed to be guarding the door?" Emily asked.

"He's receiving treatment for a blow to the head. He thought the perp was a real doctor, so he let him in. When he turned his back, he got whacked, and the kid's wife discovered him slumped over outside the door."

"Have you got some men canvassing the hospital?" asked Emily.

Sergeant Hale sneered. "What do you think, Etcitty? We're not a couple of rookies. Of course, we do. We're just a little short-handed."

"I've got a unit on the way," said Emily. "I appreciate your help, but I'd like to talk to Bobby's wife alone now if you don't mind. I think she'll feel more at ease."

"She's all yours," said the lieutenant. "We're handing the incident to you. Got other business to take care of."

The nurse finished recording Bobby's blood pressure and oxygen readings then started to remove the pillow and replace it with a clean one.

"Please don't touch anything in the room until our CSI unit has had a chance to gather evidence," Emily said to the nurse. "And save Mr. Grayfeather's gown when you change it as well. One of our men will pick up the discarded clothing after you move him to his new room."

Nina Grayfeather stiffened and jerked her body away when Emily put her hand on her shoulder but appeared to relax when she turned and saw Emily.

"Someone tried to kill Bobby," she whispered.

"But you stopped him. You saved Bobby's life, Nina."

"If I hadn't come out of the bathroom when I did . . . "

"Did you get a look at the man's face?"

"No. He wore a surgical mask. I thought he was the doctor at first; then I saw what he was doing. He had a pillow pressed down over Bobby's face." Her body shuddered as she choked back a sob.

"Tell me what you can, Nina. Was he short or tall, thin or fat? Could you see his eyes or any other distinguishing feature that might help us find this man?"

"Tall, I guess—about Bobby's size, but heavier. I don't know. He had one of those green hospital caps on his head." She paused, a long furrow bisecting her forehead. "I saw his hands pressing down on that pillow. He was wearing gloves, but the sleeves on the scrubs pulled up, and I could see his wrists. His wrists were dark, like Bobby's. His eyes too, they were black."

Emily had been scribbling notes, but stopped and raised her eyebrows. *Could the man who tried to kill Bobby be Navajo?* Before she could pursue that thought, her attention was diverted by the appearance of Raymond Martinez and Officers Begaye and Gillmore.

"We're going to have Bobby transferred to another room, and there'll be two guards at all times. He'll be safe now," she assured Nina. "If you remember anything else, no matter how trivial it seems, notify another officer or me right away."

Nina Grayfeather nodded and whispered, "thank you."

Two nurses arrived with a gurney to transport Bobby, and Emily joined her colleagues in the hallway.

"Sergeant Etcitty," one of the officers said, "Martinez found a discarded gown and rubber gloves in a utility closet."

"They're bagged and tagged," said Martinez."

"Good," said Emily. "Begaye, you and Gillmore secure the crime scene and make sure no one touches anything before CSI arrives. That utility closet too, then question everyone on this floor, all the nurses, doctors, janitors, patients, whoever. I want to know if anyone saw anything that looked suspicious or out of the ordinary. Martinez, stay here and continue the search."

"Yes, ma'am," said the rookie.

"CSI and another unit are on their way, and Farmington Police have already concluded an initial shakedown of the hospital, but I don't want to leave any stones unturned."

"Where are you going, Sergeant?"

"Back to headquarters. I want to see if a couple of our fellow officers showed up on time this morning."

"Are you referring to Officers Gomez and Talltree?" asked Martinez.

"Yes, I am. How'd you know, Martinez."

"Because they weren't at the Huerfano Station when I left. The chief was looking for them."

# 19

Apprehension swept over Emily like a tsunami, clenching the muscles in the pit of her stomach into a knot. She wanted to reach headquarters and talk to Chief Todechine as quickly as possible, but first, she had to call her mother for some reassurance that Raven was all right.

"Where's Raven, Mom? Is Will still at the school?"

"Yes, everything is fine. Will is with Raven. He told her teacher he wanted to sit in the classroom today. What is going on, daughter? Why are you so worried?"

Emily hadn't told her mother the reason for her concern, saying only that there was an escaped prisoner in the area, and that she wanted Will to keep an eye on the kids. "It's nothing, Mom. I guess I'm a little on edge today. Let me know if any problems come up."

Bertha sounded skeptical about her daughter's explanation but didn't question her further. "Of course, Emily."

Back in her vehicle, she pulled onto the highway and radioed headquarters.

"Have Gomez and Talltree shown up for muster?" she said to Sergeant Arviso.

"Gomez just arrived. Talltree called in a while ago that he would be a little late because he was having car trouble. The chief's pissed. We're short-handed as it is with that incident at the hospital."

"I wish I knew what those two are up to," Emily said to herself after she had signed off. Here was yet another coincidence: Talltree and Gomez show up late for work on the same morning that someone makes an attempt on Bobby Grayfeather's life. Nina described the perpetrator as tall, dark-skinned—like Bobby—like Talltree. Emily stepped on the gas pedal, swerved around a slow-moving truck, then turned on the emergency flashers and raced down the highway toward the Huerfano Substation.

Once at headquarters, she didn't bother to knock before bursting through the door into Todechine's office. Heads swiveled, and three sets of eyes pinned her in place.

Emily, ignoring the appraisal from Gomez's slitted eyes and the wolfish stare of Talltree, tried to control her breathing. "I need to talk to you, Chief. It's urgent."

"Can't you see I'm in a meeting, Sergeant Etcitty? Come back later and give me a full report of what's happening at the hospital."

"This can't wait, Chief. It has to be now. I'd like Talltree and Gomez to stay and hear what I have to say."

Chief Todechine rubbed his bald head. "That's interesting because these two officers happened to be discussing you just now. They both contend that you are interfering with an investigation, that you have a conflict of interest concerning your boyfriend, and that he has had more than one liaison with Malcolm Keetso. What do you have to say, Etcitty?"

Emily felt the heat rise in her face. She turned toward Talltree. "Where were you this morning?"

"I've already explained to the chief where I was," said Talltree. "I don't owe you an explanation, Sergeant."

"Why did you and Gomez harass Abe Freeman last night and break the taillights in his truck?"

"We didn't bother nobody," Gomez said. "Me and Talltree were coming back from the Checkerboard yesterday evening, saw this old junker truck driving with broken taillights, so we stopped and gave him a warning. We were doing our job—didn't even give the guy a ticket. Who would have guessed that was your boyfriend, Sergeant? Small world, huh?"

"That's right," said Talltree, echoing his partner's account. "Just some dumb guy driving around without taillights." A slight smirk curled the corners of his mouth. "We turned in an incident report last night, Chief."

A pounding in her head began as Emily's rage reached the boiling point. If she knew anything about Abe, he was the most honest person she had ever met. He didn't lie. He may keep secrets at times, but if he says something happened, it happened. "You know *exactly* who Abe is. We were all at Keetso's camp together." She grabbed Gomez's shirtfront and glared into his pig-like eyes. "Why did you threaten my little girl, asshole?"

Todechine slammed his hand on the desk and bellowed. "Etcitty, Gomez, back off! I'm not putting up with this shit. If this division weren't so short-handed, I'd put you all on a three-day cooling off period—without pay. I've had calls coming in all morning and not enough people to cover them. I need my department to work together. That means you come to work on time and do your job. So, you either put your personal grievances aside or think about handing in your badges and I'll hire some replacements. Gomez and Talltree, you are assigned to the Checkerboard area. Now, get the hell out of here."

Emily glowered at Gomez and Talltree before pivoting and striding out of the room.

"Sergeant Etcitty!"

She stopped in the doorway, without turning or responding to her boss's voice. She couldn't risk the chance that any of those men would see the tears of anger threatening to spill from her eyes.

"I want a full report of the incident at the hospital on my desk within the next thirty minutes," yelled the chief to Emily's back.

Splashing cold water on her face, Emily tried to regain her composure. She took a deep breath and strode from the women's restroom to her desk, sat down at the keyboard and punched out a detailed report including direct quotes from Nina Grayfeather and an accurate description of the crime scene. After listing all the investigative avenues that were being taken, Emily quickly read it over to see if anything had been left out. In less than half an hour, she dropped the summary on Chief Todechine's desk and turned to leave.

"Sit down, Etcitty," Todechine said. His voice sounded tired, his manner more subdued.

Emily perched on the edge of a chair and looked at her boss.

"You've got something you want to tell me, well, let's hear it."

"I know Abe," Emily said in a tight voice. "He doesn't lie. It's not in his nature. I believe everything he said is the absolute truth."

"Then tell me exactly what he said."

After Emily had related her story, Todechine leaned back in his chair and rubbed his chin. "I've assigned someone to tail those two," said the chief. "I've had a bad feeling about them for some time. This is confidential, understand. I didn't want to arouse their suspicions this morning when all three of you were in my office."

"Yes, sir," said Emily, sitting up straighter, feeling a sense of vindication.

"Someone from internal investigations will pay a visit to your boyfriend and document his version of the incident, but I don't want him coming here."

"Yes, sir, I understand. It's a hush-hush operation. I'm sorry I lost my cool, Chief."

He waved her apology aside. "I'll keep Gomez and Talltree out of your way. Be careful out there."

Emily acknowledged to herself that Chief Todechine was smarter than she gave him credit for. "Thank you, sir."

"One more thing. The report came back from forensics. The poison used in the watering hole that killed Nakai's sheep was sodium cyanide."

"Makes sense," Emily said. She knew that this particular chemical combination was extremely toxic. Sodium cyanide blocks off the supply of oxygen and even a minute amount can kill an adult in a matter of minutes. The white powder is hard to see in water, and the stench of dead sheep would have obliterated the faint bitter almond smell of the poison. "Miners use it, don't they?"

"Mostly in gold mining," said the chief, "but it has other uses. So, yeah, a mining operation has access to all sorts of chemicals, including sodium cyanide."

Emily felt the adrenalin kicking in. Things were looking up. She felt relieved that someone was monitoring the actions of Gomez and Talltree and that she might be making headway in this case. "I need a search warrant, Chief. I'm going to pay another visit to Steve Sanford and Strathmore Minerals."

"I'll see about getting a warrant, but Strathmore's offices aren't on Navajo land. Before you start on that, return to the hospital and find out if they've learned anything new, then pick up your partner, that rookie Martinez."

# 20

Abe saw the blinking light on his answering machine when he returned to his office after his first-period class. He pressed the play button and listened to Emily's voice:

"Hey, Abe. I just wanted to give you a heads up. Someone from Internal Affairs will be stopping by to get your statement. I don't know exactly when, but probably not during the lunch hour, so how about I pick you up at twelve, and we get some tacos at Chuey's? We could check if your truck's ready afterward."

"*Hmm*," he said to himself. He wondered what had transpired between Emily and her boss. So, Todechine is moving quickly on this. The lunch date was a surprise. Abe had thought Emily would have wanted to go to the school and eat with Raven. He looked at the wall clock behind his desk. Ten-fifteen. He had a ten-thirty piano class and doubted anyone from internal affairs would show up until after lunch, so he looked up in surprise when he heard the knock on his door.

"Got a few minutes, Mr. Freeman?" said the lanky Navajo man in a  blue western suit. He pulled out his identification shield and said, "I'm Ben Garza with Internal Affairs."

"Sure," said Abe. "I have ten minutes before my next class. Take a seat, Mr. Garza."

The man scribbled notes on a yellow pad while Abe rehashed the previous night's encounter with Gomez and Talltree. The investigator kept his comments to a minimum and let Abe talk rather than asking a lot of questions, but Abe saw his eyebrows rise when he mentioned the perceived threat to Raven.

"What were the officer's exact words?" said the investigator.

Abe felt the flush of anger when he recalled the sneering cop's comment. "The fat one, Gomez, said, 'I'd hate to leave a little girl like that alone. Something could happen.' And it wasn't just what he said, it was the way he said it."

A few questions later, the internal affairs investigator pursed his lips and stood. "Thanks, for your cooperation, Mr. Freeman. I'll be getting back to you once I prepare a statement for you to sign."

Shortly before noon, Emily arrived at Abe's office and found him hunched over a stack of papers. He put his pen down, took off his reading glasses, and flashed her his infectious grin, blue eyes sparkling, crinkling at the corners with his smile.

"Hi," she said.

"Hey, right on time, sweetheart. I just finished grading these tests, and I'm really looking forward to sharing some tacos with you. Sure beats a sub at the Student Union. I'm surprised you got a little free time. I heard about the attempt on Grayfeather's life."

*Naturally, the news media got wind of the story and broadcasted it all over the rez.* "I had a little break in the action and wanted to spend some time with you, that's all. Ready to go?" Her mind churned on how to keep Abe from knowing her real motive, and how best to approach the topic. She wanted to see Keetso and was convinced Abe could find a way to take her there.

Emily and Abe both ordered the combination plate: two chicken tacos, chile rellenos, and cheese enchiladas with refried beans on the side. Sipping tea while they waited for their order, Emily filled Abe in on her meeting with Chief Todechine and told him that Gomez and Talltree would be kept under surveillance.

After dousing his taco with a generous splash of salsa, Abe said, "I'm relieved that someone is keeping an eye on those two, Em, but you could have told me that on the phone. What's the real reason I have the pleasure of your company?"

Emily looked at her watch and decided she might as well get straight to the point. There wasn't much time. She had agreed to pick Martinez up at one. "I want you to take me to Keetso."

Abe held his half-eaten taco midway to his mouth, then put it back on the plate. "I can't do that. I don't know how to get there."

"But you can set it up, Abe. Either you call that number and make arrangements, or I'll do it myself, even if I have to pull some strings and arrest one of your students."

"And what if I say no?"

Emily felt her cheeks burning. "I'll have to subpoena you."

"Come on, Emily. Get serious."

"I am serious. I don't want to arrest Keetso or any of his followers. But, I think he has some critical information about the people involved in this case, and if you don't take me to him, you'll be obstructing the investigation."

"And I guess if I say no, you'll arrest me and tell me not to bother to come over tonight to see my daughter."

"I can't stop you from seeing Raven, but I may not be available."

Emily swallowed hard and averted her eyes to avoid Abe's incredulous look.

"I think I've lost my appetite. I'll pay the tab, and you can take me back to work."

"Abe . . ."

"I'll make the damn call, but I can't guarantee anything."

Emily felt her face flush. Did she actually threaten Abe with repercussions?


Back in his office, Abe slumped in his chair and pushed his papers aside. He couldn't understand why Emily had acted in such a contrary manner, and why she was so intent on seeing Keetso right now. The man would be coming to Window Rock on Friday, and she would have her opportunity. Abe felt a headache coming on, a not so uncommon occurrence since receiving a concussion years ago while attempting to save Will's life. He propped his elbows on the desk and held his head with both hands. Abe knew people considered him naïve, unworldly, and foolish for taking people at face value, but intuition told him Malcolm Keetso was an honorable man, and Abe always trusted his instincts. He sighed, picked up the telephone receiver, and punched in a number.

Emily felt like shit and mentally kicked herself. *Why was I so hard on Abe? What's my real motive in insisting he take me to Keetso? Pride? Arrogance? Jealousy because Abe was there and I wasn't? Do I really want to question Keetso and possibly bring him in?* The answer was no. She was not concerned about Keetso and the *Diné* Freedom Fighters and no longer annoyed at Abe. The truth was, Emily hoped for an encounter with Chipeta Longtooth, the fugitive Ute woman, wanted for murder, who, six years earlier, had discovered Emily lying unconscious with a broken leg. Chipeta had taken Emily to her camp, splinted her leg, and cared for her until Abe and Will had stumbled onto the campsite and rescued her. Chipeta had fled—disappeared off the face of the earth it seemed. The incident had happened seven years ago, and Emily had not heard a single word about the Ute woman since then—until now. *What will I say if and when I meet her?* Emily shook her head. She had to get her mind back on the job. She pulled into the McDonald's parking lot where her young partner, Raymond Martinez, waited out front.

Martinez dropped his Super-Sized paper cup into a trash bin and got into the passenger side of the SUV. "Hey, Sergeant. How was your lunch?" The fact that Emily didn't respond to his question and the distraught look on her face must have given him a clue that things were not so good. He didn't ask again, and Emily did not pull out of the parking lot.

"Hold on a minute. I need to make a phone call." Emily couldn't think about her job, the case she was working on, or anything else. She realized she had made a terrible mistake in pressuring Abe to set up a meeting with Keetso just so she could pursue Chipeta Longtooth. The Ute woman had finally found a place where she was accepted and felt safe, and Emily had been on the verge of destroying everything for her. She inserted the required coins into the pay phone and dialed Abe's number.

"Abe, it's me."

"All right, it's done. I set it up. Tomorrow at four. You got what you wanted."

His cold, detached voice pierced her heart. Emily chewed her lip and choked back a lump in her throat. "Cancel the meeting, Abe. I don't need to go. I don't care about talking to Keetso. I was wrong to insist you do this." She held her breath and listened to the silence on the other end of the line. When Abe finally spoke, his voice had softened.

"It was wrong of me not to tell you about my meeting with Keetso in the first place. Can it be true that two wrongs make a right, Em?"

"Maybe. Two negatives make a positive in Algebra. Why don't we try to figure it out when you pick Raven and me up tonight."

"Okay. I'll call Keetso's contact and tell him we're not coming." Another pause. "Uh, you know I love you, Em."

"I know, Abe. I love you, too. I have to go now—I'll see you later."

Emily got into the patrol vehicle and started the engine. "You asked me about lunch, Martinez. Well, the first course wasn't so great, but it got better. Tell me what you learned at the hospital while we drive back to headquarters to pick up a search warrant."

"Yes, Ma'am. Crime scene investigators are still wrapping up. They've recovered prints from the inside doorknob of the utility closet where the discarded scrubs were found, and they're going to run a DNA analysis on the hair and skin flakes found on Grayfeather's sheets and pillowcase. If the hairs don't match the victim or his wife, they could belong to the perp."

"Or to a nurse, doctor, or custodian," Emily said.

"Forensics are going to examine the inside of the gloves for skin particles. If they get a match there, we could be closer to finding our man."

"The assailant wasn't very smart to leave the gloves behind. He must have been in a hurry."

"One of the custodians I talked to said they saw a man slip out a back door exit. The janitor said he yelled at him that he wasn't supposed to use that door, it was for deliveries, but the man paid no attention."

"Did he get a description?"

"Not much. The witness only caught a brief glimpse of his back. Described him as tall, muscular, wearing a blue ballcap and Levi's with a dark shirt."

"Investigators are checking that door and whatever is outside for prints, right?"

"Yes, Sergeant. They're on it. They've got it taped off, and Begaye is keeping an eye on things. Did Gomez and Talltree show up for work?

"Yeah. Assholes were in the office with Todechine when I got there. Talltree told him some bullshit story about having car trouble. Later, I talked to the chief alone. He's pulling them off the case."

"That's good news. What's the search warrant for?"

"Strathmore Minerals. We're looking for any traces of sodium cyanide, the chemical that was detected in the waterhole where Nakai's dead sheep were found. And, hopefully, we'll find Sanford at home as well."

October was her favorite month. The sky took on a deeper shade of blue, the air turned crisp and clean smelling, and the sun had cast a golden glow over the landscape accentuating the changing colors of trees and grasses. As she drove toward the office of Strathmore Minerals, Emily pictured herself hiking through a wooded area with Abe and Raven. Her idyllic thoughts were interrupted when the patrol car radio crackled to life. A vehicular accident had been reported on Route 666 ten miles north of Twin Lakes. The driver, Earl Chee, was found dead at the scene. The victim smelled of alcohol, and an empty bottle of Johnny Walker whiskey had been found near the body.

Emily, her mouth gaping open, turned to stare at Martinez. "Councilman Earl Chee, the tie-breaking vote."

# 21

Abe puzzled over Emily's change of heart as he prepared to pay the garage bill and waited for his truck to be brought to the front. Hopefully, she would reveal the reason for her sudden reversal about wanting to meet Keetso once he got her alone tonight. He felt the heat rising in his loins as he thought about the conclusion of their argument leading to some soul-scorching love-making. A disagreement resolved with great sex was the way it sometimes went with Emily and him, and he couldn't wait. He was daydreaming about her slender, naked body when the mechanic's voice brought him back to reality.

"Looks like $163 total," said the man. That includes $70 for labor and $80 for parts plus tax."

Abe winced, reached for his wallet and vowed he'd somehow make Gomez and Talltree pay. After settling the bill, he counted his remaining cash—two twenties, a few ones, and some loose change were all that separated him from payday, and it was still a week away. The college didn't pay much, and Abe had put a lot of money into fixing up the old house he had recently purchased near the Animas River. Sighing, Abe twisted the key in the ignition and headed toward the Huerfano

Housing Complex to pick up Raven and Emily. *I still have enough to take my two favorite girls out on the town.*

Emily would be full of chatter about the case she was working on. She had called again and breathlessly told him she may be a little late wrapping things up. The day had been crazy, and news about Earl Chee's death had shaken everyone.

"The timing of the accident is too convenient," Emily had said. "Chee would have had the deciding vote against the mine."

Abe didn't mind waiting—he would have more one-on-one time with his daughter. When he pulled in front of Bertha Etcitty's house, he saw Raven and Will waiting on the porch steps. Reassured his daughter was safe and in good hands, he breathed a sigh of relief.

"Dad, dad!" Raven shouted as she ran to meet him with outstretched arms.

"How's my princess?" Abe said, swooping her up in the air.

"I'm not a princess, Dad, I'm going to be a *hataali*," Raven said. "I'm learning the songs and stories from Uncle Will, and someday I'll be a healer like him and teach everyone how to live in *hózhó*."

Abe chuckled. "Wow! You'll be the best girl *hataali* the *Dinétah* ever saw." He knew that *hózhó* was the most important word in the Navajo language. Its meaning encompassed beauty, order, harmony, humility, and balance. To live in *hózhó* meant you were at one with the world around you. For Abe, that was a noble but unreachable goal. He didn't think it was possible for *him* to reach a state of *hózhó*. Turmoil, either inward or outward, always managed to make its way into his life. He swung Raven down. "Go grab your jacket, Raven. It's going to be chilly tonight."

"Or maybe I'll be a girl warrior and chase all the bad people away," she said before going inside.

Abe sat on the front step beside Will. "How's it going, brother?"

"I'm keeping busy. Got a lot of ceremonies on the weekends. Then, after watching Raven until she gets home from school, I go out to the prison. Mike Nakai is helping me set up a sweat lodge at the jail. There's a lot of men in there suffering from addiction, anger, fear, and a shitload of other stuff. They need a good sweat and someone who will listen to them and teach better ways to deal with their issues."

"Sounds good, Will." Abe thought that after years of struggle with alcoholism, Emily's brother had managed to rediscover his sense of *hózhó*. Even with the constant demands on him as a *hataali,* Will appeared at peace. "The Nakais holding up all right?'

"They're worried about the grandfather. Mike's cousin says the old man isn't doing so well. He's depressed, won't eat, and wanders off like he's still looking for his sheep. Leonard wants to be released so he can take care of his father. Maybe they'll let him out for humanitarian reasons, I don't know, but Mike has to have a trial and do his time." Will paused, letting his eyes linger on the golden sunlight glinting off Huerfano Mountain before speaking again. "What're you up to tonight?"

"I'm taking my girls out for some fancy fast food. Want to come?"

"Nah. I'll stay here and eat with mom and head on out to the prison. Say, who's that guy hanging around the school? I don't recognize him. I was about ready to run him off, but the principal said he was all right."

"I don't know who he is. Could be that guard Emily said Todechine assigned to keep an eye on the school. He put Gomez and Talltree on administrative leave. And someone came by from internal affairs to get a statement from me today," Abe added. "If this new guy is doing his job, you should be relieved of duty, I'm thinking."

Will's rugged face furrowed into wrinkle lines. "Hmm. Funny, I don't remember ever seeing him around. If he's a cop, I should know him. I've had a few run-ins with the Navajo Nation Police myself to be on a first name basis with most of them." He chuckled, then turned serious. " Think I'll stick it out and keep an eye on things.

"Maybe he's private security," Abe said. "He give you any reason for concern?"

"Not really—just asked me what I was doing there."

The crunch of gravel diverted the two men's attention as Emily turned into her parking space in front of her mother's house. "Hey, guys," she said when she got out of her vehicle. "What are you two commiserating about?"

Abe looked at her and smiled. She was so beautiful, just looking at her never failed to leave him weak-kneed. Even when she was angry or tired and overworked, Emily enchanted him. But before he could answer, Raven burst through the front door. "Mom, are you ready to go? I'm so hungry."

"Oh, you're starving are you?" Emily said, tickling her daughter under the chin. "Well, just give me ten minutes to change clothes and wash up, then we'll go. Cheeseburger Deluxe with a strawberry shake and an order of fries for me." She gave both Abe and Will a peck on the cheek before disappearing inside the house.

They ate their burgers and fries in a local park and sat close to each other at a picnic table while Raven played on the swings. The sun hung low on the horizon, casting long shadows and painting a line of clouds in swaths of orange and fuschia before dropping behind a grove of Chinese Elms.

Emily shivered from a burst of chilly wind and Abe wrapped an arm around her, pulling her close. "It's getting cold. We should take our baby home."

"We'll go to my house. I'll make a fire and some hot cocoa for Raven." He watched his little girl pumping her legs to make the swing go higher, wanting to fly. Wisps of curls escaped from her long braid and framed her face. He loved her more than life. "Raven, time to go."

"In a minute dad, I want to go down the slide one more time."

"I made a pig out of myself tonight. Am I getting fat, Abe?"

Abe knew that when Emily felt overwhelmed, she would often turn to food for comfort, then feel remorseful for overindulging. When she was young, alcohol served as assuagement for feelings of frustration, but she had given that up long ago. That's why Abe was surprised when she had asked for the whiskey last night.

"Are you kidding me. You have an utterly beautiful and amazing body. You're working too hard. Let's go home, we can cuddle by the fireplace, and I'll make you feel better."

She smiled. Abe could be so tender. He was right—it had been a rough day. When she and Martinez returned to headquarters, the chief had told her the search warrant hadn't been approved for Strathmore Minerals. "Lack of probable cause," Todechine had said, and that puzzled her. They had the papers to search Sanford's house and plenty of justification. He had been identified as the primary suspect in the waterhole poisoning. But, when she and Martinez had driven to Sanford's, they found the place locked, untouched mail in the box, and newspapers piling up on the porch. They had run down an equally blind alley when they went to Strathmore Minerals hoping to talk to the manager. Ernest Whittington was nowhere on the premises. They lacked legal authority to search the storage shed, and everyone they tried to question clammed up. Except for a truck driver, a young Navajo, they had met on the road going out.

"Hey, man. What're you hauling today?" Martinez had asked.

"Nothing. Already done hauled it," the driver had said. "I'm parking the truck and going to lunch."

"What were you hauling?" Emily asked.

"I don't know. A bunch of unmarked crates."

"Where'd you take them?" Martinez asked.

"To the Farmington Airport—the boss's private plane."

"Whittington's? Was he on the aircraft?" Emily wanted to know.

"Yeah, but he's gone now. His plane took off right after I loaded the crates into the cargo hold. Don't know where he's headed, but I can't say I'm sorry he's gone. That white man's a son of a bitch to work for."

*Why would he leave just before the vote?* Emily wondered. *And where had he gone?*

"Emily, did you hear me?"

"I'm sorry Abe. I was preoccupied. What did you say?"

"Why don't you and Raven spend the night at my place. Raven has plenty of clean clothes there, and I can drive both of you back to Huerfano in the morning before school. I want you to stay, sweetheart. We need some time together—to talk—to make love," he ended with a devilish smile.

She didn't have to think twice before responding. Emily wanted to be with Abe. She needed his arms around her, his touch, his body entwined with hers, his sex. Everything seemed out of balance—nothing made sense. Emily had lost her *hózhó*. She had told Abe everything that had happened today, and he had listened quietly, not interrupting or giving advice, and Emily loved him for that, for letting her talk. She nodded, relieved that he had broken into her thoughts. "Yes, let's go home. Raven can have a cup of cocoa, take a warm bath, and you can read her a story before you tuck her in. Then we 'll have our time. Abe, I'm so sorry about today, about demanding you take me to Keetso. I'm bewildered by this case, and I don't know where to go from here. I have a feeling something isn't right, but I can't put my finger on it. And now that Chee is dead, what's going to happen with the council's vote—and at Keetso's protest march? It could turn violent. People might get hurt."

Emily ran a bath for herself while Abe read to Raven from a child's book of Navajo legends. She dropped in a handful of sage and immersed herself in the steaming water, feeling her muscles begin to loosen and relax. She lathered her hair and body with a blue corn soap infused with herbs and wildflowers she had purposely bought to use at Abe's house. After rinsing and drying her hair, Emily wrapped her body in Abe's terrycloth robe and tiptoed into her daughter's room. Abe looked up at her and closed the book. Raven and Patch were cuddled together, both sound asleep. The sight of her beautiful family nearly brought tears to Emily's eyes.

Abe put the book on a bedside table, stood up, and went to the open doorway where Emily stood. Taking her hand, he pulled her into the hallway and closed the door. Abe wrapped his arms around her and kissed her, then untied the sash on her robe and slid his hands inside, caressing the contours of her back, her breasts, nuzzling her neck. His hands were warm and smooth. He took care of them because of the piano.

"You smell good," Abe said.

Emily pressed her body closer, feeling his erection. "You feel good."

Abe pushed the robe back over her shoulders. "Let's go to bed," he whispered in her ear.

Emily let the robe drop to the floor and took Abe's hand, leading him into the bedroom. She pulled back the down comforter on his bed, glad it was full-sized instead of a queen or king. It meant he was never far away. She could feel the heat of his body, smell his masculinity, hear his breathing. She slipped under the sheet, watching as Abe hastily undressed. His body had remained trim but muscular, his stomach flat, his legs sturdy from a habit of daily hiking.

Abe crawled in beside her and placed his hand on her breast. Emily drew in her breath as he began to kiss her—first her lips, then her neck, her breasts, slowly inching his way lower.

"Yes," she said. "There." She gasped and cried out as she felt herself coming, forgetting for the moment everything except this rush of feeling. But she wasn't finished. She rolled over and crawled on top of Abe, straddling him and feeling his erection throbbing in her body, and she came again. Afterward, feeling spent, she knew that she could sleep. Tomorrow the stress of her job would return, but for now, she was at peace. And so was Abe, she assumed, judging by the slight upturn of his lips and the sounds of his soft snores.

# 22

Emily took a quick shower, pinned up her hair, and dressed for work. She strapped on her ballistic vest, tied her boots, and tucked in her shirt. The transformation became complete when she buckled her utility belt around her waist, but there was still enough mom in her to admonish her daughter to eat all of her breakfast and brush her teeth before Uncle Will walked her to school. Abe had left right away to attend an early morning faculty meeting but had promised to come back in the afternoon.

"I'll grab a bite to eat in town," Emily said to her mom. "I love you guys." She planted a kiss on Raven's head. "Wear your warm coat today. And don't forget a hat and mittens. It feels like snow," she said to her daughter. Before leaving the house, she snagged her heavy police-issue jacket.

Arriving at the station early, a good forty-five minutes before the shift change, Emily parked at a discreet distance and watched as a black Ford Ranger maneuvered into a parking space in front of the Huerfano Substation. Officer Gomez, dressed in blue jeans and a checkered shirt, stepped out of the pickup truck and slowly surveyed the parking lot. Emily ducked down and waited until he went inside the building before leaving her vehicle. Gomez's truck looked new, or like it had recently received a new paint job. Emily recalled that he had driven the same make and model of vehicle in the past, but it had been green. Goaded by curiosity, she decided to make a closer inspection.

The lower part of the truck felt tacky as if the paint had been recently applied. Emily squatted down and examined the undercarriage and saw a small strip of green that had been missed. She ran her hand over the surface and felt a slight crease on the passenger side fender where some quick repair work might have been done. The windows were tinted, but by cupping her hands around her eyes, she was able to look inside. Lying on the passenger seat, was a lug wrench and other tire-changing tools. Emily wondered if Gomez had been in a recent accident.

The front door of the station headquarters swung open, and Gomez stepped out. He checked his wallet, smirked, and started walking toward his vehicle. Emily dropped to her haunches and slipped between two vans until she heard Gomez drive away. *What the hell just happened?* She was also stymied by Abe's description of the Internal Affairs investigator. It didn't match up with anyone she knew in the department. It was still early, and Martinez hadn't arrived yet. She saw the chief's silver SUV and headed for his office.

Todechine stood looking out the window with his back to the door. He jerked his head around when Emily entered.

"Don't you believe in knocking, Etcitty? What're doing here? Your shift doesn't start until eight."

"Sorry if I startled you, Chief. I thought I'd come in and review some of the files before Martinez shows up."

"So, what case are you interested in, Sergeant? Aren't you busy enough with your own?"

"I was hoping to learn some details about the accident that killed Councilman Chee."

Todechine frowned and turned back to the window, not meeting Emily's gaze. "It didn't happen in our district. Window Rock's handling it. The man had a drinking problem. Why are you so interested?"

"I'm curious, Chief. I just talked to Chee the day before his accident. He seemed like someone who could handle his alcohol."

"You met him once and came to that conclusion? Bullshit. Pay attention to your own workload and don't go looking for more trouble."

"Right, Chief. But help me out with something. "Who's conducting the Internal Affairs Investigation of Gomez and Talltree?"

"Some new guy sent up from Albuquerque, and I'm not free to divulge a name. That's the way they want to handle it." Todechine sat down at his desk and shuffled a stack of papers. "I've got a shitload of work to do, Etcitty."

"Sorry, Chief. Oh, by the way. I'm pretty sure I saw Gomez in the parking lot. Kind of strange for him to be here so early in the morning."

Emily saw red creep up Todechine's neck and onto his ears, then his bald head. He glared at her. "Look. Gomez turned in his badge. He's quitting the force. Now, get the hell out of here, Etcitty, so I can do my job."

"Yes, sir. Just one more thing. My brother says he doesn't recognize the plainclothes cop who's keeping an eye on Raven's school."

"Okay, listen. I'm trying to be patient. What's with all these questions?" His face had turned scarlet. "We're fucking shorthanded, and I had to hire from a private security agency so someone could watch your kid. You want a guard or not?"

Emily felt her own temper flare. "I have some concerns, Chief. I have a right to know what's going on."

"And, I told you. If that's all, you're dismissed."

Emily sat down at her desk feeling uneasy about the explanations Todechine had given her. She picked up the phone and punched in the number for the Navajo Police near Albuquerque.

"This is Police Sergeant Emily Etcitty at Huerfano. Can you transfer my call to Sergeant Joe Hosteen?" She waited while her call was being transferred, and thought about the days seven years ago when Hosteen had been her partner. They were both competing for advancement to sergeant at that time, and Joe had beaten her out. But then he had married a school teacher and transferred to Albuquerque. They had occasionally remained in touch over the years, sharing information about cases, and Emily knew she could rely on Hosteen to be straight with her.

"Hey, Emily. Great to hear from you. How're things going out there in the boonies?" said the familiar male voice. "Are you managing to hold it together without my help?"

"I thought I was doing all right until recently, Joe. I'm working on a crazy case, and a couple of cops seem to have gone rogue on me. Do you remember Talltree and Gomez?"

"Yeah, the mean one and the fat one. Never did trust those two."

"I'm curious about the Internal Affairs Officer that was sent out here from your department to investigate them."

"We didn't send anyone from my unit, Emily. What makes you think this person came from Albuquerque?"

"Because that's what Todechine told me."

"He must have been mistaken."

"Yeah, well thanks for the info, Joe. Say hello to the wife and kiddos."

Martinez came in the door with a couple of other officers working the day shift. He poured himself a cup of coffee, and one for Emily then ambled over to her desk. "Why are you staring at the phone, Sergeant?"

"I think I've been lied to, and I can't figure out why. Thanks, Martinez," she said, accepting the steaming mug.

"But, it could have been a mistake." She blew on the hot liquid. It smelled old and burnt.

"I stopped by the hospital," said Martinez. "This morning Grayfeather opened his eyes and appeared to recognize his wife. The doctor wouldn't let me talk to him, but he said if Bobby continues to be responsive, we can pay him a short visit this afternoon. He still has an around-the-clock guard."

"Good. Are you caught up on paperwork?"

"Yes, ma'am. What's on the agenda?"

"I'm going to drive to the airport to check the manifest for Whittington's flight. Then, I know I'm going against the Chief, but I need to know what's going on. We're taking another ride to Window Rock to look at the scene of Councilman Chee's accident and examine the vehicle he was driving. After we get back, we'll question Bobby Grayfeather—see if he can tell us why someone tried to kill him."

Martinez nodded, a thoughtful expression on his face. "Do you think what happened to the Councilman might not have been an accident, Sergeant?"

Emily carried her coffee to the sink and dumped the contents down the drain, washed her cup, and filled it with water. "Too many coincidental accidents, Martinez. Finish that poison, and let's get rolling."

The day had turned cold and blustery with dark clouds building in the west, perfect conditions for the first snowstorm of the season. Emily felt glad she had opted for the warm leather jacket this morning. She looked at Martinez still wearing his light khakis. "You're going to freeze your butt off."

Martinez shrugged as if he were accustomed to being cold.

It was a short detour to the Four Corners Regional Airport a mile west of Farmington. When they found the office of the local Civil Aviation Authority, Emily presented her Navajo Police Badge and told the representative she needed to see yesterday's flight plans submitted by pilots of privately owned aircraft.

"Anyone in particular?" asked the Air Traffic Controller.

"Ernest Whittington," said Martinez.

"Easy," said the controller. "Mr. Whittington's Beechcraft took off for his ranch near Colorado Springs at two o'clock yesterday afternoon. It was the only private flight scheduled. He asked the ground crew to help him load several crates into the cargo bin."

"Did he indicate when he would return?" asked Emily

The controller scratched his head. "Friday morning—that he was expecting some good news and wanted to be on hand to celebrate."

Emily thanked the controller and gave him her card, requesting that he give her a call when he knew Whittington's approximate arrival time.

"Get on the radio, Martinez, and request a background check for Ernest Whittington in Colorado Springs, Emily said when they made their way back to the patrol vehicle. The wind kicked up a mixture of rain and snow, blowing it horizontally across the highway. While Martinez talked to Arviso, Emily turned onto the paved road leading to Window Rock. She knew the alternative route would be washed out and muddy, an inevitable outcome of road conditions on the reservation during inclement weather. The trip would take longer than expected as it was, and they couldn't risk getting stuck. A wave of anxiety swept over her as she switched on the wipers and headlights. She wanted to return home, to make sure Raven was safe while trying to reassure herself that Abe, Will, and her mother would take care of everything. Still, she couldn't shake the uneasiness she had felt since her meeting with Todechine. *Stay focused*, she told herself.

"They're on it, and will get the info back ASAP," Martinez said, breaking into her thoughts. "Jeez, look at that mess out there."

Emily nodded and concentrated on the yellow highway line. Roadside ditches were already overflowing, and oncoming oil trucks blinded her with their lights, showering the windows with muddy slush. "We'll make this a short trip. I want to examine the vehicle Chee was driving, and get back to Farmington with plenty of time to question Bobby Grayfeather."

Chee's totaled Honda Civic had been towed to the Impound Unit at the Window Rock Police Headquarters. Emily asked the desk sergeant if they could review the report covering Councilman Chee's accident. The papers documented the approximate time and location of the collision. The vehicle was traveling at a high rate of speed before impact. Measurement of the skid marks indicated that braking occurred just before contact with a tree. Emily passed the report and photos to Martinez.

"The report states drinking and high speed caused the accident," said Martinez. "Chee's clothing smelled of alcohol, and they found an empty bottle in the wreckage. But, how did they determine that the councilman was drunk? I'm assuming an autopsy was not performed due to family taboos concerning that procedure. Am I correct?"

"That's right," said the sergeant. "Chee was known to be a drinker. Everything points to that as a factor."

"Hmm," Emily said. "Do you mind if my partner and I take a look at the vehicle, Sergeant?"

After receiving permission, an officer unlocked the gate and allowed Emily and Martinez into the fenced-in impoundment area. Snow had turned to icy sleet that had washed the car clean but made their examination miserable. Emily pulled a rain parka out of her storage compartment and handed it to Martinez.

"Here, put this on. Next time, come prepared."

The entire front end of the Civic had crushed in like an accordion due to the impact with a large pine tree. Emily and Martinez made quick, but thorough, work of their inspection. After a few minutes, Emily spotted scuffing of green on the driver's side door. She snapped photos of the wrecked vehicle, concentrating on the slash of paint and corresponding dent.

Martinez made measurements, writing it all down on his notepad.

"I'd like to see the accident site," said Emily when they returned to her patrol car. The area where Chee had crashed was located on a straight stretch of highway north of town. Emily pulled onto the hard shoulder near the wreck site. A short walk took her to the damaged tree. "Call in our 20," she said to Martinez, as she pulled down the bill of her campaign hat. She didn't expect to see much considering the weather. It was more a desire to get a feel for the scene.

Fifty feet south of the concrete trestle they located the spot where skid marks began,. The vehicle had swerved to the right, slammed on the brakes and tried to correct before impact. The report indicated there had been no witnesses, and if there had been, the investigator's tracks and inclement weather had obscured any signs. *Same as the Bobby Grayfeather incident. A conversation with him may turn out to be incredibly revealing.*

# 23

"I don't know for sure—it was dark," said Grayfeather. The young Navajo man looked up from his hospital bed at the two police officers standing over him and shook his head. "I'd had a bad day, so I stopped for a couple of beers. But I was okay and getting close to home thinking about how I was going to break the news to my family that I'd lost my job. Someone with their brights on came up right behind me. Next thing I knew, they had pulled up close to my side and flashed a searchlight in my eyes—like the kind they use for spotting deer." He looked at his wife who sat clutching his hand, nodding silently. "I couldn't see anything, and then, I guess I lost control. The truck went over a ledge and rolled over, and I blacked out. That's all I remember up until I woke up this morning." He looked from one face to another and blinked his eyes, appearing confused.

"You were employed by Strathmore Minerals. Is that correct, Bobby?" said Martinez.

"Yes, that's what I've been told."

"Can you tell us why you were fired?" Emily asked.

"I...I'm not sure. I overheard some men talking, and I got mad. I...I told them you can't do that."

"What were they talking about, Bobby?"

The young man squeezed his eyes shut and shook his head. "I can't remember."

"Do you know why anyone would want to harm you?" asked Martinez.

Grayfeather shook his head, a puzzled look on his face.

Nina Grayfeather caressed her husband's cheek and brushed back his hair. "It's okay, Bobby." Turning to Emily and Martinez, she added in a hushed voice, "Please go. You're upsetting my husband."

"Yes, of course," said Emily. "I apologize. Thank you for allowing us this time, and please call my number if you or Bobby remember anything else."

Emily and Martinez met the brain trauma doctor, a small East Indian man with a neatly trimmed mustache, in the hallway as he was about to enter Grayfeather's room.

"What is your prognosis, Doctor?" asked Emily. "Do you think he'll regain full cognition and memory?"

"Yes, probably, but it will take specialized therapy and time. Tomorrow I am transferring Mr. Grayfeather to a rehabilitative center in Albuquerque that specializes in traumatic brain injuries."

"You do know there was an attempt on his life, don't you?" said Martinez.

The doctor drew his eyebrows together and frowned. "Yes, I'm acutely aware of that. The staff at the rehabilitation center will be informed of the situation, and a guard will be assigned to monitor his room."

Abe paced the floor in his small office, his agitation growing by the minute. He had been trying to call Bertha Etcitty's home and then the school for the past hour. But, due to the high winds and accompanying torrential rains, electric and telephone lines were down at Huerfano, and he had no way of reaching Emily. Abe punched in Bertha's number and once again heard the interminable busy signal.

Afternoon classes had been canceled to give students who traveled the remote dirt roads the opportunity to get home before dark. The light in Abe's office flickered. He felt an uneasy lurch in his stomach, and the need to verify for himself that his daughter was safe. Grabbing his coat and hat off the rack, he locked his office door and went outside into the wind-driven sleet.

Gale winds screamed and lashed at his truck as Abe swerved around fallen branches and debris. The windshield wipers proved ineffective at dealing with the sideways rain mixed with ice pellets strafing his pickup. Abe grasped the steering wheel to keep the vehicle steady while he made his way through town and onto Highway 44 toward Bertha Etcitty's house. *Surely, they sent the kids home*, he thought as he took note of more than one overturned box trailer along the highway's edge.

Bertha's car was not in the driveway, and no one in the darkened house responded to Abe's repeated pounding on the door. Although the school was a mere two blocks away, Abe knew it would be faster to take his vehicle. His building anxiety told him something other than a storm had happened.

He spotted Bertha's Honda in the parking lot and rushed inside. The school lay in total darkness except for one room. Students, teachers, and parents had all gathered in the cafeteria-auditorium where a small generator powered the overhead lights. The room was in chaos as teachers attempted to calm the students and parents scurried around calling out their children's names. Abe spotted Bertha hustling from group to group. He did not see Will or Raven anywhere in the crowd. "Raven!" he shouted over and over as he went from one group to another. Unable to spot her, he joined Bertha. "Where's Raven? Where's my little girl? Will was supposed to be watching her. What the hell happened to them? Where is that fucking guard?"

Bertha trembled, and her voice broke when she spoke. "He had gone to his truck to smoke just before the power went off—said he thought it would be okay because Will always ate lunch with Raven. Will said he came right in with a flashlight as soon as he saw the lights go out. They're both out looking for her now. Everything went black for about five minutes. The teachers brought everyone into the cafeteria, and all the children have been accounted for," she said, wringing her hands. "Except Raven. I've called her again and again." Bertha's eyes glistened with tears. "Maybe Will found her and took her home."

The blood drained from Abe's face—he felt like he'd been gut-punched. "No. I just came from there. Bertha, drive to police headquarters and report her missing. And, tell someone to radio Emily. I'm going out to look for my baby."

"Let's break for lunch," said Emily. "I missed breakfast this morning, and I'm feeling it. We can grab something at a fast-food place."

Martinez patted his flat belly. "I'm ready."

*He looks like the kind of guy who could eat six times a day and never gain a pound, unlike me*, Emily groused to herself. She was beginning to notice a small spare tire hanging around her middle, and she had to pull a little harder to button her pants. She sat up straight and sucked her stomach in.

Martinez looked out the window at the storm. The rain and wind buffeted the Blazer. "Temperature's dropping. This is all going to turn into ice and snow."

Blake's Lotaburger was located on the next corner. Emily switched lanes and entered the parking lot then drove to the drive-through lane. "What do you want, Martinez? I'm buying today, so why not go for the combo."

"With chili cheese fries?" He paused when he heard the static on the radio. "Just a minute, Sergeant. We've got a call coming in."

The dispatcher's voice sounded tight. He didn't bother with codes but went straight to the point. "Emily, do you read?"

"Ten-four, Arviso. What's happening?"

"You better get over to the school. We have some lines down, and power's out here, so phones don't work. Uh—the lights went out at the school when everyone was in the cafeteria. When they got the generator going, your little girl turned up missing. Bertha says Will and Abe Freeman are out looking for her."

Emily tensed, turned on the flashers and siren, sped through the drive-through lane, crossed over the intersection, and landed back on the highway to Huerfano. She raced through red lights, cursing any vehicle that slowed her down. Luckily, traffic was light. Unfortunately, she couldn't see a car until it was ten feet in front of her. Halfway to the school she swerved and braked attempting to avoid a semi-trailer that fishtailed back and forth directly in front of her. The Blazer spun around on the icy surface, finally stopping with a jolt. They were high-centered on an embankment with the rear tires embedded in a ditch and the front tires in the air.

"God damn it!" Emily yelled pounding her fist on the dash as the semi straightened and plowed ahead leaving Martinez and her stranded. She looked at the rookie sitting next to her. He had lurched forward then slammed his head back against the headrest. "Are you all right, Martinez?"

Martinez rubbed the back of his neck. "Yeah, I think so. It's a good thing for seat belts. I'll check the tires," he said jumping out of the SUV

The dim headlights of an approaching car caught Emily's eye. "There's a car coming, Martinez. Try to wave it down. We've got to get out of here." She turned on the emergency flashers and tried to radio headquarters, but as close as they were, all she got was static.

With his arms waving frantically, Martinez positioned himself in the middle of the road. The oncoming truck blasted its horn but made no attempt to stop and offer assistance.

Martinez jumped out of the way as the truck driver rolled down his window and shouted, "That's karma for the speeding ticket you gave me, pig. Hee Haw," he snorted." He blew on the horn once more before disappearing from view.

"Fucker!" Martinez yelled. "Sergeant. You got a shovel?"

Emily jumped out of the disabled SUV and opened the rear tailgate. Inside the storage compartment, she found two folding shovels and a pick, standard issue equipment for reservation roads. She passed a shovel to Martinez and kept one for herself. Her heart pounded like a jackhammer on steroids. The wind-driven sleet felt like gravel sandblasting her face and body. Emily shuddered, thinking of her daughter possibly out in the storm. She took a deep breath and plunged the shovel blade into the sludge under the vehicle. "Hurry, Martinez. I've got to find my little girl," she said, digging ferociously.

Rain and wind had erased any tracks from Raven, as well as those from whoever had taken her. Abe cupped his hands around his mouth in a desperate attempt to shout into the storm. "Raven, Raven, honey, where are you?"

He ran from one car or truck in the parking lot to another, banged on the door, and tried to peer inside. But they were all empty, shrouded in an icy glaze, awaiting owners who had come to retrieve their children. Abe pivoted around, looking in all directions, and called again. The wind had died down, and the storm had broken. Patches of blue appeared in the eastern sky, and a perfect rainbow arched in the west. Near panic and not knowing what to do or where to go, Abe beseeched his long-abandoned God not to let anything happen to his daughter, and his plea reverberated through the emptiness. "Stay with me. I feel so lost. If you are there, God, help me find her, please!"

Not knowing where to go, Abe ran toward a cluster of junipers near the schoolyard. The deafening silence was broken only by the whistle of the wind and clomping of his boots in the soft mud. After twenty minutes of searching, he heard a noise—the deep rasping cr-cruck, cr-cruck, cr-cruck call of a solitary raven signaling his mate. This cry was answered shortly afterward by a similar sound. The pair had perched on a fence line, both cawing loudly until they were joined by a flock of young bachelor ravens.

Abe recalled hearing that a group of ravens was called an 'unkindness.' *Is this the message that God has sent me? Do I deserve this unkindness because I have turned my back on you?* Abe thought. "Damn you!" Abe shouted. "You can't take her from me."

He cursed and waved his arms, running toward the line of ravens perched on the fence. The young birds flew away, but the pair remained close. They swooped low over his head while gliding in concentric circles, then did a curious thing. One of them dropped something. When Abe bent down to see what it was, he stared in disbelief at the object, then picked it up. It was a button, a shiny shell button that Bertha Etcitty had made for Raven's coat. *My girl, my smart, beautiful girl*, he thought. *She left me a clue.* He looked up at the corvids, their black feathers glossy from the cleansing rain, their beady eyes staring at him over curved beaks. Abe swallowed the lump in his throat. "Thank you," he said. "You know where she is, don't you? Can you lead me to her?"

# 24

Emily tried to rock the SUV then gunned the engine in frustration. The back tires spun, covering Martinez in mud and slush as he pushed the patrol vehicle in a futile attempt to get it back on the highway. There were few drivers on the road, mainly oil and gas trucks, but none so far had stopped to offer assistance. *Either they hate cops, or they hate Indians or both*, Emily thought. Each passing moment brought her closer to panic, and she was ready to start walking when a rusty pickup came to a shuddering halt behind her.

"*Yá'át'ééh shi'kis*," said the elderly Navajo in the driver's seat. "You need some help?"

"Yes, please," said Emily. "I need to get to the Huerfano School right away."

Two teenage boys who had been riding beside the old man jumped down from the pickup and joined Martinez.

"Give it all you got," said Martinez, and with one mighty heave from the three young men, Emily was out of the ditch.

"*T'áá íiyisíí ahéhee'*. Thank you so much," said Emily to her rescuers.

The teenagers returned to their pickup, smiled shyly, and waved. *"Il hózhó,"* the old man said as they drove off.

*He has given me a blessing*, Emily thought. *Hózhó. May the ancestors provide me with strength and protect my daughter.* "Jump in, Martinez. Let's get moving."

The ravens flew a short distance ahead of Abe and landed on the bare branch of a dead juniper. Abe followed, and each time he approached them, the birds took off again. Abe didn't believe in magical thinking. His rational mind told him that a pair of ravens couldn't possibly take him to his daughter, but he persisted. It was all he had to go on.

The wind started to howl again, but the clouds were dissipating, exposing patches of bright blue sky. The birds perched on another tree and called to Abe in their croaky voices, as if waiting for him.

"What is it? What do you want?" he yelled. "She's not here. Keep going."

Still, the birds remained in place.

Abe recalled how his daughter interacted with these strange birds. She would give them corn, and they, in turn, would bring her gifts—trinkets of colored beads or stones, shiny paper, brilliant pieces of glass. He had no corn to give them. Abe dug through his pockets. A handful of loose change, a package of chewing gum, car keys, and a few paper clips was all he could come up with. He tossed a dime in the bird's direction, and they cocked their heads, eyeing the coin as it sunk in the mud. One of them flapped its wings as if annoyed.

"Wait," said Abe, as he unwrapped several sticks of gum and rolled the foil into a ball. "Look at this. You know you want it?" he said as it tossed the shiny orb in their direction.

The two birds flew to the ground and walked around the foil ball examining his offering as if to decide it this trinket was worthy of their effort. After a moment, the smaller one of the pair bent forward and picked it up before both took flight once again.

Abe, trudging and slipping through the mud, tried to keep up with the birds. Whenever he thought he had lost them, he would hear their call and find them waiting in a nearby tree. Once they passed through a wooded area, he stumbled upon a dilapidated tin building. The mated pair of ravens perched on the roof of the shed and dropped the ball of foil.

A bolted lock secured the heavy wooden door of the tin shed. Abe looked in all directions and saw no one. A single set of footprints, embedded deep in the mud led to and away from the door to a narrow dirt road. Deeply eroded ruts indicated that someone had driven in, turned around, and drove out. His mouth was dry, and he licked his lips, then swallowed hard. He approached the door and banged on it. "Raven? Are you in there, baby?"

No one responded. Abe glanced around. He must have walked at least three miles from the school. It was hard to discern if there was a nearby road or not, but Abe recalled the deep indentations of recent tire tracks. He tried again. "Raven, it's daddy. Let me know if you are in there, baby, please."

Abe pressed his ear to the door, hearing only the sound of his labored breathing. He sunk to his knees and dropped his head, sobbing.

A soft rustle, as if leaves were blowing in the wind, but there were no leaves, got his attention, and he pressed his ear closer to the door, barely breathing, listening.

He heard it again, then a whimper. Something or someone was in the shed. "Raven?" He pounded on the door again and pushed with all his weight against it. "Can you hear me? Raven, it's daddy. I'm here, sweetie."

"Daddy? Daddy, please get me out of here. I'm scared," the child sobbed.

At the sound of his little girl's voice, a rush of adrenaline soared through Abe's body. "I will, baby. Just hang on. Are you hurt?"

"N-n-no. But I'm scared, and I'm cold."

Abe worked himself into a frenzy trying to break into the shed. There were no windows to peer in, and the bolt with the combination lock would not budge. Oblivious to the pain and the cuts to his hands, he tried ripping off the rusty sheets of tin from the wall, but they were riveted together. Abe cursed in frustration, then slumped against the wall and spoke to his daughter.

"Listen, sweetheart, I've got to go for a little while to get help and some tools. Be daddy's brave girl. I'll be back in no time, I promise."

He pressed his ear against the door once again and heard his child wailing. "But, Daddy, what if the bad man comes back? Where's mommy? I want my mom. Don't leave me here alone."

"I'm coming right back, Raven." Abe turned away, and with his heart in his throat and the sound of his daughter's sobs echoing in his ears, began running as fast as he could. Backtracking the way he had come, bogged in mud up to his ankles, he reached the school in time to see Emily's patrol vehicle screech to a stop near the front entrance.

Emily jumped out, leaving the SUV door open, and rushed inside the school before Abe could get her attention, but Martinez evidently heard him and turned his way. It must have been difficult to recognize the mud-splattered figure with blood-smeared hands, but after a moment, Martinez said, "Freeman?"

Abe leaned back against the Navajo Police vehicle, holding his side and gasping for breath. "Get Emily—and a toolbox, bolt cutters, some blankets. I found Raven," he gasped. "Hurry up damn it."

Seconds later, Emily came running outside with Bertha close behind.

"Where is she? Is she all right?" Emily said.

"She's okay—about three miles from here. She's locked in a tin shed. I couldn't break the door open without help. Follow me, and hurry. I'll take you there."

Martinez returned carrying a large metal toolbox. "I know that place," he said. "There's an old dirt road behind the school

We can make it out there in the Blazer—if you let me drive, Sergeant Etcitty."

Emily paused for only a moment before she nodded. "Let's go."

"I'm coming with you," said Bertha, as she hustled out of the building carrying a bundle of blankets. She and Abe clambered into the back seat, and Emily took her place on the passenger side.

While Martinez navigated the police vehicle to the back of the school and to the dirt track that led to the abandoned maintenance shed, Emily grilled Abe with questions about Raven. "Are you sure she's not hurt? What did she say? Oh, my poor baby."

"She's frightened. Hell, she's scared to death. I'm going to kill the bastard who did this," Abe said.

"Is Will with her?" Bertha asked. She peered out the window and wrung her hands. "He should be with her."

"I haven't seen Will," said Abe.

"Martinez steered around a bend in the road, managing to avoid the deepest ruts, then slowed down. A white pickup, headed in the same direction they were going, was mired in the mud directly in his path. Will stood off to the side while the driver attempted to rock the truck free."

"I don't want to stop," said Martinez. "We might get stuck as well. I'm going to try to go around them."

"Jump in, Will," said Bertha as she opened her side door.

Will squeezed into the police Blazer seconds before Martinez accelerated, leaving the driver fuming behind the wheel.

"What the fuck! You just going to leave me out here?"

"Who's that you were with, Will?" Abe asked.

"That's the security guard. He picked me up a while ago. Said he knew about an old maintenance shed we could check out. Where're we going?"

"To get my granddaughter," said Bertha.

After the men had cut the lock, Abe pulled the door open and rushed inside. He lifted Raven and carried her to Emily who waited outside the opening. Emily reached out her arms and held her crying daughter tightly while Bertha draped the child with dry blankets, and wrapped her ample arms around her daughter and granddaughter. It wasn't only the women and child who cried. Some of those tears shed were of joy and relief, some out of fear and trauma, others of rage. No one said much on the trip back as Raven burrowed in her father's chest and clutched her mother's hand.

The white pickup, now abandoned by its driver, was still mired deeply in mud by the side of the road.

# 25

The wind had subsided, and the clouds had cleared exposing a breathtaking cerulean sky. Emily told Martinez to drop them off at the school so they could get their own vehicles and then for him to proceed with the investigation on his own.

"I'm taking a couple of days off, so, in the meantime, you're in charge of this inquiry. I'll put the word out that the patrol vehicle will be assigned to you. Get whatever information you can find about that security guard. And listen, Martinez, you report to me and no one else, that applies to the chief as well."

When Martinez's raised eyebrows formed question marks, she offered a vague explanation. "Something is going on, and until I find out what it is, I don't want anyone else in the department involved. Radio headquarters that Raven has been found, and I'm going home with her."

"Okay, Sergeant. Do you want me to pursue any other angles?"

"If you come up with something, yes, but let me know first." Before Officer Martinez drove away, Emily cautioned him. "Watch your back, Raymond."

Bertha retrieved her car, and Emily carried Raven to Abe's truck. They were going to Bertha's house to clean up and decide what to do next.

"I'm taking Raven to my house," Abe said. "I don't want her out of my sight." No one put up an argument, so that much was decided.

Will had parked his Indian Chief in a protected niche at the side of the school building. "I'll ride on out to Abe's house later," he said as he began walking toward the motorcycle. "I want to let Manuel know what's going on, then I'll meet you all over there."

Manuel was Will's partner—possibly lover. They had teamed up four years ago, and he stayed with Will at Grandfather Etcitty's old Airstream helping with the sheep and taking care of things when Will traveled to perform a ceremony. Everyone knew by now that Will was gay, and most people didn't care. In Navajo tradition, three separate sexes had always been acknowledged. But before Will got on the bike, Abe pulled him aside.

"Bring your granddad's old rifle when you come back, Will," Abe said in a tight voice. "I might need it. You don't have to mention this to Emily or your mom."

Will gave Abe a long look, then nodded.

While Raven took a warm bath and changed into dry clothing At Bertha's house, the adults huddled, speaking in hushed tones, and making plans. Raven and Emily would move into Abe's house until the child felt comfortable and safe enough to return to school. Abe would take a medical leave of absence so that he could be with his daughter at all times. He had a graduate student who was more than able to follow his lesson plans. At any rate, with his injured fingers, playing the piano would be out of the question until they healed. Bertha stated that she would pick up all of Raven's school assignments from her teacher and bring them to her so that she wouldn't fall behind.

Emily packed a bag for Raven and herself. "I can come back for more things we might need later. This will be enough for a couple of days," she told her mother as she fastened a suitcase. "I need to help Raven get ready now, then we can go."

Abe flinched as he washed his hands in the kitchen sink and doused them with peroxide. Some of the cuts were deep, still bleeding, and his fingers were beginning to swell.

"Abe, you need to go to the clinic to get stitches and a tetanus shot. I can take you," said Bertha.

"I'll be all right, thanks. I'm making a mess is all. Do you have something I can wrap them with?"

"Stubborn man," Bertha mumbled as she left the room. She returned a few minutes later carrying rolls of gauze, tape, and a bottle of mercurochrome. "Here, let me see those hands." When she had finished, both hands were swaddled in bandages.

"Guess I won't be making music for a while. But, my primary concern is not my hands, it's Raven. Bertha, you're welcome to stay at my place as well. I know you are used to having Raven around all the time, and you love her as much as we do. There's a rollaway bed I can put in Raven's room—it might be a little tight in there. . ."

"Well, maybe for just a few days," said Bertha, her face lighting up. She gave Abe a quick hug. "I better gather up a few things for myself."

Abe stared at his hands, but he wasn't thinking about the pain or the scars he might have. His thoughts were on Raven and the person who had taken her. Although he was dying to ask the child what she knew, he and Emily had agreed to go slowly on the questioning. Raven had suffered enough trauma for the moment. "I'm going to kill the bastard who did this to my little girl," he said under his breath.

A bright fire crackled in the wood stove warming the house and delivering the sweet scent of piñon. They ate a light supper, and Abe set up the rollaway for Bertha. Raven didn't want to eat. She had remained quiet and prone to quick tears, refusing to leave her mother's lap. She wanted to go to bed but was afraid to be alone, so Emily crawled under the covers with her and held her close. Abe lifted Patch onto the bed as well, since their aged three-legged dog was too old to jump anymore. Patch snuggled up close to Raven and Abe kissed his daughter, assuring her she didn't have to be afraid anymore. She was safe. When he checked on them a short time later, all appeared to be sleeping. While Bertha busied herself with the dinner dishes, Abe went out to the barn to help Will with the horses.

They cleaned the stables and laid down fresh straw for bedding. Abe filled the water trough and gave the horses hay and oats. At least the animals had enough sense to come under cover when the storm had begun. Red, Raven's sorrel pony, whinnied and tossed its head as if looking for the girl. Abe took the curry comb and spoke quietly to the horse as he proceeded to groom its mane and neck. His horse, Jessie, appeared to be only interested in eating.

"Pull up a bale," said Will. "Let's rest a while." He sat down and opened his *jish,* then pulled out his prayer pipe and a packet from the medicine bundle. Will prepared the pipe with *dzil natoh,* the sacred tobacco that comes from the mountains. He drew on the stem, held the smoke in his lungs for several seconds, then, exhaling, handed the pipe to Abe. While Abe smoked, Will chanted a prayer song.

Abe exhaled a cloud of smoke. The tobacco was pungent but comforting. "What are you singing about, Will?"

"It is a protection prayer song for my niece and you, Abe." He took the pipe and puffed. "I thought you didn't like guns. The last time we took Grandfather's gun, it was for revenge against someone who had done harm to my family. You didn't want any part of weapons then."

Abe tightened his jaw. He recalled the incident, years ago, when Will had taken the rifle and convinced Abe to help him track down a brutal motorcycle gang member. Abe had told him then that he would go with him, but he wouldn't ever shoot anyone—that he hated violence of any kind. "This is different. It's protection for Raven. Did you bring the rifle?"

"It's here in the barn, behind that last row of straw bales. There's a box of shells with it. The old rifle needs to be cleaned and oiled. It hasn't been shot since before Grandfather died."

"You miss him, don't you?"

Grandfather Etcitty had lived long enough to see his only great-grandchild born. After that, he stated he was content and ready to join the holy ones. He wanted Will to have his *jish* with all his sacred paraphernalia and to carry on the tradition of a *hataali*. He had been grooming him to follow in his footsteps ever since Will was a young boy. One morning, the old man walked off with his sheep and didn't return. When Will went looking for his grandfather, he found the old man's body on a high boulder overlooking the grazing sheep. And though it had taken him many years and missteps, Will had found his calling.

"Of course, I miss granddad. But I have comfort in knowing that when he made his last step on earth, the holy ones carried him to the entrance of Old Age People so they could prepare him to be born again. Life is never-ending. Memories are treasures of a person's life."

"Memories?" Abe said. "I have plenty of those. Some, I'd just as soon forget."

Will passed the pipe back to Abe. "Let me tell you why we smoke this tobacco. When we become stressed, overworked or need guidance *dzil natoh*, mountain herb, is smoked to release tensions, worries, and concerns. The *Diné* traditional pipe is made from clay, kneaded by hand, and shaped into the proper form. Then it is burned in a mixture of sheep manure and mud and covered with piñon tree gum. One is able to connect with the earth, water, fire, air, heaven, and the mountains when we smoke. The smoke that rises from the pipe is a signal or message made from the mouth of the person smoking to the holy ones around and above us. They shape our prayers into a formation of clouds. In return, when the holy ones receive our prayers, they answer through the clouds, the wind, the rain, and animals." He paused, drew on his pipe stem and exhaled a cloud of smoke. "Abe, how did you know where to look for Raven?"

Abe shook his head, a look of bewilderment on his face. He was a romantic, but also a pragmatist. "You won't believe this, Will—it was a pair of ravens that led me to her. They would move ahead, then call and wait for me. Then, one of them dropped something near my feet. It was a button from Raven's coat. I felt bewildered, and I didn't know where else to go, so I followed them. The damn birds took me right to the shed. It was the craziest thing."

Will closed his eyes and grinned. "Not so crazy. Ravens belong to the inner world, that place where we protect the part of us that's often injured. When troubles arise, they can become a powerful ally. They have a natural connection to your daughter because of the love she shares with them. The raven is her spirit animal. Did they request something from you?"

"A ball of foil," Abe laughed and scratched his head. "But, I still don't understand." Just as quickly, the smile disappeared from his face. "I want to know who took her, what was his purpose, but she's not ready to talk about it, and I don't want anyone coming around questioning her."

Will nodded in agreement. "Raven will let you know when she's ready." He looked around the barn. "You built this with your own hands—nice work, the horses are happy. Now you need a few sheep and goats if you want to become a real member of *dinétah*."

"Shearing, butchering—no, I don't think so. These battered old hands are pretty full, Will." He stood and looked at his bandages. "I guess we'd better go in and keep your mom company."


The aroma of freshly brewed coffee filled the kitchen. Bertha was sitting at the table holding a steaming mug. Abe washed the parts of his fingers that were not taped and took two cups from the cupboard, then filled one for Will and one for himself.

"Sit down," said Bertha.

Emily's mother's hair had grayed in the last few years, and she had slowed down some. Still, she remained in good health and had managed to maintain her strength and a cool head when troubles arose. Tonight, she appeared tired and tense.

"How're we going to find this monster and punish him?" Bertha said to the two men.


Emily may have appeared to be sleeping, but she was wide awake, her brain spinning like a top. If it weren't for the fact that her daughter needed her, she would be out tracking down the asshole who did this, and she had a pretty good hunch where to start. Gomez and Talltree had issued a threat against Raven, though it seemed odd that they would be so brazen, knowing the finger of guilt would be pointed directly at them. Chief Todechine was acting strange, but he had always been prone to moodiness. Emily had worked under the chief for fifteen years, and he had been her mentor. Still, she never knew what was behind those hooded eyes. The security guard was conveniently out of the building when the lights went out. Emily tossed on her side. She could hear her mom and Abe talking in the kitchen. She turned over gently, so as not to wake her daughter and started to get up, but Raven whimpered, "Mommy," and she stayed. "I'm right here."

# 26

Early the next morning, while everyone sat around the table and waited for Bertha to serve a favorite of Raven's, blue corn *atole* with honey and cinnamon, the telephone rang.

"It's for you, Em. It's Martinez," Abe said.

"Sorry, but I've got to take this," Emily said. "Go ahead and start without me. She carried the cordless receiver into the bedroom and closed the door. "Hey, what's happening?"

"Hope I didn't get you out of bed, but I did some snooping around the school this morning,"

"No, we're all up and about here. What'd you find?"

"That power outage didn't occur due to natural causes, Sergeant. The line was cut at the main switch box."

Emily let this bit of information sink in before she responded. "You saw this?"

"Yes, ma'am. It was no accident. I snapped some pictures."

"Okay. The private security guard was outside at the time. Have you questioned him?"

"He's not around. The school principal said the guy's name is Frank Miller, and he had been hired by the police department, so they didn't have any paperwork on him. He didn't supply the name of the firm where he was supposedly employed."

Emily blew out a long breath. She knew she would have to question Chief Todechine again, and dreaded the confrontation. "I need to stay with my daughter today, but I'll be in tomorrow. Check out all the private security agencies in the area and see if they have any employees named Frank Miller. It's only logical that you would be investigating this incident, so keep asking questions. But remember, if you find out anything, keep it to yourself." She didn't want to admit to the rookie cop that she had a growing mistrust of someone at headquarters.

"Right, Sergeant Etcitty. And when I write my report . . . ?"

"When you log in your report, make it routine. Conduct a couple of traffic stops. There's always someone around committing a minor violation, and you can write up that incident. You're doing a good job, Martinez. I've got to get back to my family, so I'll see you in the morning. You can report to me tomorrow unless something urgent comes up beforehand."

"Okay. Anything else?"

"Go back to Strathmore Minerals and talk to a few employees. See if you can learn anything about what Bobby Grayfeather was referring to now that Whittington is out of town. Remember to be careful."

Later that morning, after Bertha had gone to the school to pick up assignments, and Emily was straightening up the house, Raven asked her dad to go outside with her. They walked along the path that led to the barn. Raven's small hand clutching at the fingers that protruded from Abe's swath of bandages.

"I want to get some corn for the birds, dad. They must be hungry. And I'm bringing apples for the horses. Do you feed them when I'm not here?"

"You mean the horses? Of course, I feed them, but I don't always give corn to the crows and ravens because I don't think they like me as much as you. And I figure they're smart enough to find their own food when you're not around. But I think I will bring them something from now on."

They stopped at the corral fence, and Raven stroked the horses' long noses before giving each a chunk of apple.

"How come you changed your mind about feeding them?" Raven asked as she dipped an empty cup into the bin of corn.

"Come and sit down beside me for a minute," Abe said. "I want to show you something."

After they had settled on a wooden crate, Abe pulled the shell button out of his pocket. "Do you recognize this?"

"It's the button from my coat! You found it, Dad."

"I had some help. Your buddies, the ravens, brought it to me. They helped me find you, sweetheart. I'm very grateful. The least I can do is give them some corn."

As they walked to the pasture, Patch hopped along beside them, struggling at times to keep pace. Raven wanted to scatter corn kernels for the birds, and Abe debated with himself as to whether he should try to gently seek more information from his daughter. A flock of large black birds called to each other in the distance. "Ravens or crows?" he asked to break the ice.

Raven grew solemn as the birds drew closer. "Those are crows," she said. "See how their tails spread out like a fan."

"You know, that was a smart thing you did, leaving your button for the ravens. How'd you manage that?"

After a long minute of silence, she squeezed his fingers and tears welled in her eyes. "I want to tell you about the bad thing, Dad."

"Are you sure. Do you want Mom here?"

She shook her head. "Just us for now." She tightened her grip on his fingers. "This is what I remember. Uncle Will was sitting at our table, and I was in the lunch line getting my tray when the room went black. Then someone put a piece of tape over my mouth and something over my head. I got picked up and carried away. It was raining hard. I couldn't call Uncle Will, and I couldn't see anything."

Abe forced himself to appear calm while his mind burned with rage. He unclenched his jaws and kept his voice soft when he spoke. "Did anyone hurt you?"

"No. It only hurt when I pulled the tape off my mouth."

"What about the button?"

"My hands were tied together in front, but I could feel my button, so I kept pulling on it until it came off. When the truck stopped, and the person took me out, I dropped the button."

"And the ravens found it and brought it to me."

"They must have been watching. I could hear the birds cawing."

Abe wrapped an arm around his little girl and drew her close. "After that, can you tell me what happened?"

"I got put in a dark, smelly place, and my hands were untied. I heard a voice then, it was a man. He said, 'Don't take that sack off your head until you count to one hundred. Someone will come and get you out of here if you do as I say.' I started counting to myself, and I heard the door slam shut and the truck drive away."

"Did you ever see this person?"

"No, I was too scared." Tears welled in her eyes and ran down her cheeks.

Abe wiped them away. "Raven, honey, you are the bravest girl in the world—a true warrior."

Once she made sure Abe and Raven were out of earshot, Emily picked up the phone and punched in the number for the Huerfano Police Station.

"Arviso, this is Emily. Connect me to the chief." She chewed her lower lip while waiting for Todechine to pick up. His voice sounded wary when he answered.

"Todechine."

Skipping formalities, Emily got straight to the point. "It's Emily. I'm taking another day off to stay with my daughter, Chief. Don't send anyone around to bother her with questions. She's been through enough."

"I heard there was a problem at the school. Is your little girl all right?"

*A problem*, Emily thought and felt her blood boil. Without answering his question, she said, "Is Frank Miller the name of that security guard or is that an alias."

She listened while her chief stammered and stalled. "Uh, well, yeah. It's Miller, Frank Miller. He's not a local, though, and I heard he took off."

"Who did he work for, Chief, and what was he hired to do?" Emily tried without succeeding to control her voice. "Traumatise my daughter, leave her locked in a cold dark shed, terrified and alone? Or is there more to it?"

"I don't know what you're talking about, Emily. He had credentials. He was doing his job. He didn't hurt your little girl."

"Bull shit, Chief! Something is going on, and you're not straight with me. That so-called Internal Affairs investigator that talked to Abe did not come from Albuquerque. I spoke to Joe Hosteen. Their office didn't send anyone up here. That asshole at the school was not protecting my daughter. Gomez and Talltree are dirty. I saw Gomez counting a wad of money after he left your office. This hurts me to question you like this—I've always looked up to you. What are you hiding, Chief? What the hell is going on?"

Todechine's sigh sounded more like a moan, a man in pain. "You got it wrong, Emily," he said in a guttural voice. "Hosteen doesn't know anything. Nobody would have hurt your little girl. There's a lot of things you don't understand."

"Well, explain them to me then," said Emily, her voice rising, "because you're right about me not understanding." She paused before asking, "How much are you involved in this, Chief?" She waited, her breath caught in her throat, for him to answer, but all she heard was a buzzing noise at the end of the line after the phone went dead. Emily replaced the receiver and sat down. She held her head between her hands and cried, resolved that she had not only been betrayed by her boss but had lost respect for the man she had considered a father figure after her own father had died of cancer due to uranium poisoning.

The rattling of the door and Abe's hushed voice brought her back, and Emily composed herself. "Hey, you guys. What have you been up to?" she said, quickly drying her tears.

Raven let go of her father's hand and ran to her mom, hugging her tightly. "We fed the horses apples and gave the birds corn," she said. Then, in a whispered voice, "Dad and I talked about the scary thing."

A look flashed between the parents. Emily saw Abe's lips curl into a small grin, and she felt reassured. She would question him about their discussion when the two of them were alone. "That's good," she said to Raven, stroking her hair. For the moment, she would push the conversation with Todechine out of her head and devote all her attention to her child. But tomorrow, with the help of Martinez, it would be a different story. Emily cupped Raven's chin in her hand and smiled at her. "I'm thinking of making sugar cookies. I sure could use some help."

While Emily and Raven busied themselves in the kitchen, Abe took a box of cotton pads from the medicine cabinet and walked back to the barn. He pulled Grandfather Etcitty's rifle from its hiding place, dripped some oil on a square of cotton fabric and attached it to the end of a slender rod. He ran the rod through the bore of the gun several times, then repeated the process with a fresh pad. When he had finished, Abe loaded the chamber. "You bastards show your face around here," he muttered under his breath. "I will blow your fucking heads off."

# 27

That night, after their daughter had been read three stories and finally fallen asleep, Abe told Emily about his conversation with Raven. They stood at the edge of the deck, the stars twinkling above them in the crisp night air. While Abe spoke, Emily swallowed hard to keep the lump in her throat from turning into a sob. When he had finished, they remained silent for a moment, holding each other, while Emily blinked away the tears escaping her eyes, replacing her sorrow with anger. *How could anyone inflict such fear and trauma on an innocent child, and why? Why my daughter?* Emily felt sure it had something to do with the case she was working on and that Chief Todechine knew more than he was telling.

"Did Raven get a look at the man's face?" Emily asked.

"No. The asshole ordered our little girl to leave the sack over her head until she counted to a hundred. She was afraid to disobey him, but Raven is pretty sure there was only one man. It's Gomez or his partner I'll bet, and if I find them around here…"

"Maybe those two had something to do with it, or maybe it was the security guard Todechine hired. And what will you do if you find Gomez and Talltree, Abe? Get yourself in trouble or hurt? How would that help Raven or me? Let me handle this. Martinez is trying to track down the security guard. I'll stay with our little girl tomorrow. She might remember something and tell me—some detail about her abductor. But, the next day I'm going to the station. I'll find out what the chief is hiding and why he's giving money to Gomez."

Abe sighed. "I know you have to do this, sweetheart. Try not to worry about Raven. I've requested a month's emergency leave, and it's been approved. I won't let her out of my sight."

The following day, both parents spent the entire time with their daughter. They brought a picnic lunch and rode the horses along a trail that bordered the river. Patch perched on the saddle with Abe, while Raven and Emily doubled up on the broad back of the sorrel, Red. Emily had packed Raven's favorites—peanut butter and chokecherry jelly sandwiches, sliced apples with raisins and nuts. She included a jug of lemonade and some of the sugar cookies they had made the day before and even corn for the birds and squirrels that might decide to join them. When they reached the majestic cottonwood that hugged the riverbank, Emily spread a blanket on the thick bed of bright yellow leaves while Abe tied the horses near a patch of dried grass. The weather had turned sunny and warm with a slight cooling breeze. It would have been perfect, if not for the circumstances that kept Raven out of school and brought them to this place.

Raven still showed signs of trauma. She was not her exuberant, bubbly self, and instead of running off to find treasures in the woods, she stayed close to her mother and father. After eating, they stood at the edge of a quiet inlet pool formed by the river. Abe tried to show Raven how to skip stones on the water's surface, causing Patch to run along the bank, barking as if he wanted to fetch the rocks.

"I can't do it, dad," Raven whined after a few unsuccessful attempts. "I can't do anything right." She burst into tears and ran into her mother's arms.

"That man, he said he would come back for me if I told anyone," she sobbed.

"No, sweetie. Daddy and I will never let anything bad happen to you again, I promise. You can tell us anything."

"His hands were rough and smelly, mom. They smelled like tobacco, but not like Uncle Will's. It was like stinky cigarettes." Raven continued to sniffle while Emily stroked her hair. "I was so scared."

Abe took a clean handkerchief from his pocket and dried the tears from her face. "Mom's right," he said. "No one will ever hurt you again." His mind flashed back to the search for Raven. *What was it that Will had said about the security guard? He had gone outside for a cigarette.*

The digital clock on the bedside table blinked from 2:11 to 2:12. Emily had slept only a couple of hours, a restless sleep filled with disjointed dreams that left her feeling unsettled, but that she could no longer recall. She listened to Abe's even breathing, then quietly slipped out of bed, wrapped herself in his robe, and tiptoed into Raven's room. Her child looked at peace as she slept curled on her side, clutching her favorite stuffed bird. Patch sat up, but when he saw it was Emily, he wagged his tail and lay back down in the small of Raven's back. Emily sighed, wondering if her little girl would ever fully recover from her experience, wondering, in fact, if she, herself, would. Her thoughts drifted back to the child she had lost, and the hole that had remained in her heart. She slid open the patio door and stepped outside under a crescent moon and a sea of stars. The cold air helped her to think clearly, and Emily realized what she had to do. Todechine was never going to be honest with her no matter how much she ranted and raved. He was hiding a dark secret. She would have to defy his orders and find the truth on her own by secretly investigating her boss. She thought the heavens must agree with her, the way they twinkled, especially Alpha Centauri, the bright star closest to the solar system. Emily recalled the legend her grandmother had told her of how the sun, the moon, and the stars were created. The Milky Way, sweeping through the night sky, illuminated the pathway for the spirits to travel between heaven and earth. Before she went inside, Emily offered a prayer of thanks to the holy ones, and to coyote for tossing a blanket into the dark skies and creating the stars. One of those stars is my son, she told herself. "Good night, Christopher, my sweet boy," she whispered before entering the house. Emily crawled into bed beside Abe, being careful not to wake him. A sense of calmness had settled over her as she drifted off to sleep. She would have the weekend to spend with her daughter before returning to work on Monday morning.

The Huerfano Substation Officers were either gathered around the coffee machine or talking in small groups while they waited for Chief Todechine to show up for the morning briefing. When Emily arrived, she stood off to the side, leaning against the wall, studying the faces of the others. Raymond Martinez glanced her way, and she beckoned to him with a tilt of her head. He held up an empty mug, and Emily smiled, mouthing, "yes, please." He carried two cups of coffee and walked over to join her.

Todechine arrived a few minutes later looking as if he hadn't slept in a week. Emily had not entered his office with a friendly greeting as was her usual custom, and now, he would not meet her eye. Without any preliminaries, he addressed the officers.

"I've heard rumors, there's going to be a large group of trouble-makers in Window Rock on Friday. If the Council rules in favor of Strathmore Minerals uranium exploration, they're planning to get people riled up and stage a protest march. An ex-con by the name of Malcolm Keetso is their leader. Some of you may remember him as a known trouble-maker and criminal from way back. I want everyone here to concentrate on finding and arresting Keetso before this charade gets started. Track him down and bring him in along with any of his followers. I'm assigning the following officers to be in Window Rock no later than eight o'clock Friday morning, and I want that demonstration squelched." He looked up and caught Emily's eye before he named the officers. "Begaye, Gillmore, Tsosie, Martinez, Etcitty, Rodman. Any questions?"

Martinez raised his hand before Emily's elbow to his ribs could stop him.

"Yeah, what is it, Martinez," said the Chief.

"Uh, I was just wondering if I could switch with someone and take Friday off. It's my kid's birthday."

"Are you fucking kidding me?" said the chief. "That's it. Get out of here and do your job, and leave me alone. I don't want to be disturbed by anybody's whining and complaining. I've got work to do." Slamming the door behind him, he locked himself in his office.

"That was a pretty lame question you asked Todechine, Martinez," Emily said when they were seated in the patrol car. "You weren't actually considering taking the day off, were you?"

"Sorry, Sergeant. I had to come up with something quick after you jabbed me."

"What had you planned on asking?"

"Just wondered what would be the basis for arresting protesters if they had acquired a lawful permit."

"No basis. We could probably drum up some charges against Keetso for holding us at his compound, but I told him we wouldn't. That's not the reason the Chief wants him out of commission." A brisk wind chased puffy white clouds across the deep blue sky and sent a clump of tumbleweeds skittering along the roadside. Emily didn't share her growing suspicions concerning Todechine with Martinez, that the chief, for reasons unknown, was doing everything in his power to guarantee the approval of uranium mining on the reservation. Five miles outside of Bloomfield, she turned onto a gravel road. "Did you learn anything new while I was out."

"There's no record of a Frank Miller having been contracted by any private security agency in New Mexico. I checked all the sources. There are two Frank Millers in Farmington, but neither is the man we're looking for. The school didn't have any employment information on him. Since he was hired by the department, the principal took him at his word. No local address, telephone, or acquaintances."

"A mystery man," Emily said. "Did you talk to any employees at Strathmore Minerals?"

"Yes, Sergeant. I ran into that driver and a couple of other guys on their break. They agreed to talk if I don't mention their names. Scared of losing their job, but they told me, Whittington had been pressuring employees to go to Window Rock on Friday and break up any demonstrations."

"Threatened again with losing their jobs if they refused, I bet." Emily made a right turn onto a dirt driveway that led to a territorial style adobe house tucked into a grove of piñon and juniper. The sprawling structure sat in front of a hogback ridge. A windmill creaked as the blades turned in the brisk breeze.

Four horses grazing near a shed lifted their heads and whinnied when they saw the approaching vehicle.

Raymond Martinez raised his eyebrows. "Say, isn't this Chief Todechine's spread?"

"Yep, I thought I'd pay his wife, Daisy, a call. I haven't seen or heard from her in a long time." She felt a pang of guilt. She had once been very close to Daisy Todechine. If she thought of the chief as a second father, then Daisy was a second mother. Why had she stayed away so long?

"Want me to call in our 10-20?"

"Uh-uh. This is a social visit. Rumors were going around a while back that Daisy wasn't doing well, but I never heard anything more about it. I assumed she got better. I guess I should have called sooner."

The house had been constructed of thick adobe bricks, stuccoed over and painted a warm beige. Thick square wooden columns supported a long narrow front porch or *portal* as it was commonly called. The large wooden front door cracked open, and a slim teenage girl with a worried-expression stepped out. She was wearing a faded pair of jeans and a black tee-shirt with the words *Diné Pride* emblazoned in turquoise lettering across the front. Her long hair was tied in a loose pony-tail.

"That's Daisy's niece," Emily said to Martinez. She rolled the window down to offer a greeting before getting out of the vehicle. "*Yá'át'ééh*, Gladys. It's Emily Etcitty with my partner, Raymond Martinez. We just dropped by to see Daisy. Is she up for a visit?"

"*Yá'át'ééh abini*, Emily. You and your friend are welcome. Come on up and have a seat here on the porch. I just made tea." The girl shyly ducked her head and offered her hand to Martinez when he alighted the steps.

"*Aoó, ahéheé*," Emily said, thanking the young woman.

While Gladys fetched the tea, Emily and Martinez settled into matching wooden rocking chairs. "She's probably staying here to help Daisy with the housework," Emily said. "It's a big place to keep up, and there are the horses to take care of."

Gladys returned a few minutes later carrying a tray loaded with three mugs and a plate of store-bought sugar cookies. She placed the tray on a small round table and sat down on a canvas chair.

Martinez scooped up a handful of cookies and began eating like he hadn't just finished off a couple of donuts. Emily picked up a cup and inhaled the familiar aroma of Navajo Tea before taking a sip. "Mmm. This smells so good. Grasping the cup with both hands, she looked over the rim at Gladys. "How is Daisy?" she said over the top of the mug. "Is she resting?"

Gladys' face took on an even more somber aspect, and the corners of her mouth turned down. "Uncle hasn't told anyone, has he? He said I wasn't supposed to talk about Auntie."

Emily placed her cup on the table and leaned forward facing the girl who appeared to be on the verge of tears. "What is it, Gladys? You can trust us."

Gladys hesitated and averted her eyes before speaking. "Auntie's not here. Uncle had to take her to the hospital, but he didn't like the care she was getting there or later at the cancer center in Albuquerque. They told him Auntie was going to die, that there was nothing more they could do for her but try to keep her from having too much pain and that he should take her home."

Hit with shock and disbelief, Emily realized her mouth was hanging open. Cancer! Whenever she had asked Chief Todechine how Daisy was doing, he always answered with something like, "Great," or "She's keeping so busy," or "Daisy sends you her love, Emily."

Martinez had stopped chewing. He swallowed and brushed the crumbs from his mouth with the back of his hand. "Where is your aunt, now, Gladys?"

Gladys shook her head and looked at the floor. "I can't say. I promised Uncle."

A wash of guilt swept over Emily. Daisy was dying. She grasped the girl's hand. "Please, Gladys, I need to know where Daisy is. The chief will never know you told me, I swear, and Martinez will keep your secret."

Martinez, looking solemn, made a cross over his heart, and the girl allowed her lips to curve into a sad smile before she sighed and dropped her head again.

"She's in Las Vegas, Nevada. Uncle refuses to accept the fact that Daisy is going to die. He had read about a doctor in Las Vegas who claims to have secret cures for cancer, so Uncle took her to the man's private clinic, and that's where she is now. Uncle leaves every Friday to go see her, and he doesn't come back until early Monday morning. He's been doing this for the past two months."

"It's nearly five hundred miles to Las Vegas from Farmington," said Martinez. "Do you mean to tell me he's driving that round-trip every week then showing up early for work Monday morning?"

"That's right," Gladys said. "But it's getting to him. He's so angry and sad. He hardly eats or sleeps anymore. I am worried about him, but I don't know what to do. Uncle won't talk about it, and he won't let me tell anyone in the family."

"Well, that explains his bad mood." *But it doesn't account for the payoff to Gomez or the hiring of the phony bodyguard*, Emily thought. "Gladys, do you know the name of the doctor, the one who is treating Daisy?"

"No, but there's an envelope that came in the mail today from Las Vegas. I put it on Uncle's desk."

Emily desperately wanted to talk to Daisy now—both because of her grave concern for the woman's well-being and her instinctive distrust of a likely charlatan.

"Will you let me see that envelope, please? I'd like to know that doctor's name and address so I can get in touch with Daisy."

"I'm not supposed to mess with the mail. I just pick it all up and put it on the desk, but the letter from Las Vegas was on top of the stack, and I couldn't help noticing." Gladys said, then stared at the wall and nervously chewed at a hangnail on her thumb.

"I'm not going to open it, and you can put it right back where it was."

After hesitating a bit longer, Gladys stood up. "Okay, but hurry, Uncle might come home to check the mail." She left the room, returning a moment later and handed a white business envelope to Emily.

Emily read the sender's information, quickly committing the name and address to memory. "Thank you," she said after handing the envelope back. "And as far as anyone is concerned, Martinez and I were never here."

"Write this down," Emily said to Martinez when they were back on the road. "Dr. Lawrence Kingsley ND, Vitapure Wellness Center, 1831 Spring Mountain Road, Las Vegas, Nevada, and run a background check on the doctor."

Martinez pulled a notebook and pen out of his shirt pocket and scribbled out the information. "What's the ND?"

"Naturopathic Doctor. I know we use herbs and natural cures all the time here on the rez, and a lot of times they work, but we don't claim to cure cancer. If we could, my dad would still be here. Todechine is smarter than that. I can't believe he would fall for this scam."

# 28

America West Express had daily flights to Las Vegas and back out of the Four Corners Regional Airport. When she had read through the summary of the background check on Kingsley, Emily made a quick decision to see the man in person. She could leave early this afternoon and return by ten this evening.

"Martinez, you're the only one on the force who knows I'm taking this trip, and I want it to stay that way, understood? You're going to be on your own today. Keep trying to track down Frank Miller and Whittington. Give me a number I can reach you at. After I call Abe, drop me off at the airport."

"Got it, Sarge. Anything else?"

"Watch your back."

"Some phony doctors build up people's hope and con a lot of money out of them."

"I know, and Indian Health Services won't pay for that shit."

Before Martinez dropped Emily off at the airport, she grabbed the backpack with a change of civilian clothes, a small handbag, and a traveler's assortment of toiletries that she kept in the back of the SUV. She gave Martinez some final words of advice and headed for the women's restroom. Dressed in black slacks, a white blouse, and low-heeled black pumps, Emily examined herself in the mirror. She brushed her hair out of the tight bun she always wore to work and added a touch of pale pink lipstick. Satisfied that she no longer displayed a policewoman's persona, Emily took the handbag out of her backpack and found the ticket agent. The plane for Las Vegas would depart in thirty minutes, giving her enough time to look up the number for Kingsley and set up an appointment. She stressed the urgency of meeting today to the receptionist and was told the doctor was a very busy man, but she would try to squeeze her in at two.

The flight time of slightly over an hour allowed Emily the opportunity to develop her approach to the man in charge of the Vitapure Wellness Center. She would tell him her sister had been diagnosed with incurable lung cancer—that the doctors gave her no hope of recovery, then feign interest in the possibility of having her admitted to Dr. Kingsley's Center. She planned to ask for a description of treatment programs, cost, and other pertinent details, and request a tour. Once inside, Emily would find her way to Daisy Todechine.

When she stepped out of the terminal, it felt as if she were entering a blast furnace. The temperature in Las Vegas hovered around the hundred degree mark. A Yellow Cab stopped in front of her, and she jumped in, grateful for the slight cooling from the air conditioner. After giving the driver the address of the clinic, she checked her watch—over an hour to kill. Emily leaned back and took in the view of garish casinos and hotels. Zombie-like crowds of tourists and gamblers wandered the sidewalks like insomnious nomads. Gambling had never appealed to her—she hated losing. But she was keenly aware of the stranglehold it had on some people. The taxi turned onto a quieter side street lined with respectable-looking businesses—banks, law offices, financial consulting firms.

One more turn and they were on Spring Mountain Road, a busy commercial street lined with chain restaurants, a Walmart, auto parts stores, and donut shops. When the businesses thinned, large complexes hidden behind high fences appeared. The cab pulled into a long palm tree-lined driveway and stopped in front of a sprawling white stuccoed building.

"This is it," said the cabbie. "You sure this is the place you want?"

The Vitapure Wellness Center was designed in the Moorish style with blindingly whitewashed walls, arched passageways lined with tropical plants, mosaic tiles, and fountains.

Emily checked the time. "Yes, I'm sure," she said, handing the cabbie a twenty. She was still early, but it gave her a chance to investigate the building and grounds. Emily followed a tiled pathway that led past tree-shaded benches, picnic tables, and a pond complete with a pair of swans. A Japanese gardener tended the meticulous lawn and flower beds. The whole scene provided an impressively peaceful atmosphere, an oasis in the dry desert, but there was no one outside to partake of all this beauty. *Too hot?* Emily wondered. *Or is this all for show?*

Eventually, the meandering path led to an ornate wooden door. The refrigerated air inside carried the scent of freshly-picked flowers. On a marble table, a large vase of long-stemmed roses and a container of iced drinking water shared space with crystal glasses. Funeral home came to Emily's mind.

"How may I help you?" asked the smiling blond receptionist in a sugary sweet voice. She sat behind a teak wood desk and adjusted expensive-looking designer glasses on her slender young nose.

"I'm Rita Yazzie. I have a three o'clock appointment with Doctor Kingsley," Emily said giving the fictitious name she had used when she sat up the meeting.

Fastidiously manicured fingernails clicked over a keyboard. "Ah, Miss Yazzie. Yes, I see you are scheduled for two o'clock."

"I know I'm a little early, but my flight just arrived from Phoenix. Could you tell me where to find a bathroom?"

"Certainly. The ladies room is located at the end of that hallway. It will be the last door on the left."

The marble and brass-fixtured ladies room was as sumptuous as the rest of the building. After stepping into one of the stalls, Emily checked the miniature camera-recorder located in her purse, then flushed the toilet. Satisfied the recorder was working, she stepped back into the hallway and looked in both directions. Not seeing anyone, she headed away from the reception room and turned the corner. Both sides of the corridor were lined with windowless doors. Emily knocked lightly on the first one. When she didn't receive a response, she turned the knob and found it locked.

Reaching into her purse, Emily fished out her lock-picking tools: a tiny tension wrench and lockpick. She inserted the wrench into the bottom of the keyhole and the pick at the top. While applying slight torque with the wrench, she rubbed the pick back and forth in the keyhole until she heard all the pins set. Before turning the knob, she checked the hallway. Not a soul in either direction, so she quickly stepped inside.

The room was vast and devoid of furniture other than ceiling-high shelves lining the walls. A dolly and an electric ladder lift leaned against a stack of crates. Emily examined the items on the shelf. Some appeared to be specialized diets or types of herbal remedies. Many of the box labels were in Chinese or German. Emily tapped the camera button on her recorder, taking pictures that she could research later. Another row of shelves held different kinds of devices using some version of electric treatment: She read the labels and snapped photos of devices with bizarre names like Bioresonance Therapy; Electrophysiological Feedback Xrroid; and something called a Rife Frequency Generator that claimed on the label to cure cancer by transmitting radio waves.

One shelf contained rows of boxes labeled, "Clark's Cure For All Cancers," another with something called Hoxey Therapy, and a third, Kelley Treatment. Emily was so busy snapping photos, she almost didn't hear the footsteps outside the door. She crouched behind the crates just as the door swung open.

"Did you leave this door unlocked?" a male voice said.

"No, I swear it was locked when I left," said another. "Someone else must have been in here."

Emily held her breath while the two men haggled. She wondered what she would say if they found her, or, something she hadn't thought of—if there was a video camera in the room.

"The hell with it," said the first voice. "Leave it for now and let's get those other crates moved in so we can go to lunch."

When she could no longer hear the fading footsteps, Emily cautiously opened the door and peered out before stepping back into the hallway. She took a deep breath to compose herself and walked back to the waiting room.

"Please help yourself to a beverage," said the smiling receptionist. "The doctor will be with you shortly."

"Thank you." Emily let the ice-cold liquid slide down her throat, picked up a *Smithsonian Magazine*, and sank into one of the plush oxblood-red leather chairs. She thumbed through the magazine while the list of questions she had for Kingsley ran through her head: *What is your specialty? Where did you receive your training? How much do you charge? And, most importantly, Where is Daisy Todechine?*

"Miss Yazzie?" said the tall, distinguished man standing at the head of the hallway. Curly black hair turning silver at the temples had been carefully cut to provide a polished professional look. She caught sight of a white slash of perfect teeth when he smiled at her and extended his hand. Only his eyes, gun-metal gray, remained disengaged.

*A real lady killer*, Emily thought. She stood and accepted the two-handed clasp—hands that were too soft for a man and that had probably never seen a day of hard labor. A whiff of aftershave, an expensive brand, breath mints, hair mousse, and something else—something she couldn't put her finger on got her attention. Something funereal.

Kingsley led Emily into his "consultation room" and invited her to sit on one of the two brocade chairs facing his desk. After settling himself in his matching swivel chair, he propped his elbows on the polished cherry-wood desk, made a tent with his fingers, and leaned forward, staring intently into her eyes. "Now tell me about your sister, Miss Yazzie," he said, his modulated southern accent dripping with concern.

Emily forced herself to meet his gaze and related her fictional story, even allowing her voice to break when she described her sister's symptoms and about the doctor's pronouncement of 'only two months to live.' "Do you think you can help her, Dr. Kingsley?"

"Absolutely. After a thorough exam and diagnosis, a program can be implemented to put your dear sister on the road to recovery," he smooth-talked. "We have tools at our disposal in the clinic that are not available to the mainstream medical establishment." He handed Emily a glossy brochure that featured colored photographs of men and women with testimonials to their newly regained health.

Emily glanced at the smiling faces of people she doubted had ever been diagnosed with a life-threatening disease. "It's a Miracle!" one of the captions proclaimed. "Dr. Kingsley Brought Me Back from Death's Door!" said another. She let her eyes rove over the diplomas and certificates lining the wall, the awards that claimed Kingsley was tops in Holistic Neuropathy.

"But, the equipment is costly, as are the rare special herbs and tinctures. My clients are required to stay at our facility during the treatment stage. We offer commodious private rooms with all the amenities and a special diet individually prescribed to fit the patient's particular issues."

"Money is no object. My family has recently come into a large sum due to an oil lease with the government, and we would pay anything to save Jeannie's life." Emily noticed a flash of light in the man's dead eyes at the mention of money. "How much are we talking about?"

"It depends, of course, on which tier or personalized combination of treatment procedures are required after a diagnosis is made. There is a price list on the second page of that brochure that describes the different levels."

The numbers were staggering. A quick calculation added up to more than $180,000 for one month of treatment, and that was the cheapest option. Emily tried to keep the shock out of her voice and said in a thoughtful manner. "I see. But, how can I be sure you will actually cure my sister, Dr. Kingsley?"

"You have read the testimonials of my former patients, and there are more if you need proof," said the man.

*Those testimonials are undoubtedly fake, and the dead don't talk*, Emily thought. "Yes, I'm very impressed and amazed," is what she said instead. "Now, I'd like to see the patient's rooms, if you don't mind."

"No problem at all. Naturally, we can't invade the privacy of patients who are undergoing treatment, but I do have a vacant room I can show you."

The showroom that looked as if it had never been inhabited could only be described as richly luxurious. Located in an adjoining wing of the clinic, it overlooked a rose garden and the fountain. Filtered sunlight reflected off a crystal water pitcher and glass. A pair of comfortable-looking upholstered chairs were placed on either side of a glass table. The walls were a warm peach, and the bed was covered with a plush floral-patterned comforter.

"Beautiful," Emily said. Her roving eye noted the lack of medical equipment, and she asked the doctor about that.

"We want our patients to feel as much at home as possible and not as if they are in a dreary hospital, so all equipment is movable and only wheeled in when necessary." Kingsley led Emily out of the room and closed the door.

"I'll discuss this with my parents, explain the costs and everything. I'm sure we'll be contacting you soon about bringing my sister in." In truth, Emily was surprised that the man had not asked more questions or requested that medical records be sent. She followed Kingsley back to the reception area, lagging a few paces behind. There was a half-dozen more doors along this hallway, all closed. As she passed one, she heard a moan, a few words in *Diné Bizaad*. A nameplate on the door read Daisy Todechne. Emily froze then quickly turned the knob and pulled the door open. When she saw the figure lying on the bed, she drew in a sharp breath and clasped her hand over her mouth to keep from crying out.

Kingsley quickly closed the door. "You must not impose on the privacy of my patients," he admonished, his voice changing from the cajoling, honeyed tones of before to a taut guttural snap.

Emily kept her mouth shut, but she couldn't erase the image of the desiccated skeletal figure with sunken eyes that lay strapped to the bed. Daisy had once been a plump vivacious woman, quick to make a joke, always on the go and ready to help whoever needed it. *I'll get you out of here, Daisy*, she swore to herself.

# 29

"Who was that on the phone, dad?" Raven asked looking up from her homework.

"That was Mom, sweetheart. She has to work late tonight, but she'll be here when you wake up in the morning."

Raven's lower lip pooched out and trembled. "I don't want her to work late," she whined.

Bertha gave Abe an inquisitive look, but Emily had insisted Abe tell no one of her plans. He lifted Raven onto his lap and brushed a tear from her cheek. "There's nothing to worry about. You know, police officers don't always get to come home right on time. She's fine, just has to finish up a job. Dad, Grandma, and Will are going to stay here with you. Now, how about we saddle up the horses and take a little ride down the river trail?"

Later that evening, when the dinner dishes were cleared, and Raven was bathed, and in her pajamas, Abe stood on his deck in the darkness looking down on the reflection of the moon on the rippling waters of the river. He had plenty of unanswered questions himself, about Emily's sudden flight to

Las Vegas. She had been vague concerning her reasons for leaving so soon and about the need for secrecy. *I have to interview a possible witness,* she had told him. *I'll explain more when I get home. I don't have time right now, the plane leaves in twenty minutes, but I think I'm on to something. Kiss our baby girl. I love you guys.*

At this time of night, when all was quiet, the craving for a cigarette was intense—the stinky kind, as Raven called them. But he had given up smoking for good when his child was born, except for an occasional puff with Will on some of that sacred tobacco or taking a hit of some good weed whenever Will scored.

Abe listened to the crickets chirping, the gurgle of the river flowing over rocks, and the call and answer toots of a pair of Western Screech-owls. It was a rare tranquil moment until something seemed wrong. The crickets had stopped, their chirps replaced by snorts and whinnies from the horses. Abe listened, first to the ensuing silence, then to a rustle of movement in the underbrush near the barn. Like the hackles of a dog, it felt as if the hairs on the back of his neck were standing on end. Abe ducked behind the railing and slowed his breathing, listening for anything out of the ordinary. He thought it could possibly be a coyote or even a bear snooping around the barn in search of a free meal, but with the recent events, he had to be sure. A twig snapped, and he heard the crunch of feet on gravel. Animal? Man?

Still crouched, Abe crept down the steps of the deck and circled around until he was behind the barn. He inched his way along the west wall, treading as softly as possible. The horses snorted again. He reached the front wall and poked his head around the corner. The partially hidden moon cast a faint glow on the figure of a man holding something in his hand—a container of some kind.

*Shit*! Abe thought as he watched the man toss a glass bottle into the barn door. The glass shattered and Abe caught the whiff of gasoline. He lunged at the figure, but not in time to stop the man from throwing a lit book of matches onto the gas-soaked wood. The front of the barn was immediately engulfed in a wall of flame. The intruder, who had been knocked down, stood and began running away, but Abe couldn't give chase.

His first thought was for the animals trapped inside. He knew there was a fire-extinguisher attached inside the door, but he would have to break down the door and run through the flames to reach it. There was no time to call for help or to fetch protective covering. Abe held a handkerchief over his face, then kicked open the door and rushed inside. Despite the full moon, the smoke was so dense he could hardly see, so he felt for the spot where the fire extinguisher was attached. As soon as his hand grasped the metal cylinder, he pulled the pin and squeezed the handle spraying the door and surrounding wall. He could hear the horses stomping and snorting, and Will, somewhere outside the barn calling his name. Abe made his way through the smoke to the stables and let the horses out of their pens. A whack on the rump sent Red galloping toward the exit with Jessie, the Appaloosa, close behind. Choking on smoke, and still unable to see, Abe found his way to where he had hidden the gun. He grabbed the rifle and a packet of ammo, slipped a shell into the chamber, then dropped to the ground and crawled toward the exit, trying to steer clear of the white fire-extinguisher foam.

A gush of water sprayed over and around him, quenching any remaining flames, then Will put down the garden hose and pulled Abe to his feet leading him away from the barn.

"Raven?" Abe gasped between coughs.

"She's fine. Mom wanted to come out, but I told her it would be better if she stayed with Raven. She was already asleep, so she doesn't know anything about the fire. I heard a vehicle spin out of here, then I saw the flames and came running. You all right?"

"Yeah, a few minor burns on my hands, a little smoke inhalation. I put the fire out before it got inside. "Did you see the son of a bitch who did this?" Abe coughed between gasps for air. He spun around, swinging the rifle and looking in all directions.

"No. Taillights from a pickup is all. He was halfway down the road when I came out. I was more concerned about you than chasing down whoever was out here."

"Yeah, thanks, Will. The bastard's gone, and if I'd fired, Raven would have woke up scared to death." Abe inhaled deeply, replenishing his lungs with the clean night air. "The horses okay?"

"They're in the corral—no damage that I can see—spooked is all. I gotta tell ya, though, Abe." Will used the back of his hand to wipe sweat from his burn-scarred face. "Seeing a fire like that again freaked me out. Flashbacks had me paralyzed for a moment there. If I'd been quicker…"

"Hey. You did the right thing, man. We're even on that score. Wish I could have caught the son of a bitch, though." He ran his fingers lightly over blisters forming on the back of his right hand and grimaced. "Why do you think he tried to burn down my barn Will? "

"Someone is trying to send a message. Seems like certain people want to scare Emily off this investigation. Maybe she's getting too close to something. Hell, I don't know."

"Right." Abe rubbed his hands again, the gauze covering his cut had nearly burned away.

"You must have got scorched pretty bad busting through that door. Let mom take a look at those hands."

"I'm okay. I want to check the barn and try to clean up this mess before Raven sees it."

Will pulled a pair of gloves out of his back pocket and put them on. "You gonna call this in?" he said as he stomped on a few embers near the door.

"No. I'll talk to Emily when she gets back from Vegas. See what she says. She's not sharing much with her boss, or anyone else right now, and I guess she's got her reasons. Shit, what next?"

The damage to the barn door and wall was minimal since Abe had arrived on the scene so quickly. He and Will hosed the area down to make sure there were no glowing embers, then swept the floor and left the door open to air out the barn. Abe put fresh hay in the horses' stalls and clean water in their troughs. After securing the barn, he noticed something lying on the ground near the entrance. Moonlight caught the glint of the silver shaft of a ballpoint pen. He squatted down and picked it up. The logo printed in black letters on the pen read *Strathmore Minerals – Excavation, Exploration, Energy Development.*

Raven slept in a fetal position, her thumb in her mouth. It had been a long time since she had given up sucking her thumb. Abe figured it had something to do with the stress, and it broke his heart to see her sweet vulnerability. Patch raised his head and wagged his tail when Abe tucked the covers around his daughter. "Keep a close watch on her, boy," he said before closing the door.

After Abe cleaned up and changed out of his smoky clothes, he applied ointment to his burns. They were minor, but another obstacle to piano playing. He only gave it a passing thought. There were too many other things on his mind.

"I'm going out to the barn," Abe said to Bertha and Will. He retrieved his mat and sleeping bag. "Just in case someone tries to come back to finish the job."

"Want me to join you?" Will asked.

"I'd feel better if you stayed in here and helped Bertha watch over Raven."

Bertha carried her coffee cup to the sink and rinsed it. "I'll be right in the room with her."

Abe placed the loaded rifle next to his sleeping bag on the clean hay near the door and sat down. From his vantage point, he had an unobstructed view of the road and driveway. He knew he wouldn't be sleeping, but if anyone came near his place, he would be ready.

# 30

A pair of headlights danced through the juniper lining the driveway. Abe picked up the rifle and ran to the sheltered side of the barn—a place where he could see but not be seen by an approaching vehicle. He remained in place, barely breathing, his finger on the trigger until he recognized the familiar shape and insignia of the Navajo Nation Police patrol SUV. Emerging out of the shadows and into the moonlight, he waved her down.

Emily parked in front of the barn close to him and stepped out, softly closing the cruiser's door and ran to where Abe was standing. "What are you doing out here with grandpa's rifle?" She sniffed at the acrid air. "I smell smoke. What happened? Is Raven all right?"

"She's fine." Abe leaned the gun against the wall and wrapped his arms around Emily. He felt her pounding heart. "Someone tried to set the barn on fire, but I got out here before too much damage was done," he said in a hushed voice. "Raven slept through the whole thing, and Bertha's with her. I was waiting for the asshole to come back."

When she pulled herself back so she could look at his face, Abe saw anger and trepidation in her eyes.

"Did you get a look at the person?'

"No. All I saw were tail lights when the vehicle rounded that last curve, but I'm pretty sure it was a pickup, and I can make a guess at who the driver was. He left a calling card—a pen with the Strathmore Minerals logo."

"Abe," she said, still staring intently into his eyes. "What were you planning to do with the gun?"

"Shoot the bastard if he came back. Come on," he said, taking Emily's hand and pulling her through the barn door. "Let's talk inside, so we don't wake anyone. I want to hear what happened to you today."

They sat side by side on the sleeping bag Abe had spread over a thick layer of clean hay, their backs leaning on a blanket-covered bale. "Talk to me," Abe said as he draped his arm over Emily's shoulder. He felt her shudder before she spoke.

"I caught a glimpse of Daisy. She looked like a corpse. Her skin was yellow, her eyes sunken into her face. If I hadn't heard her speaking in Navajo, I would have sworn she was dead, she was so thin and withered. They had strapped her to the bed and attached some kind of electrodes to her head and different parts of her body. It was terrible. I wanted to run in there and free her, take her home with me, but I knew I couldn't. . ."

"Because only her husband can sign for her release," Abe finished. "Why would he leave her in such a place?"

"The oncologists in Albuquerque told him it was over—there was nothing else they could do, but Todechine couldn't accept the fact she's dying, and he would do anything if he thought there was a chance to save her. This place she's in is a huge rip-off. It caters to the wealthy and charges a fortune for false promises. I know the chief doesn't have that kind of money, so he's indebted to someone."

"And, someone wants you to back off from any further investigation of Strathmore Minerals. That fire tonight was meant to intimidate you."

"I think you're right. No one knew I was in Phoenix except you and Martinez, so it must have been planned for me to see."

Emily shivered again, and Abe pulled her closer.

"I called Martinez to pick me up when I landed in Farmington. He had some news for me. This evening, a woman herding sheep discovered a body at the bottom of a rocky cliff outside of Chinle. The Feds think it's Steve Sanford. It looked like he had been there a couple of days, but they couldn't be sure. The actual cause of death is still unknown."

"An accident or was he becoming a liability?" Abe asked.

"I don't know, but I intend to find out." Emily snuggled deeper into the crook of Abe's shoulder. "Did you call anyone about the fire, Abe?"

"No. Will helped me put it out, and Bertha knows. That's all."

"Good. Let's keep it quiet."

Abe used his free hand to caress the contours of Emily's face. He loved the feel of her high cheekbones and smooth skin. "Do you remember the first time we made love in Sally's barn?"

She chuckled. "How could I forget."

He tilted her chin so that she was facing him and kissed her long and hard. "I think it's time for a repeat performance."

"Yes," Emily whispered. "Only hold that thought. I need to see for myself that my baby girl is all right."

Abe nodded and helped her to her feet. "I'll be waiting."


Everyone in the house was sound asleep. After tiptoeing into Raven's room and assuring herself that her daughter was okay, Emily went into the bathroom to freshen up. She splashed cold water on her face in an attempt to wash away the day's events, brushed her teeth then returned to the barn. Stripping off her clothes, she crawled into the sleeping bag and Abe's waiting arms. Pressing herself against his warm naked body, she was able to forget, if only temporarily, the horrific vision of Daisy.


Emily called the dispatcher the following morning saying she would be checking in at ten. She wanted to spend some time with Raven before starting back on the case. Next, she called Martinez, relaying the same information.

"Where do you want me to go, Sarge?" asked Martinez.

"Stay in the office until I get there. Catch up on paperwork, study the manuals, whatever to look busy. Any new information on Sanford's cause of death?"

"Not yet. Sanford's sister has been notified, and she's coming in to make a positive identification. The victim's in the morgue at the Farmington Hospital. They're going to transport the body to Albuquerque for the autopsy at five this afternoon.

"We'll get over to the morgue when I come in. I want to get a look at the body and hear what the preliminaries say." Emily waited through the pause that followed before the rookie cop's perfunctory, 'yes ma'am.' She was acutely aware of the Navajo's reluctance to view a corpse, especially that of a non-native who had died on reservation land. The belief among her people was that the viewer would be cursed with "ghost sickness" and bad luck would follow them wherever they went. Just the same, police work took you down paths you didn't want to go. It was part of the job. She changed the subject, asking, "Do you have any information about Kingsley, that doctor in Las Vegas?"

"Yes, Sergeant. I found a goldmine of info on him. Let me get my notes."

Emily noticed how his voice had perked up, how animated and eager he was to get his mind off the dead *bilagaana* and share his findings. She heard a rustling of paper.

"I did some research at the library after I finished my shift. It took a while, but I got the goods on Kingsley, Sarge. An investigative reporter from Miami, Florida helped fill in a lot of the details."

"What did you find out?"

Martinez cleared his throat. "First off, Kingsley is not his real name. He was born Alfred Johnson to sharecroppers in Mississippi but has used a variety of aliases throughout the years. He was a smart kid, and after graduating from high school, he received a scholarship to the University of Alabama Medical School but was caught cheating on his exams and expelled in 1980. Smart, but crooked from the start. He served time in prison for various shady deals: extortion; fraud; blackmail. By the time he was released, he had worked out a new scheme—marry rich widows and soak them for all he could get. With his good looks and smooth talk, I guess it was easy to seduce vulnerable old ladies. They all died on him, and he made sure he inherited their fortunes. His degrees are fake, like him."

Emily was impressed. "Great work, Martinez. Get the paperwork verifying this information, and we'll be able to shut down that torture chamber. Send copies of your report to the Nevada Attorney General, Las Vegas Chief of Police, and FBI headquarters in Nevada. Is Todechine in his office today?"

"Yes, ma'am. Looks like our chief hasn't slept in a week."

"Be careful Todechine doesn't get wind of what you're doing. He's too personally involved to be objective."

"Right, Sergeant."

"Okay, I'll see you at ten."

After she had hung up the phone, Emily sat in the quiet alcove off the living room thinking about the implications of her actions. The chief would be furious, but Daisy would be brought home, and at least she could die in *Dinétah*, her ancestral land.

Filtered sunlight danced through the sheer curtains, and she could hear the sounds of water running in the kitchen, and pots and pans rattling as Bertha started breakfast, then the pattering of small feet.

"Mommy, mommy, where are you?"

"Right here, sweetheart. Come and give me a hug."

Autopsies to determine the cause of death on the reservation were conducted in Albuquerque by a state-appointed forensic pathologist out of the Office of New Mexico Medical Investigators. The Navajo Nation had a small forensic team with a specially trained and certified Field Deputy Medical Investigator who was commissioned to conduct investigations and gather information wherever the body was found, but that was it. Additionally, when an autopsy was deemed necessary by the Navajo Nation, the FBI had to be called in on the investigation. That meant Emily was forced to take a backseat while the Feds horned in on her case.

"Why does the FBI have to be involved?" Martinez asked. Emily had let him drive to the Farmington Hospital Morgue where the body of Steve Sanford was being held before transporting it to Albuquerque.

"Because we don't have the trained personnel, the facility, or the financial means to pay for autopsies, and the Feds will pay for it. All we can do is a preliminary investigation, but in suspected homicide cases, the Feds are always called in, and they often cover costs. I'll warn you in advance. When we do meet them, they won't let us forget they're paying the bill. We're going to have to deal with some condescending attitudes from the swell-headed black-suits, but in the meantime, the team in the morgue is our guys."

The county morgue was located on the ground floor of the hospital. Emily noted Martinez's hang-dog expression as he trailed behind her in the lobby. They entered the elevator, and Emily pressed 'B.'

"Don't look so miserable. I know it's bad luck to gaze on the dead, and I don't relish the idea either, but we're not going to see any slice and dice. The Anglo pros will do a forensic autopsy in Albuquerque. We're going to take a quick look and try to get some info concerning the cause of death from the preliminary team."

"It's a dead white man, " Martinez said.

"If you're going to be a cop, it won't be the only *bilagaana* corpse you'll run up against. Pull yourself together, Martinez."

A whoosh of cold air greeted them when they stepped out of the elevator. Emily walked up to a green door and rapped her knuckles against the metal surface.

Navajo Chief Field Investigator, Bob Haske, cracked the door open, peeked out, then beckoned them inside when he saw Emily.

"Hey, Sergeant Etcitty. How's it hanging? Brought your little brother along, I see." Bob Haske had been with the department for over twenty years. His lined face and lanky limbs had taken on the gray hue of the dead he worked with on a daily basis—some natural deaths, some accidental, some suicide, and some murdered.

"Hanging in there, Haske. This is my new partner, Raymond Martinez. Got time for a few questions?"

"I can make time." He indicated a cabinet near the entrance that contained shower caps, gowns, rubber gloves, and booties. You've met Sanford before, right? When you're suited up, come and take a look. Make sure we ID'd the right guy."

"What's this for?" Martinez asked as he pulled a shower cap over his hair.

"Keeps you from contaminating the body and screwing up the evidence, like depositing some of your hair or skin flakes," Haske said.

"Got it," said Martinez and slipped the plastic booties over his shoes.

The other two members of the team were standing over a metal gurney holding a body with a white sheet draped over it. Emily nodded in their direction, and they gave her a tilt of the chin in greeting. Amy Goldtooth, the squat, chunky photographer, pulled back the sheet and resumed snapping pictures of the body from different angles, while Jimmy Atsa, youngest of the three and sporting a wispy mustache, scribbled notes onto a clipboard. The county coroner, who had declared the victim deceased at the scene, and who probably had the least training of anyone in the room, sat at a desk shuffling through a stack of papers, nominally overseeing the preliminaries.

A sickening odor, as if someone had tried to cover the stench of rotten meat by spraying it with perfumed air freshener, permeated the room. Emily shivered in the refrigerated air. She saw Martinez swallow hard, his Adam's apple bobbing up and down. "Let's get this over with," she said.

Though the back of the head had been caved in, the face, remained recognizable—definitely Sanford. A slight green coloration tinted his skin and swollen abdomen, but due to the cold outside temperature, decomposition was not advanced.

"What's your take on the time of death?" Emily asked.

"We can't be sure without analyzing the liver," Haske said. "Rigor mortis is complete. But, considering the cold temperature lately, the moment of death could have happened sometime within the range of eighteen to twenty-four hours prior to the discovery of the body. We'll know more when the state forensic officer takes a look inside."

Martinez had looked at the body then turned away, stealing occasional quick glances.

"Cause?" Martinez asked.

Goldtooth and Atsa carefully rolled the cadaver on his side, and the camera began clicking once again.

"Blunt trauma to the head. See this indentation with the bruising and edema?" Haske said, forcing Martinez to focus on the caved-in back of the skull.

The rookie cop paled but didn't turn away.

"Would that kind of wound happen in a fall?" Emily asked.

"It could, but not likely. What got my attention is the soil samples in and around the wound are different from the soil in the canyon at Chinle where the body was discovered. I think he was struck on the head from behind with a heavy object, like a tire iron, and the body was moved."

"Can you determine where the soil sample on the wound came from?" asked Martinez.

"Maybe. We'll compare it with our soil analysis chart and let you know," Haske said.

"Did you find anything interesting in his pockets?" Emily asked.

"No. he had no identification and nothing in his pockets."

"Strange," Emily said. "Maybe whoever did this didn't want the body identified. What made you think it was Sanford?"

"That wound to the shoulder," said Haske, pointing to a prominent laceration. "It's older than the other contusions but still relatively recent. Not caused by any fall—more likely, gunshot. I remembered my team investigated the crime scene out by that stock pond about ten days ago, so I checked the incident report. Everything pointed to the deceased and Sanford being the same guy. His sister will be here soon to make identification conclusive."

"Nice deduction on the part of you and your team, Haske. Fax me a copy of your report when you're done."

"Gotcha, Sergeant," Bob Haske said as he turned to the task of scraping and preserving evidence from under Sanford's nails.

The San Juan County medical examiner, old Mort Sullivan, looked up from his desk while Emily and Martinez were stripping off their protective clothing. They dropped everything into a Sterilite Trash Bin and were buzzed out. "Keep up the good work, Mort," Emily said over her shoulder while thinking to herself, *the old fart's probably been napping the whole time.*

Back in the elevator, she gave Martinez the once-over. Some of the color had returned to his face. "You survived your first close encounter with a body. Now that wasn't so bad was it?"

His Adam's apple bobbed, but his face remained noncommittal. "No, ma'am."

# 31

Abe watched as Bertha helped Raven with her math homework. His daughter appeared more like her bouncy self and showed no sign she knew of last night's fire. Early this morning as the sun burned through a tangerine sky, he and Will had walked the perimeter of the ten acres looking for anything out of order. They had checked and double-checked his property, but had found nothing other than the skid marks in the driveway from the truck that had sped away in the dark.

Indian summer had returned to the Four Corners of New Mexico, melting all remnants of the earlier snowstorm. Despite the warmth, Abe felt a chill. He knew too well the unpredictability of New Mexico weather, and that freezing temperatures could return at the whim of Mother Nature. Will had stayed in the barn to smoke his pipe and practice his protection prayer songs for Raven. Ostensibly, he was also keeping an eye out for intruders.

Abe paced the house, stopping to look out the door and check the driveway every few minutes. Restless and edgy, he wanted to do something, like go after the perpetrator who had threatened the sanctity of his home, but he felt reluctant to leave Raven. He made a decision to contact Malcolm Keetso.

The same young woman who had answered the first time he called picked up on the second ring.

"Yes?"

Abe recognized her voice, knew her name from his class roster, but he didn't use it. He identified himself and said he needed to make contact with Keetso.

She paused. "Mr. Keetso's busy, but I'll see what I can do."

He heard the disconnect on the other end and hung up. Today was Tuesday, only three days before the Navajo Council's vote on the proposal to allow Strathmore Minerals to mine uranium on the reservation. Keetso would be getting his followers ready for the protest demonstration in Window Rock. Abe wasn't sure how he would approach the Native American activist if he did call back—maybe just get straight to the point. A half an hour later, the telephone rang. He took the cordless receiver into his bedroom and closed the door.

"Freeman, this is Keetso."

"Hey, how's that piano working out?'

"Unfortunately, I haven't had much time to practice, but that isn't why you called."

Abe took a deep breath. "I've got a favor to ask."

"What's this about?"

Abe told Keetso about the abduction of Raven and her rescue from the tin shed. He mentioned his suspicions about the security guard at the school. "Last night someone tried to burn my barn down. I have an idea who it was, and I want to find him, but I need your help."

"Do you think it was the security guard that tried to burn your place?"

"No, but he did disappear right after Raven was kidnapped. I'd like to find him because I believe he did take my little girl and lock her in that shed, but I think someone else set fire to my barn, and you might have enough connections to help me find him."

"Yeah? Who we talking about?"

"An ex-cop you had the pleasure of meeting, or more precisely, two ex-cops."

"I've run against a lot of cops in my day. Anglo or *Diné*?"

"Former Navajo Nation Police Officers—Gomez and Talltree."

Silence on the other end of the line while Keetso seemed to be putting his thoughts in order. "Those are the two that came out to my camp with your girlfriend. A pair of assholes. You said 'former' cops?"

"Yeah. They were both put on probation after harassing me and threatening my daughter. Shortly after that, they quit the force and haven't been seen. You know a lot of people. Can you ask around and see if anyone knows their whereabouts?"

"I can do that. Have you checked the homes of record?"

"I don't want to leave my daughter, even though her grandmother and uncle are here. I promised Raven I would stay and protect her. Also, being a white man, I'd draw a lot of attention if I started asking questions on the rez."

"Understood." After a moment's hesitation, Keetso added, "I'm familiar with those two. They fired on my men at my first camp, and I know they've been trying to get at me ever since. I'm going to send two of my men out to guard your place. Give me the directions."

Abe thought that over. "They'll keep a low profile? I don't want anything that might spook my little girl."

"Nobody will even know they're around, but I guarantee they won't miss a move. Leave it to me."

"Okay. I owe you."

"You give piano lessons?" Keetso asked.

"Yeah, sure, we'll work something out."


After Abe had returned the receiver to its cradle, he sat down at the kitchen table across from Raven. His daughter glanced up from her workbook and grinned at his wink.

"How's the math going?"

"It's too easy, dad. I already know this stuff."

"Okay, then, recess time," said Abe. "Why don't we go out in this beautiful sunshiny morning and find some crows to feed. Bring some corn and sunflower seeds.

A big smile lit up his daughter's face. "Ravens, dad. They're ravens, remember. Let's go. I'll call them."

Bertha stood, her arms crossed over her chest. "Abe Freeman, you are a bad influence on this child's studies."

"Bertha," Abe said. "You know there are more lessons to be learned in nature than in any workbook."

Bertha sighed and nodded her head, her voice was light and playful when she teased, "Go on and get out of my hair you two."

They stopped at the barn to invite Will along on the walk and listened in silence as he chanted a beautiful blessing prayer:

*"Mother Earth may there be beauty where you lay a foundation of stability. Father Sky, my father from up above, bless my niece. Mountain Woman, grandma, serve as her guide today. Water Woman, grandma, nourish her spirit. White Shell Woman, mother, bless her with beauty. Father Sun bless her with warmth. May she travel among her relations with humility, love, and safety. May they look upon her with the same regard. May all the animals greet her as their relative. May there be sunlight upon her feet, body, palms, heart, shoulders, tongue, ears, eyes. I wish all my loved ones to be restored to good health. May they walk in beauty."*

When Will had finished, he beckoned to Raven. "That prayer was for you, little one. Come closer. I made something, and you gotta carry it with you at all times." He took a small deer-skin pouch with a rawhide drawstring and tie and draped it around Raven's neck. The hide had been worked until it was as soft and smooth as a baby rabbit's ear. "This is where you will keep your *tádídíín*, corn pollen, gathered by your grandmother. Now you can offer a pinch to the gods—the mountains, streams, sun, and moon. And to the animals for their blessings and protection."

"Thank you, uncle," said Raven. Her voice was filled with reverence and awe, and the sweet innocent belief in magic potions as she clutched the pouch in her small hand. "Can I offer *tádídíín* to the ravens too?"

"Of course. Those birds are your sacred protectors, and they'll always be watching out for you if you honor them."

"Come with us, Will. We're going bird-watching. If we're lucky, we'll find some of those 'sacred protectors.'"

They followed a meandering path from the barn until it reached the trail that bordered the bank of the Animas River three hundred yards below Abe's house. Acorns and brown oak leaves crunched beneath their feet. The water moved swiftly, augmented by recent snow and rains, tumbling over aggregations of boulders. Yellow cottonwood and willow leaves swirled in the light breeze and floated like armadas of tiny ships on the water's surface. Raven made a clicking noise with her tongue, communicating in her secret language with the birds. Soon her calls were answered by low gurgling croaks.

"There they are," Raven said, pointing to the black silhouettes of two large birds perched on the limb of a dead willow above the river's edge. Their dark forms contrasted with the chimerical robin's egg sky. Raven began talking to them in earnest, and they, in turn, answered with short clicks and caws, cocking their heads as if listening intently.

Abe held back while his daughter approached the birds. He let his eyes roam over the surrounding woodlands, scanning the landscape for anything or anyone that didn't belong. But the land was undisturbed and quiet, except for the raucous shriek of a mountain jay. "Don't get too near the edge of the river," he cautioned Raven. She had stopped ten feet in front of the tree, opened her pouch and took a pinch of corn pollen.

"Thank you for protecting me," she said as she stretched her arm toward the corvids and released the pollen. The pair of ravens shifted their weight from one leg to the other and looked at her as if expecting more. "Now, I'm going to leave you some food." Abe handed her the bag of corn and sunflower seeds, and she poured some on the ground in a neat pile.

The birds side-stepped along the branch until they were closer to Raven, twisted their heads to get a better look and emitted a series of hoarse coos before spreading their wings, dropping their feet like landing gear and swooping to the ground.

Abe swallowed the lump in his throat, wanting to believe in protection prayers and magic pollen—wishing that trust in imaginary, unseen gods could actually protect his family. But, he lacked the faith the Navajo held for their sacred ancestors and prayers. His Jewish belief had been shattered when Sharon died, and he no longer believed in the God of Judaism. *If only it were that simple, no harm would have ever come to the people I've loved,* he thought as his eyes darted in the direction of the sound of a snapping twig. The gray squirrel scampered up a piñon tree, but Abe did not cease his watchful vigilance.

# 32

It took two hours to cover the distance between Farmington and Chinle, Arizona, putting Emily and Martinez at the scene where the corpse had been recovered. The woman who had reported the body was reluctant to return to the site or to discuss the deceased, so they had followed her directions, hiking close to three miles along a high ridge until reaching the yellow tape that marked off the crime scene. Emily understood why the woman did not want to revisit the scene and the desecration of sacred land. She and Martinez stared down the canyon where Sanford had been found. The landscape was dotted with deep gorges and beautiful red sandstone spires. In the Navajo language, Chinle meant "the place where the water runs out" referring to nearby Canyon de Chelly. It would have been a fantastic hike with Abe and Raven under different circumstances.

Despite the rough terrain, passage would not be impossible with the right vehicle. Emily thought the trail they followed could have been accessed by jeep or ATV. The distance between the tracks was narrower than a standard pickup, and the twelve-inch tread of a four-wheeler's tracks confirmed her suspicions. She didn't take out her camera, knowing that Haske's team would have taken photos and measurements and that she would receive a full report of their findings. But, out of habit, she needed to view the site in person. It helped her form perspective and provided a starting point for the investigation.

"See if we can follow these ATV tracks to wherever they left the main road," she said to Martinez. "I didn't notice any near the woman's trailer."

"Looks like they came and went this way," Martinez said. "See the broken sage stems and how the grass is pushed down."

They lost the trail on solid rock surfaces but picked it up again wherever there was vegetation or bare soil. Veering away from the sheepherder's camp, Martinez spotted the starting point where the ATV had left Highway 7, a few hundred yards from the entrance to Canyon de Chelly.

"Must have had a four-wheeler in the back of a truck," Martinez said.

Emily nodded, noting the tread marks where a vehicle had parked alongside the road and the telltale signs of the smaller ATV. This time she did snap some shots, getting close-ups of the truck's tread pattern. "Take measurements of these, then let's go on to the Visitor's Center, get something to drink. Maybe the ranger noticed a pickup parked out here and can give us a description."

Martinez took off his hat and wiped his brow with a handkerchief. Even though it was late October, the day was warm, and they had hiked over five miles in the midday sun. "Sounds good. I could use something cold."

The Canyon de Chelly National Monument was located entirely on Navajo Reservation land and managed jointly by Navajo Parks and Recreation and National Park Service. Emily introduced herself and Martinez to the Navajo park ranger, exchanged some small talk, and the two were invited into his office.

"Have a seat. Can I get you some cold water?' asked Ranger Tom Bedonie. "You two look mighty thirsty."

"Thanks. Water would be great, We're investigating a crime site near here, and we've been hiking the canyon looking for evidence," said Emily.

Bedonie extracted two bottles of water from a small refrigerator. "Word gets around. I heard about the body found near here. You think it wasn't an accident?"

Emily unscrewed the cap and took a long drink before answering. "That's what we want to clarify."

Martinez emptied his water bottle and set it on the floor. "We're wondering if you saw anything out of the ordinary?"

"Like what?" Bedonie asked. "We get a lot of people through here."

"Like a pickup truck parked alongside the road near the park a few days ago," Emily said.

Bedonie leaned back in his chair and closed his eyes. "Three days ago, after I closed the center and left for home, I noticed a truck on the shoulder. I thought the driver might be having engine trouble, so I stopped, but there wasn't anyone around. Next day, when I came to work, it was gone."

"Can you describe the truck and approximately where you saw it?" Martinez pulled a pad and pen out of his shirt pocket and gave the ranger an expectant look.

"Black. I always thought black was a terrible color for a truck out here. Gets too damn hot and shows all the dust. I noticed it was a Ford and the tailgate was down. Might have been an F-150, newer model. I'm a Chevy man myself. It was parked about 600 yards from the entrance."

Emily felt a surge of adrenalin, a drumming in her heart. Out of the corner of her eye, she noticed that Martinez was scribbling furiously on his notepad. She caught his eye, and a look of acknowledgment passed between them. "Are you certain about the date?"

"Absolutely. It was my anniversary, and my wife and I had plans to go out. Didn't want to be late."

Emily rose, followed by Martinez. "You've been a big help, Ranger Bedonie. Here's my number if you think of anything else. We'll be getting in touch with you."

"Glad to help," said Bedonie. "Hey, you guys want me to run you back to your vehicle? The National Park Services Ranger can handle things for a few minutes while I'm gone."

"Appreciate it," Emily said. "One more thing—would you be willing to testify in court?"

"Hell, yes. We try to keep things nice and calm out here. Don't want to drive away the tourists."

"You do a great job," said Martinez.

"You gonna issue a warrant for Gomez's arrest?" asked Martinez when they were back in the squad car. "That sure as hell sounds like his truck."

"Not yet," Emily said. "I want the charges to stick when we throw the cuffs on him, and there's Talltree to deal with. I think they're both involved. We'll play it safe and keep digging up more info. And, Martinez, don't talk about this to anyone." *Especially the chief*, she thought. It made her sick to think about her boss being involved in a murder case and in sabotaging her investigation.

"Where're we goin' now?" asked Martinez.

Emily needed a break, time to think, and Martinez was always ready for a meal. "Garcia's Restaurant right off the highway in Chinle. They've got good tacos."

"I hear ya, Sergeant."

# 33

Abe roamed from room to room trying to appear calm for Raven's sake but felt too keyed up to relax. The attempted burning of his barn and the possible loss of his animals angered him more today than it had last night when he was busy dealing with it. Waiting made him nervous. His burnt and bandaged hands made it impossible to play the piano, his usual escape from stress, so he paced in anticipation for a phone call from Keetso—watching for uninvited visitors—keeping an eagle eye on Raven—wondering what new evidence Emily had uncovered.

"Dad, would you sit down on the couch with me and I'll read you a story. You look stressed."

He had to smile. A child too perceptive for her age. "Okay, sweetheart." But, he no sooner sat down than the telephone rang.

Abe jumped up and grabbed it before Bertha could and took the receiver into the bathroom.

"I've got something for you," said Keetso.

"I'm listening."

"It's about those two ex-cops. Harold Talltree has a reputation as a bully and meth user. After beating up his wife and abandoning her and their three kids in Ojo Amarillo, he moved in with a prostitute in a rundown trailer park outside of Kirtland—place called Piñon Park Playland. I hear he makes a habit of knocking around women when he's high and anyone else he sees as weak, so the woman he's shacking up with probably gets the same treatment, especially after she's scored a client and he wants the money."

"Talltree's a real piece of work," Abe said, remembering the incident when he and Gomez attempted to intimidate him.

"Yeah, I'd like to spend five minutes alone with the asshole. But no one was around when my sources checked, and Talltrees wasn't hanging out at Shorty's Bar where he pimps for his girlfriend. Since he lost his job, he spends a lot of time there. No one has seen him today."

That thought gave Abe a reason to pause. *Maybe Talltree is hanging around near here waiting for an opportunity to come back.* "What does he drive?"

"A white Dodge Ram. It has a dent in the left fender. Don't worry. Two of my guys are watching your place right now. If he shows up, I might get my five minutes before I hand him over to you."

"They must be invisible. I've been looking my place over all day, and I haven't seen anything."

"They are," said Keetso. "Now, as for Gordon "Gordie" Gomez, he lives alone and recently rented a small cabin a block from the *Diné* Baptist Church in Waterflow. That's right off

64. A black Ford truck is parked out front. Want my men to bring him in?"

"No, but if you can spare a man, I'd like someone to keep an eye on him, tail him if he leaves, and find out where he goes."

"I can do that. What about if my men catch either one of them around your place, do you want us to hold them for you?"

"I don't think they'll risk coming back here until night. I need to work something out so that my daughter is in a safe place  and no one here gets hurt."

"Okay, but my two guys aren't leaving until I give the word. If there is any trouble, they'll be on top of it. Are you coming to the protest march in Window Rock on Friday?"

"I wouldn't miss it, but isn't there a warrant out for your arrest? And I heard Todechine has it in for you."

"Charges were dropped, I'm not worried. I'll be there."

Thanks, Keetso. I'll call you back after I talk to Emily. I owe you."


After Abe hung up, he tried to think of a way to move Raven into a secret hiding place where she would feel safe, even if he were not there.  In a few minutes, it hit him. Raven loved spending time at the sheep ranch Will had inherited from his grandfather. She and Patch could pass hours with the sheep, helping Manuel move them to new grazing land and driving them to water holes, especially if she had her horse. If Emily agreed, Raven, Bertha, and Will would load up the horses and sneak out to the isolated trailer behind Huerfano Mesa where there was only one way in and one way out. It might be a little crowded with everyone there, but Will had added extra living space to the old silver Airstream when his partner, Manuel, had moved in with him. Another plus was the fact that Raven loved and trusted Manuel as if he were another uncle, and Manuel would protect her with his life. Abe would feel comfortable with his daughter in their care, and he, with the help of Keetso's men, could set a trap for Gomez and Talltree. He'd have to clear it with Emily first, of course. Maybe he would just mention the move to Will's place and leave out the detail that he planned to stay behind and get even with the two assholes who had wreaked so much havoc on his family.

Martinez bit into his goat and roasted green chile taco and smiled appreciatively. Garcia's Diner was busy with a mix of tourists and local natives, the former eyeing the menu with some trepidation, and generally opting for the proven safety of a cheeseburger. Emily guessed blood sausage would not find its way to the visitors' plate. She had played it safe herself with a Navajo taco loaded with plenty of beans and chile.

She dabbed at her mouth with a napkin and pushed her empty plate away. "Did you ever break into a house, Martinez?"

"Uh, just my own when I couldn't find my key. Why?'

"I know the investigators have gone through Sanford's place, and it's taped off. But, I'd like to take a look. Are you up for it?"

"Are you trying to get me fired before I make it past rookie?"

"We should be able to talk our way inside if there's an officer posted, but if not, we'll have to break in. You can say no—I won't hold it against you."

"Did the FBI conduct the initial search?"

"No, it was our officers."

Martinez wiped up the last of his beans with a piece of fry bread and stuffed it in his mouth. "I'm ready when you are, Sergeant."

Sanford's rented bungalow was located in a sparsely populated residential area on the north side of Farmington.

"Drive past the house and circle the block a couple of times, Martinez. If no one is around, we'll park in the alley."

Yellow tape stretched across the gate, and a sign stating 'Criminal Investigation – No Trespassing' was tacked to the front door, but there was no sign of police presence. Martinez parked the cruiser beside a dumpster in the alley a half-block from Sanford's. The backyard appeared to have never been maintained. Emily and Martinez checked the alley for onlookers then crouched low to the ground as they made their way to the back door. Shrub oak and juniper filled the dirt lot, allowing good cover for the two cops.

"Put these on," said Emily. She pulled out a pair of gloves for Martinez and herself. "Screen's latched," she said, pulling on the unyielding door.

Wielding a pocket knife, Martinez made a thin slit in the screen and pushed the lock upwards with his knife blade. "Not anymore, but the back door is locked."

"Let me at it. It's a simple push-button lock. I guess Sanford wasn't expecting a break-in." Emily took a credit card out of her side pocket and slid it in the door crack where the lock was. She pushed the card toward the doorknob until she felt it slide in more, then bent it in the opposite direction. After the second attempt, she heard it click. "Got it."

They ducked into the kitchen and closed the door behind them.

An overturned cup of coffee sat on the table beside an ashtray filled with cigarette butts. The sink overflowed with dirty dishes. Kitchen drawers and cupboards spilled their contents onto the floor. Whoever had already conducted a search left a mess.

After a quick survey of the house, Emily said, "We'll work together. Start in the kitchen, then the office alcove, the bathroom, the bedroom, and living room. Be thorough—don't forget closets, toilet tank, picture frames, freezer. You know the drill. Put everything back the way you found it."

"Okay, Sarge. What exactly are we looking for?" Martinez asked.

"Paperwork or anything else that appears suspicious or incriminating or some clue that whoever has been here before might have overlooked. Let's get started."

They were working the bedroom when Martinez ran his hand along the underside of the headboard.

"There's something here that feels covered with tape. Hold on, let me get it." He peeled duct tape away and handed a plastic object the size of a matchbox to Emily.

"Bingo. Nice work. It's a mini audio recorder. Sanford must have thought he needed insurance. Keep looking—there may be more." Emily dropped the recorder into a plastic bag and went back to riffling through the already disarrayed desk drawers. An hour later, after not turning up anything revealing, she called it quits, and made sure the upheaval in each room looked the same as it did when they had entered.

They were headed for the back door when a thudding sound from the front of the house froze them. The lock clicked, and the front door swung open casting bright sunlight toward the kitchen. Martinez plastered his body to the side of the refrigerator, while Emily ducked behind a counter, barely breathing.

A man's voice, harsh, angry, and familiar broke the silence.

"God damn it! It has to be here. Go back and check every room in this dump. Don't quit until you find it or all our asses will be on the line."

Emily shuddered as recognition hit her. *Todechine.*

She couldn't risk him finding her. She and Martinez had to leave.

An irritated male voice said, "Fuck it, Chief. We looked everywhere. There's nothing."

Then, a roar, "Start all over!"

The sound of footsteps faded into the bedroom, and Emily nodded at Martinez. They crept to the door and slunk out as quiet as flies on a feather duster, taking a moment to secure the lock behind them.

When they reached the cruiser, Emily slumped down in the passenger seat. Martinez gave her a questioning look.

"Not now. Let's go." It was neither fear nor adrenalin that caused her rapid breathing to compete with the pounding in her chest. Emily felt like her heart had been pierced with a poisoned arrow. *What else are you involved in, Chief? It keeps getting worse.* "Take me home, Martinez."

"Do you want to play the recorder first?"

"Later. We're calling it a day. Go spend some time with your wife and kid."

# 34

Abe noticed the stricken look on Emily's face the moment she entered the house. "What happened, sweetheart? You look like you lost your best friend."

Emily shook her head and sunk into Abe's arms. "I think I did. I wish—Oh, never mind. Where's Raven?"

"She's taking a nap. Bertha laid down with her, and Will's in the barn. Tell me what's going on."

"I will, but first, fix me a drink, Abe—whiskey on the rocks? Get one for yourself, too, and let's go sit out on the deck. I need to relax."

When Abe returned with two tumblers filled with ice and amber liquid, the late afternoon sun had dropped low in the sky casting Emily's face in dark shadows.

Abe had been surprised by her request for a drink. She had made a point of cutting back on alcohol, stating that she didn't really like to drink anyway.

"It's been a rough week," he said, handing her a glass. He watched as she tossed the drink back then leaned against the chair cushion and closed her eyes. Abe sat across from her, sipped at his whiskey, and waited. When it seemed she wasn't ready yet to talk about what was on her mind, he decided to tell her about his proposal to temporarily move the family to the Etcitty sheep ranch.

"Not many people know where it is and it'll be safer for everyone out there, including the animals. We won't have to worry about Raven. You know how she loves the ranch. Your mom, Will, and Manuel will be with her at all times, and you can sleep there at night. It's closer to the station."

Emily stared hard at Abe and blinked as if she were just now comprehending his words. She sipped her drink then put the glass down. "What about you?"

"I'll stay here to keep an eye on my place until things settle down. I want you to go with Raven, Emily. She'll feel better if you're with her."

Emily nodded. "I know. It makes sense. When do you think we should leave?"

"Today, as soon as we finish packing. I've already talked it over with Will and Bertha. They think it's a good idea."

"Will brought the horse trailer over here, didn't he?"

"You gotta be prepared."

"Pretty sure of yourself, weren't you?"

Abe grinned, hoping he could coax a smile out of Emily, but all he saw was a slight loosening of the tension lines in her face and acceptance in her eyes. "I thought you might see the advantages." He hesitated, watching her face. "Before we start packing, do you want to talk about what's on your mind?"

Emily took a deep breath and slowly blew the air out of her mouth. "Martinez and I learned that Sanford didn't die from a fall. His skull had been bashed in with a blunt object, and his body had been moved. I broke into Sanford's house today to look for evidence, and Martinez found a mini recorder hidden behind the bed headboard—small like the kind used by spies or undercover agents. He must have been recording meetings he had with someone. Then, while we were there, Todechine showed up at the house with two men. I never got a look at them, so I don't know who they were. I heard the chief order them to search the house again. He sounded extremely agitated and desperate. I think they were looking for that recorder."

"Have you listened to it?" Abe asked.

"No. I've been afraid of what I'll find out—that the man I've looked up to all my life is not only involved in corruption and bribery but is possibly a murderer." Emily finished her drink, tossed the ice cubes over the deck railing, and stood. "I can't deal with that right now. Thanks for listening, but don't try giving me advice. I need to focus on my family—get things together and head for the ranch. You're right about it being safer for Raven out there."

Abe stood as well and held her in a long embrace. "Everything's going to work out, you'll see," he whispered. "Keep your chin up. You're a good cop." He heard her sigh, felt the release of tension in her muscles, her warm lips on his.

"I love you, Abe. Promise me you won't do anything crazy when you're here alone."

"I'll be fine. You know you can count on the piano man. I just need one more kiss to hold me over for a while."

They laughed and pulled apart at the sound of the sliding door being opened and a small but belligerent voice.

Raven looked at them with her hands on her hips. "Mom, Dad. Are you guys kissing again? And why is Grandma packing all my things?"

When everything, including Patch, the horses, the stuffed animals, and Raven's books had been loaded, and everyone was ready to go, Raven threw her arms around Abe's neck. "Why can't you come to Uncle Will's ranch with us, Dad?"

"I'll be out there as soon as I can, sweetie. Don't worry about me. Take good care of your mom and Patch, help your grandma, and don't forget to feed the horses and the crows."

She giggled. "Ravens, Daddy. How many times do I have to tell you?"

Abe watched the truck and trailer pull away until he could no longer see Raven's small face gazing back at him, then he went inside. The house felt desolate and forlorn without his family. Although Abe was often alone, he had grown accustomed to Bertha's benign bossiness and the camaraderie of male companionship with Will. The absence of his wife and daughter was especially hard, and he felt overcome with a sense of dread, almost wishing he hadn't sent them away. They'll be better off at Will's, Abe reassured himself, and if Gomez, Talltree, or anyone else showed up, he would be ready. He made a pot of coffee then filled a thermos with the fresh brew and fried a couple of eggs, slathered mayonnaise on bread, and threw together a couple of sandwiches. It was no gourmet meal but would satisfy his hunger. After eating one, he wrapped the other and put it in his knapsack along with a flashlight, a hunting knife, gloves, skull cap, and a down-filled jacket. The barn provided a better view of the road and driveway. When night crept in, Abe left a lamp on in the house and headed for the barn. His sleeping bag was still on the bed of straw, the rifle and ammo tucked in the hayloft where he had hidden them. Abe was not aware of the two men with red headbands watching him with binoculars and tracking his every move.

A high wind gusted from the north, and the waning moon played hide-and-seek with scurrying clouds. *Another storm coming*, Abe thought. After dropping his backpack beside the bedroll, he loaded the gun and stood by the barn window watching for any unexpected movement. The temperature had taken a  sharp drop when the sun sunk in the western sky, and the chill crept into his bones. Abe zipped up his jacket, donned his hat and gloves, picked up the rifle, and walked outside. Not wanting to give his position away, he didn't turn on the flashlight he carried in his right hand. The trees moaned in protest to the wind's unrelenting assault, making detection of any sounds out of the ordinary difficult, if not impossible. Abe jumped, then crouched down when he heard a branch snap, pointed a beam of light in the direction of the noise, then continued his patrol of the fence line. From a high point at the far corner of his lot, he could watch the occasional headlight of a car or truck on the frontage road, but each one passed by his driveway without slowing down.

He had walked the perimeter of his land and was headed back to the barn when a dark shape stepped out of the brush. Abe drew in a deep breath and swung the rifle toward the figure.

"Stop right where you are, and put your hands on your head where I can see them!" He cradled the stock in the crook of his left arm and kept his trigger finger on the trigger guard. "Who are you and what are you doing here?"

The man, not showing any sign of apprehension stopped and raised both hands. "Easy, man. *Diné* Freedom Fighter. You can call me Slim, and put the gun away. You won't be needing it. Keetso sent my buddy and me out here to keep an eye on you, and we found something you might be interested in."

Still pointing the rifle with his left hand, Abe beamed the flashlight at the face of a tall, muscular Native American, his long dark hair held in place with a red headband. "Okay." Abe lowered the rifle. "It's not smart to sneak up on someone with a gun. I could have shot you. Why didn't you let me know you were here?"

"Because 'sneaky' is what we do best. Keetso told you we'd be around, didn't he? Now, follow me."

"Where're we going?" Abe asked.

"Not far. Keep that flashlight on. It's as dark as a coal mine out here with that cloud cover. If you hadn't turned your light on a while back, I might not have found you."

Abe followed Slim through a thicket of oak brush. He could hear the churning of the river and knew they were getting close to the water's edge. They hiked the river's bank for ten minutes, then Slim stopped and whistled a high-pitched mimic of a nighthawk. He waited for an answering whistle before proceeding.

"Why don't you just tell me what you've got?" Abe asked.

"You'll see for yourself. We're almost there." They came around a bend and reached a clump of willows when Slim whistled again. "Hey, Little John, we're coming down."

Another man, not little at all, but a massive giant appeared in the glare of Abe's flashlight.

"It's about time. I was tempted to make a fire. I'm freezing my balls off out here. You must be Freeman," he said squinting in Abe's direction.

"That's right, and you're. .?"

"Call me Little John. Everybody else does. " He kicked a lump wrapped and bound in a blanket with the toe of his cowboy boot. "And this thing is known as 'Pile of Shit."

Abe heard a groan, saw movement, and realized the pile of shit was a man.

"Who is it?" Abe asked.

"Didn't give us his name," said Slim. "He came down the river in a skiff and left it a little way upstream from your place. Had some homemade explosives in his pack—Molotov cocktails, gasoline, and other crap with him, including this gun." Slim pulled a small revolver out of his parka.

Abe felt a tightening in his chest and a rush of blood to his face. "Let's take him to my barn and hear what the asshole has to say," he said through tight lips.

With his round face, the crinkled skin around his eyes, and close-cropped gray hair, Will's partner, Manuel, resembled a Budha. He broke into a broad smile and stretched out his arms when he spotted Raven emerging from Will's truck.

"Little Bird," he said, using his pet name for her, "come here and see me." He lifted her above his head. "You've grown so much, I can hardly pick you up anymore."

Raven squealed with delight. "Uncle Manuel, you're so silly. Do you think I've really grown? It has only been a couple of weeks since I saw you."

"At least two inches and ten pounds." He feigned fatigue and put her down. "You gonna visit us for a few days?"

"Yes. Can we play checkers? Remember, I won the last game."

"Sure. But first, let's get your things put in the new room. You, your mom and your grandma get to sleep in there. I got it ready for you with sheepskin pallets and nice warm blankets."

Raven smiled when she entered the cozy room and rushed over to place her stuffed bird in her chosen sleeping space. The add-on served as both a workroom and showplace for Manuel. He was a skilled weaver, unusual for a man as most weavers were women, and his brightly colored blankets covered the walls. A large loom occupied space in the center of the room. In front of the loom stood a stool and a small table with handcrafted battens, combs, needles, and other paraphernalia used in weaving. Numerous skeins of natural-dyed yarn in brilliant colors hung over a line near the back of the room. A fire blazed in a corner kiva fireplace.

When everything had been put away, the horses settled in their stalls, and Raven immersed in a game of checkers with Manuel, Emily said she was going outside for some air.

Bertha gave her a questioning look but caught her daughter's eyes, and nodded.

Emily zipped up her jacket up and pulled a cap over her hair. A blustery wind bit at her face as she made her way along the path to the sheep shed. A myriad of stars danced in the darkening indigo sky then disappeared behind scurrying clouds. She reached into her pocket, feeling for the small recorder she had placed there earlier. When she entered the shed, the comforting, familiar smell of sheep, goats, and straw greeted her. The animals bleated in alarm, and she began speaking to them in a soft voice until they became accustomed to her presence and settled down.

Drawn by the open space and the smell of crushed sage as her pony trampled the silver-gray foliage, Emily had loved herding sheep and goats with her grandfather when she was young. A rueful thought ran through her mind. *I should have never left sheepherding to become a cop.*

The three-legged stool used for milking nanny goats was hanging from a nail right where she remembered. *There's no point putting this off any longer*, Emily thought as she pulled down the stool, sat and braced her back against the wall. After taking the recorder from her pocket, she took a deep breath and pushed the play button. She listened again, then a third time, and finally returned the recorder to her pocket and buried her head in hands. The final words on the recording were, "swear no one gets hurt." Well, it was already too late for that with two men dead and her daughter the victim of a kidnapper.

"I was watching that moon and thinking about singing a horse song," said a voice near the entrance. "Remember how we used to ride as far as daylight would let us, and I would have to make you turn around and go home? You never wanted to get off that spotted pony."

"Will. You startled me. I didn't know you were out here." She chewed her lip. "I miss those days."

"You've got some heavy business on your mind, little sister."

"How much did you hear?"

"I was looking at the sky, watching clouds, thinking about other things. I didn't mean to eavesdrop, but I couldn't help it, especially when I heard Chief Todechine's voice. There were others I didn't recognize. Do you know who they were?"

"My guess is Gomez and Talltree. I can't prove it. Sanford is dead because of what he knew. When they couldn't find the recorder, they probably killed him."

Will came into the sheep shed and squatted on his haunches beside Emily. "I was getting ready to smoke some *dzil natoh*. Want to join me? It'll help put your mind at rest, and maybe we can talk about this bad business afterward."

Will filled his pipe, lit it, and passed it to Emily. She drew the aromatic smoke into her lungs then exhaled through her nose. A feeling of warmth and a loosening of the tension in her muscles swept through her body. "I haven't done this in a long time," she said, taking another puff. Looking at the sky through the open door, she watched the moon make a brief appearance before ducking behind a cloud. "Hello moon, my old friend," she said.

After his turn, Will put the pipe away and waited in silence for Emily to be ready to continue.

"Sing that horse song, Will. The one grandfather used to sing to us when we went out with him to get the sheep." She closed her eyes and let Will's deep baritone chant take her back in time.

"Thank you for remembering those songs and stories and not letting our history die," she said when he finished. "Those were better times, before the uranium mines, the gas and oil drillers, the fucking powerplant."

"Times and people change, Emily."

"I never thought the chief could be corrupted."

"Something must have triggered him. Something so big he couldn't deal with it."

Emily watched the moon slip through the clouds again. "Daisy is dying. The chief thought he could save her by taking her to this expensive clinic in Las Vegas. Turns out it's run by a quack. I think Todechine needed money to pay the bills— he's probably in debt over his head, and that's where Whittington comes in."

"So, Whittington offered to bail him out if Todechine made sure the uranium contract passed?"

"Sounds like a likely scenario, doesn't it, Will? Won't be the first time money has passed under the table so some *bilagaana* corporation could move in and poison our land."

It was Will's turn to be quiet. After a few minutes, he stood and faced Emily. "It's a sorry mess. How come I didn't know about Daisy? If Todechine had come to me, I could have helped him. What are you going to do, Sis?"

"There're others involved. Think about it. Someone kidnapped Raven, tried to set fire to Abe's barn, nearly killed Bobby Grayfeather. Now a tribal councilman and an EPA contractor are dead. The FBI is going to be all over it if they can get their heads out of their bureaucratic asses." She stood as well. "I have to clean up this mess, Will. But, for now, we better get inside before Mom comes after us. She doesn't like it when supper gets cold."

"You're right. Don't forget to say a prayer and offer some corn pollen to your good friend up there. Mother Moon is watching out for you."

# 35

A series of muffled moans emanated from the tightly bound blanket when Little John threw the lumpy load over his shoulder as if it were a fifty-pound sack of beans. Guided by the beam of the flashlight, the three men walked in single file back toward Abe's barn.

"What did he have to say for himself?" Abe asked.

"I didn't give him a chance to say anything before I stuck a rag in his mouth and tied him up. Figured you'd ask the questions."

"He's got a lot to answer to," Abe said when they entered the barn. "Put him down and untie the blanket so I can see the fucker's face."

"You got it," said Little John unceremoniously dumping his load on the ground.

Abe lit a lantern casting shadowy shapes over the interior of the barn as Little John began untying the ropes.

Slim had noticed the thermos beside Abe's sleeping bag. "You got coffee in there?" he asked.

"You're welcome to it, but first hold that revolver on this dirtbag, so he doesn't try anything." As the blanket started

296

unrolling, first the legs and then the torso of a man appeared. Abe stared down at a person of average height and weight with a face he couldn't place right away but looked vaguely familiar. The man spat the rag out of his mouth and looked at his captors with darting eyes.

"You," Abe said when recognition hit him. An eruption of fury surged through his body. He bent down and grabbed the man by the shirt front, pulling him until their faces were within inches of each other. "You're the  security guard that was supposed to be protecting my little girl." Abe put his hands around the man's neck and slammed his head back onto the barn floor. "Why? Why did you do that to my daughter?" he said squeezing tighter. "Why are you terrorizing my family and trying to burn my place down? Who put you up to this?"

The man clawed at Abe's fingers. "Get him off me," he gasped.

"Easy man," said Slim. "You don't want to kill him."

Loosening his grip, Abe backed off and stood upright. He felt no pain in his burnt and bandaged hands as he made tight fists and glared down at the crumpled body. "Answer me, or I swear, I'll kill you."

Little John was off to the side, arms crossed over his chest. "You don't want to do that, man. Let me take care of him."

"No," Abe said. "This is personal." He delivered a swift kick to the man's ribcage. "Answer me. Who hired you? Was it Todechine?"

"Stop!" croaked the security guard, as he tried to crawl away. "Todechine knew about it, but he didn't hire me. He made me swear no one would get hurt. I kept my word. I didn't harm the kid. I would have rescued her myself if you hadn't come along. It was just to put a scare in your wife, make her back off the investigation."

Abe smoldered, but his voice was cold. "What investigation?"

"Strathmore Minerals was afraid they would lose the uranium contract if . . ."

"If what?" Abe said. "Was it Whittington who paid you?"

"I swear, I don't know who handled the payoff. I picked up an envelope with cash in it from Todechine's office. That's all I know."

Abe felt a wave of nausea rising from the pit of his stomach. He had never resorted to this kind of violence against any living thing, human or animal. *What am I turning into? I'm no better than him.* "Little John, do me a favor. Tie this piece of shit back up and put him in that horse stable. Throw the blanket over him, so he doesn't freeze and keep an eye on him. I need to call my wife."

Abe walked outside into the bracing night air, leaned over the fence, and vomited until there was nothing left in his stomach. After catching his breath, he wiped the bile from his lips, went inside, and washed his face with cold water. When his nerves had settled, he dialed Will's number.

"Emily. I've got him here in the barn, tied up—the one who took Raven. I almost killed him, Em."

"Wait, slow down, Abe. What are you talking about?"

"It's the security guard. Keetso's men were watching my place. They caught him, and we took him to the barn. I tried to strangle him."

"Don't do anything. Stay away from that security guard. I'll be right there."

Abe returned to the barn, saw that the guard was secured to a post in the stable and the rag had been stuffed back in his mouth. Slim and Little John looked at him with raised eyebrows.

"Now what?" asked Slim.

"My wife's on her way. You guys can come inside and get warm, have some coffee."

"Thanks for the offer," said Little John. "We done drank your coffee and ate your sandwich. Don't want to meet up with any cop, man or woman, so we're going to head on out. You'll find all your evidence in a small boat tied to a tree about 500 feet upstream."

Abe nodded. "Tell Keetso, I owe him. I won't forget what you did."

"Weren't nothin'," said Slim.

The two men lumbered out of the barn and disappeared into the darkness. Abe gave his prisoner a quick look, felt renewed anger rising like a ball of fire in his stomach, then, oblivious of the cold wind, walked outside to wait for Emily.

Twenty minutes later, he saw headlights turn into his driveway. The Bronco screeched to a stop, and Emily jumped out.

"Abe!"

"Over here."

Emily rushed over to where Abe stood by the barn entrance. "What happened? Did you harm him in any way?"

Abe shook his head. "Nothing permanent. He admitted to kidnapping Raven, Em. I wanted to kill the bastard, but Keetso's men stopped me. He's in the barn, hogtied in a horse stall. I think he's all right."

"I'm going in there, and I want you to stay out, okay, Abe? Promise me. I feel the same way you do about this shitbag, but I can't let personal feeling obstruct police procedure. He's going to have information we can use to incriminate others, and we can't let his testimony be jeopardized. I have to do this the right way."

"I get it. I'll be outside, but if that creep tries anything, I'm coming in."

"Stay put. I'm going to make sure the prisoner doesn't need medical assistance and read him his rights. I won't need any help." Her eyes were black obsidian when she clutched his arm and met his gaze. "The Feds are on their way. You're going to have to tell them what happened, Abe. Including the names of Keetso's men. What the hell were they doing here, anyway?"

"I called Keetso and told him about Raven's kidnapping and the fire. He sent two guys over here to keep an eye on my place. I don't know their names, but they're the ones that caught that dirtbag tonight."

"You keeping secrets again?"

"I'll explain later, Em. That son of a bitch in there had explosives with him."

After Abe's call, Emily knew she would have to contact Harrison and Monroe, the two FBI field agents assigned to the reservation, and hand the prisoner over to them. It would be hard to explain why she was unwilling to arrest the security guard and book him at Navajo Police Headquarters, but she didn't trust herself to remain impartial with her daughter's abductor, and, she didn't want to alert Todechine. That meant sharing more information with the Feds, but there was no way to prevent it. With the murder of an Anglo on Navajo land, the FBI was already involved. She had given Harrison directions to Abe's place and said she would meet them there.

Abe was still standing in the same place when Emily emerged from the barn. "He's not hurt," she said. "I untied him and left him cuffed to a railing, and took that rag out of his mouth. He clammed up after I read him his rights. Said he wanted a lawyer."

"He spilled his guts to me," Abe said.

"You can tell me what he said, but we can't use it. Anything said to you won't hold up in court. They'll claim coercion, and it's his word against yours."

"I have witnesses."

"Did he tell you who hired him? Did he give you his name?"

"He picked up his payoff at Todechine's office."

"Let's go inside. The prisoner's not going anywhere. I want you to tell me exactly what happened here before the Feds arrive."

"Well," Emily said. She folded her arms across her chest and watched Abe put water in the coffee pot and fill the basket with fresh grounds.

"Sit down, Sweetheart. Those agents are based in Window Rock, right? We've got time."

When the aroma of strong, freshly brewed coffee filled the kitchen, Abe poured them both a cup and sat across from Emily at the table. He held the cup with two hands, letting the warmth soothe his aching fingers, and studied Emily hoping to read understanding and acceptance in her expression, but her face was a blank slate. Sighing, he sipped from his mug and began.

"After you and Raven left, I waited until dark then went outside to patrol the grounds. That's when I ran into Keetso's men. They said their names were Slim and Little John, obviously fakes ."

He finished the story and set his cup on the table. "And that's how it came about that the kidnapper of our daughter is tied up in my barn."

Emily had listened without interruption. "That still doesn't explain why you called Keetso in the first place."

Abe tapped the table while he considered his answer. Shrugging, "Okay, I wanted him to help me find Gomez and Talltree."

Emily narrowed her eyes. "This is police business, Abe. What the hell is wrong with you?"

Abe's voice took on an edge. "It became my business when they went after my family." He placed both palms on the table and leaned forward, his intense blue eyes staring into hers. "At one time you wanted my help."

"That was before we had a child." Emily glanced away, turning to face the window. "My job is dangerous, Abe. Every morning when I get suited up, I pray I'll come back home to you and Raven that night. If something should happen to me, I want to know you are going to be there for our little girl, not out risking your life playing cops and robbers."

Abe reached across the table and took Emily's hand in his. "Don't you think I worry about you every day? What would we do without you?"

"Okay, enough of this, the Feds should be here any minute. We both knew what this job entailed. I'm careful, and Martinez is smart. He's going to make a good cop."

"You haven't been able to find Gomez and Talltree have you?"

"We haven't looked, too busy with other things."

"I can help you with that."

"What do you mean?"

"I know where Gomez and Talltree live and the places where they hang out."

Emily's raised eyebrows formed question marks. "How. .?" Before she could finish, the crunch of tires on gravel announced the arrival of Agents Richard Harrison and Jack Monroe. "We'll talk about this later, Abe. The Feds are here."

Abe remained seated at the table, drank his coffee and thought about how to talk to the FBI without giving away Keetso.

# 36

Harrison, the older agent, had a compact body, swarthy complexion, and piercing green eyes. He wore his gray hair in a close crewcut, thin lips set in a tight line, his movements quick and purposeful. The younger Monroe, tall, blond, and loose in the joints, walked with a swagger and wore a perpetual smirk on his ruddy face.

Abe watched through the window as Emily met the agents at the car. They stood talking for several minutes before entering the barn. A half hour later, they emerged with Frank Miller, if that was his name, walking between the two men, his hands cuffed behind his back and Emily bringing up the rear. They placed Miller in the back seat behind the security screen, and both agents turned their attention to the house. *This is it*, Abe thought, licking dry lips. *I better get my story straight.*

"Have a seat," Abe said after introductions. "Want some coffee? I just made it."

"Can't handle caffeine this late," said Harrison. "Keeps me awake."

Monroe tilted his head and gave Abe an appraising once-over. "Thanks, don't mind if I do. Then we want you to tell us what happened here last night."

Abe recounted the events as he remembered them, omitting Keetso's involvement. When he finished, Harrison scratched his head and stared out the window.

"These two men who you say apprehended the perp, give me their names again."

"I don't know their full names. They went by Slim and Little John." Abe knew he sounded like a liar and forced his tapping foot to be still. "That's all I know about them."

"What puzzles me," said Harrison, "is how these two happened to show up on your property at just the right time. Are you sure you never saw them before?"

"I'm sure," Abe said truthfully. "They told me they were walking by the river and they saw this guy pull up to the bank in a little skiff. They checked his boat, saw a backpack full of explosives, and decided to follow him. When they saw him approach me, they jumped him, found that revolver, and took him to the barn. Then they left." A partial truth.

"Give us a description of the two men," said Monroe.

Abe hesitated before answering. "They were Native Americans. One was tall and muscular. The other was huge, about three-hundred pounds maybe." This was true.

"Did they happen to mention why they were out walking along the river at night?"

"Nope. But I'm glad they were there. Someone tried to set my barn on fire a couple nights ago, and this guy had flammable material in his backpack and in the boat. I figure he came back to finish the job."

"Where is that rowboat he came in?" asked Monroe.

"I never saw it, but I was told it was tied about five-hundred feet upstream. I could find it for you."

Monroe put his cup down, and the two men stood.

"Take us there," said Harrison.

Emily felt a part of the massive load she had been carrying had been lifted after handing over the security guard to the FBI. Let them do the background check on him, whoever he is, she was glad the man who had abducted Raven has been caught, and he wouldn't be skulking around Abe's house any longer. She also felt grateful to Abe, even though she knew he had managed to avoid mentioning Keetso's name. Driving to work the next morning, her mind focused on the challenge she would have to face today—how to approach her longtime boss and friend. When she stepped into the Precinct Station, a chill ran down her spine. Her fellow officers were huddled in small groups, talking in hushed voices and Captain Tom Littleben from Shiprock stood near the front of the room. He cleared his throat and conversation stopped as they turned their attention to him. The captain, grim-faced and unsmiling, his gray-streaked hair combed straight back, met the eyes of his audience. There was no sign of Chief Todechine.

"We've received sad news concerning your chief's wife, Daisy," said Captain Littleben, his long, deeply creviced face appearing more sorrowful than ever. "It is with great regret that

I have to share this news with you. Late last night Chief Todechine's niece informed me that Daisy had passed away. The chief has taken a leave of absence to claim her body and bring her home."

The squad's chatter turned to silence and shocked expressions, as one by one they removed their flat bill caps and looked down at the floor. Emily felt a lump in her throat and swallowed hard, even though she knew this news was coming.

"I can see that you're as surprised and dismayed as I am," Littleben continued. "My wife and I have been friends with the Todechine family for many years. Your chief and I attended the Police Academy together, and we have been close ever since. Yet, I was not even aware of Daisy's illness. I have been temporarily assigned to the Huerfano Precinct until your chief has had the opportunity to proceed with a traditional burial ceremony and mourn for his wife of forty years. I'll be in the office reading reports this morning. If you have any concerns, bring them to me. That's all I have, for now, you're dismissed to go about your duties."

Emily felt as if a heavy stone had dropped in her heart. Her eyes welled as she turned to join Martinez, but before she could leave, Littleben called her name.

"Sergeant Etcitty, can I have a word with you?"

"Yes, sir." Emily wondered what the captain had on his mind. Although she knew Littleben 's reputation as a thorough professional and trusted him, she was not ready to confide her suspicions concerning Todechine's involvement with

Strathmore Minerals. And this was not the time. She entered her old chief's familiar office and waited for Littleben's lead.

The captain looked up over the rimless reading glasses perched on his nose. "Sit down, Emily. I'd like to offer my personal condolences to you. I know you were very fond of Daisy, and this has come as a blow to all of us."

"Thank you, sir."

Sliding his glasses up with his index finger, he met her gaze. "The truth is, I don't know what to think. I've been concerned about Chief Todechine for some time now. His behavior has been erratic, he didn't return my calls, and he had never once said a word about Daisy. I don't even know where he is."

"He must have gone to Las Vegas to claim his wife's body, sir. I had dropped by the chief's house a few days ago to visit Daisy. His niece told me, even though her uncle had advised her not to mention it to anyone, that her aunt was being treated in a private clinic there. She also informed me that Chief Todechine spent all his spare time traveling to be with Daisy in Las Vegas."

Littleben' eyebrows shot up. "Las Vegas, Nevada?"

"Yes, sir. I have to admit I was surprised too, so I did some checking on the clinic, a place called Vitapure Wellness Center run by a Dr. Kingsley who claimed he could cure any form of cancer. The cost to stay this place is exorbitant, way beyond the means of the chief. It's a scam run by a con man." Emily paused, wondering if she had said too much, but continued. "I believe Chief Todechine is under a lot of stress, Captain, what with Daisy's illness, huge money problems, fatigue…"

"Did you speak to him about your concerns?"

"I haven't seen him since I obtained this information."

Captain Littleben rubbed the back of his neck. "I came in here two hours early to review the paperwork and familiarize myself with current cases. This office is in shambles, there's nothing in the files. It appears Chief Todechine hasn't done anything for the past couple of months. I need for you to bring me up to date, Sergeant."

"Yes, sir. The officers in this precinct keep a folder containing copies of the reports they've submitted. I'll tell them to prepare a new copy for you. I'll also write a summary of the cases the Huerfano Substation is currently working on and have it on your desk by the end of the day.

Littleben nodded. "That's good. But, before you get started, give me a quick overview."

There was no way Emily could provide a coherent summary of her investigation into Strathmore Minerals—still too many convoluted twists and turns for her to make sense of it. "I'm coordinating a murder investigation with the FBI," she said. "The victim was an EPA contractor who was shot and wounded while testing a reservation stock pond on October 10. I was the first officer on the scene. A couple of nights ago, his body was discovered at the bottom of a canyon near Chinle. Preliminary forensics indicate that death was caused by a blow to the head with a blunt instrument, and soil samples suggest the body had been moved after death."

"Do you have a lead?"

*How to proceed*, Emily thought. "I'm looking at several different angles, sir, and as I said, the FBI is in charge now. My partner, rookie officer Raymond Martinez, is assisting me." Wanting to escape the captain's scrutiny, Emily said, "I probably should inform the squad to get busy on those copies and bring them to you before they head out, and I want to write the summary. I have a full agenda, sir. I have a meeting with a potential witness at one o'clock, so if you have no further questions, may I be excused?"

Captain Littleben scratched his head. "Okay—for now. Make sure no one leaves the building until they get their reports to me. Maybe things will become clearer after I've read the paperwork. I just don't understand why Ben Todechne left his office in such disarray. He's always been topnotch."

"I know, but he's under a lot of pressure, Captain."

Back in the precinct room, she took a breath before addressing her fellow officers then called Martinez to her desk.

"What's up, Sergeant?'

"The captain needs a copy of everyone's paperwork. Get on yours right away before the machine is jammed up and we get stuck here. I'll give you a couple minutes headstart before I address the troops. When you're done there, pull up the photos of the tire tread marks at Councilman Chee's accident scene and those for Bobby Grayfeather. Compare them with the shots we took near Canyon de Chelly."

"Right. You think the tracks were made by the same vehicle?"

"If they were, we've got our suspect. I'm placing a call to the Sheriff's Department in Clark County, Nevada. I want to know how things came down at the Vitapure Clinic. Then, I need to talk to Abe so he can tell us where to find a couple of people."

"Abe? Your 'boyfriend'?"

"Yes, the one and only Abe Freeman. He has some information he hasn't shared with me."

Emily told the troops not to leave until they had taken copies of the last two month's reports to Captain Littleben. She knew how much her fellow officers hated paperwork and heard the groans. Next, she found the number to the Clark County Sheriff's Department and dialed. While waiting for her call to be transferred to the sheriff, she watched Martinez carry a folder to the one copy machine and began placing his papers inside. After spending several minutes on the phone, she hung up and massaged her forehead—a tension headache coming on. Kingsley had managed to flee before the raid on his clinic. The patients were left unattended, too weak to move on their own. Daisy was already dead when they arrived, but they were able to find her contact information in the receptionist's files and had notified Chief Todechine. The FBI had an APB out for Kingsley, and the sheriff assured her he wouldn't get far.

Martinez was gathering his papers and moving toward the chief's office. Emily picked up the phone again and dialed Abe's number.

"Abe, you said you knew where to find Gomez and Talltree."

Abe answered with an audible yawn. "No hello? How's it going this morning? Where are you, Emily?"

"I'm at work, Abe. Did I get you out of bed? Sorry, I woke you, but I'm not messing around. If you know where those two live, give me their addresses."

"Come by and pick me up, and I'll show you. You might need backup when and if you find those dickheads."

"No, damn it, Abe. I have Martinez, I don't need your assistance. Tell me how to get to their place."

"You always need me. I'll be waiting out front," Abe said before hanging up.

"You stubborn fool," Emily mumbled.

"Take a look at these, Sergeant," Martinez said. A series of photos were spread across his desk. Emily bent over and squinted, thinking she probably would need glasses sometime in the near future.

"See these cuts on the right front tire," Martinez said, using a pencil to point out a series of marks. "There's an identical pattern on this other set of photos."

"What are these shots from?" Emily asked. She picked up each photograph and studied it carefully.

"The first one here was taken at Chee's accident scene and the second from those you took the other day out near the Canyon park entrance. The tread marks are identical, too. But, look closely. The tire tracks from Grayfeather's accident don't match."

"Hmm. Doesn't surprise me. Weren't Gomez and Talltree the first on the scene when Grayfeather crashed?" The question triggered a memory—a tire iron in the front seat of Gomez's newly painted truck. "Let's go, Martinez. You drive."

The truth was, Abe couldn't get to sleep after the FBI and Emily had left last night. The security guard was no longer a threat, but Gomez and Talltree were still out there. With all that had transpired during and after the apprehension of Frank Miller, Abe had forgotten to give Emily the locations of the two former cops. He knew his family was safely ensconced at Will's remote sheep ranch, so he decided to take a pre-dawn drive on his own.

It had been easy to find the simple wooden frame house where Gomex lived situated an empty lot away from the Baptist Church. A black Ford F-150 sat in the pot-holed driveway. Neighbors were scarce and scattered in this neighborhood. Abe parked in front of an empty lot next door to Gomez's house and turned off his headlights. The dwindling moon had slipped behind gathering clouds providing a cover of darkness as Abe left the truck and crept toward a dim glow from the front window. An infomercial flashed across the television screen while Gomez, his mouth gaping open, snored from a recliner. Beer cans littered the floor. *It would be easy to get rid of that fat-ass ex-cop once and for all. He'd never know what hit him.* Abe tried the doorknob, found it locked and let the urge to beat the hell out of the sleeping man pass. He walked around the house checking for another exit, found a back door and a wooden shed. He tried opening the shed, then, startled by a snarling pit bull chained to a nearby post, jumped back and hurried to his truck. The guard dog was an unforeseen problem, but it didn't phase Gomez.

Piñon Park Playland on the outskirts of Kirtland turned out to be a tougher challenge. It was a sprawling jumble of mobile homes parked in no particular order. Most were in a sad state of disrepair with sagging steps, faded paint, and draped windows. The only option Abe had for finding Talltree was to drive around until he spotted a white Dodge Ram, and unlike Gomez's dark neighborhood, the trailer park buzzed with activity. Heavy metal music blasted through the open door of a nearby trailer. A man staggered out to the front stoop and relieved himself. Raucous laughter followed him from within. A woman screamed from another hovel. A group of youths huddled near a dumpster passing a joint. They turned to stare at him with narrowed eyes. Abe knew he could end up getting hurt in this labyrinth where no exact roads existed, and he had no allies present. After taking numerous turns to avoid curious onlookers, he wasn't sure he could find his way back to the main road. It was while driving around one of the twisted roadways, that he encountered someone driving a white Dodge Ram. Abe pulled behind an abandoned trailer and watched until the driver parked and stumbled out of the truck. He had lost weight and jerked his head around with a nervous twitch while cursing to himself. But there was no doubt in Abe's mind, the man he watched was Harold Talltree. Talltree tripped over the trailer step, swore loudly, and flung the trailer door open. Once he was inside, Abe backtracked and sped out of Piñon Park Playland. It was past three when he reached home and crawled into bed.

After talking to Emily, Abe took a quick shower, felt the stubble on his chin and cheeks, then said 'the hell with shaving.' He quickly dressed and heated a cup of leftover coffee in the microwave, and put a handful of Patch's doggie biscuits in a plastic bag. When Martinez turned into his driveway stirring up a cloud of dust, he prepared himself to face Emily.

# 37

"All right, Abe, give me those directions and stop being a jerk," Emily said from the rolled-down window.

"Can't," Abe said. "I have to show you." He tried the door to the back seat and found it locked. "You gonna let me in?"

Emily scowled. "You mean, 'won't tell me,' Pop the damn lock, Martinez." After Abe crawled into the backseat, she added. "You're staying in the car."

"How're you doing, Raymond?" Abe said from behind the cage. "Does this lady give you a bad time, too?"

The rookie cop steered the vehicle back to the main road. "Uh, no sir, not at all."

Abe saw the flush of red creep up Martinez's neck. "Head on over to Waterflow. You know where that little church is off 64? That's our destination. I'll tell you where to go from there."

After Martinez parked the police cruiser behind the '*You Can't Enter Heaven Unless Jesus Enters you*' sign, Abe pointed to a small clapboard structure. That's Gomez's house. His truck's not out front, so maybe we can take a look."

Emily twisted around in the seat and glared at Abe. "Not 'we,' Martinez and I."

Ignoring her, Abe continued. "I know the layout. There's a shed in back, and a pit bull chained near the door. I'll distract the dog while you two check out the shed. We better hurry before Gomez comes back. You'll need something to pick the padlock, and you might want to grab a camera. Now, please open the damn door so I can get out."

Martinez exchanged a quick look with Emily. Abe heard her sigh, mumble a curse, then the click of the lock.

Following Abe's lead, they circled around to the back of the house. The brindle pit bared his teeth, saliva dripped from his mouth. He snarled, jerked on his chain, and lunged at the intruders. Emily and Martinez held back while the dog continued to growl and block the doorway. While speaking in a soft voice, Abe moved to the other side of the shed.

"Here, boy. That's a good dog. Come on, good boy. Here, you want one of these?" He pulled a dog biscuit from the plastic bag and tossed it in the direction opposite of Emily and Martinez.

The pit bull turned his attention from the two cops and concentrated his attack on Abe. Another biscuit landed in the dirt in front of the dog.

"Come on, fella. You know you want it."

Finally, the pit stopped growling and sniffed the treat before devouring it.

"Atta boy, that's good stuff, huh. I bet you don't get many treats," Abe said, moving closer. He reached out his hand with another biscuit. When the dog took it from him, Abe scratched him behind the ears, talking all the while in a soothing voice. Without changing his tone, he added, "Okay, Em, go for the door now."

Emily popped the lock, and the two cops ducked inside.

Abe kept an eye on the main road for any sign of Gomez's truck while he continued to distract the dog. Several minutes later he saw a black pickup turn off Highway 64. "Time to go. Gomez is on his way. Let's make a run for the church." He gave the dog the remaining treats and patted him on the head. "Thanks, fella. You've been a big help."

Martinez pulled the door shut and replaced the lock before all three made a run backside of the *Diné* Baptist Church and hunkered down behind the sign.

"He went inside, and all the blinds are closed," said Abe. "Let's get out of here before he opens them and notices the cop car."

Back on the main drag, Abe said, "How about stopping for breakfast."

"You got away with this one, Abe," Emily said. "How about you tell us where Talltree lives and we take you home."

Abe shook his head. "Uh-uh. You can't take a Navajo Nation Police vehicle in there. It would draw too much attention. What'ya find in the shed?"

"A set of tires. That tread sure looked familiar—especially that one with the cut marks on it," said Martinez. "Looked like those tracks over by Canyon de Chelly. He had a bunch of other junk—tire-iron, some paint-splattered overalls, boxes of something we didn't have time to check out."

"I took pictures of everything. We'll know if those treads match when we compare the photos with the ones we have on file. You got the measurements, right?"

"Yes, ma'am."

Emily turned around to look at Abe. "We'll drop you off, go back to headquarters, and get my Bronco. So, what's the address?"

His blue eyes twinkled as he gave her his most winning grin. "Too hard to explain, sweetheart. It's a twisted journey. I'll have to go along to show you. You should change out of your uniform, you know. Hey, anybody up for breakfast?"

"I could sure go for some *huevos rancheros*," said Martinez.

Emily puffed up her cheeks and exhaled a stream of exasperated air in surrender. "Okay, okay. I'll change at your place, Abe. Talltree knows your truck, so we'll go back to headquarters and get Martinez's Jeep Wrangler instead. You better not be putting me on, is all I've got to say."

Abe smiled. "I wouldn't do that to you, Emily. Hey, Charlie's Diner has good breakfast burritos, and it's close. Why don't we stop there, and I'll tell you what I've learned about Talltree. I think he's on the skids."


Abe and Martinez were close to the same size, so Abe had Martinez change into a borrowed pair of jeans and a denim shirt. The pants were a couple of inches short, but they'd do in a pinch. Emily threw on some of her own jeans and a black hoodie then strapped her Glock and gear under the bulky sweatshirt. The sky had turned a milky gray, and the temperature showed no sign of warming up, so Abe grabbed a couple of jackets and two wool beanies before they left for the station.

Abe sat in the back seat of Martinez's Wrangler surrounded by a jumble of candy bar wrappers and chip bags. However good a cop Martinez might be, tidiness did not rank among one of his attributes. The car had a rusted floorboard and an odometer reading of over 250,000 miles from what Abe could see, but it cranked over when he turned the key, and the heater worked.

"Gets okay mileage, too," said Martinez.

"Piñon Park Playland is about five miles west of Kirtland," Abe said. "I don't know where Talltree hangs out."

"You mean Shorty's Bar?" said Emily. "I'm familiar with the place. We've done a few prostitution busts there."

"And if we do find Talltree? What are you going to do? You don't have a warrant, no proof he was involved."

"Ask some pertinent questions," Emily said. "And apply a little pressure."

A cruise around the trailer park failed to turn up either Talltree or his girlfriend, so Emily gave Martinez directions to a seedy-looking, out-of-the-way building at the end of a dirt road. Shorty's had been tossed together with sheets of tin and scrap wood. No flashing neon lights advertising beer brands welcomed visitors, but a hand-scrawled sign on the door read, 'Private Club – Members Only.'

"Stay out of sight, Abe. 'Members Only' is Navajo for 'No White Men.'" Emily pulled the hood over her head, putting her face in shadows. "It'll be so dark inside that if Talltree is in there, he may not recognize us." She patted the gun holster under her bulky sweatshirt. "Do you have quick access to your weapon if the need arises, Martinez?"

The rookie tugged his cap down to his eyebrows and turned up his collar. "Yes, Ma'am."

"We don't want to make a scene, so keep your gun out of sight. If Talltree is in there, I'm going to walk him to the car, and we'll take him somewhere on the rez for questioning." She and Martinez got out, but before she closed the door, she looked at Abe. "Since you're unarmed, move to the front, duck down in the seat, and stay out of sight. I'll get in the back with Talltree."

Abe made a fist and rubbed his rough knuckles with the other hand. The cuts and burns were slowly healing, but they still throbbed with pain. "Be careful, Emily. If I hear gunshots, I'm coming in, member or not." Once in the passenger seat, he slid down, but not so low he couldn't watch who came and went through Shorty's door.


It took a minute before Emily's eyes adjusted to the dimness of the smoke-filled bar, and after a cursory glance from Shorty, no one paid much attention to the two cops. Less than half the stools were occupied, and a few desultory-looking men hunched over their beer bottles, lost in a haze of alcohol, cigarettes, and the lyrics of a country song about bad luck and betrayal. At the far end of the bar, a young woman in a tight-fitting short skirt and skimpy top blew a cloud of smoke at the new arrivals then turned her head toward the man seated beside her. Emily could only see his profile, but she nudged Martinez and tilted her head in the direction of the couple.

"Martinez, that's him, and she must be the woman he's pimping. Get a stool at the other end of the bar and order a drink for the lady. When she comes over, keep her occupied while I move on Talltree, and make sure your face is turned away from him."

Emily stood back in the shadows until she saw the woman settle on the stool beside the young cop. Even in the semi-dark, it was impossible not to notice the bruises on her cheek and arms. Heavily mascaraed and pencil-lined eyes gazed blankly at Martinez, even as the woman, more a girl, attempted to smile. She was thin, more pathetic than sexy, and young. Emily clenched her jaw and swore to herself that she'd find a way to get that child out of here and into rehabilitation. Talltree watched the couple, showing no interest in Emily nor recognition of Martinez. He appeared glassy-eyed and woozy. Emily figured he was high on something, which could make his apprehension easier or more challenging, depending on how he reacted. She sauntered over in his direction then stopped behind his stool.

"If you say anything or make any sudden moves, Talltree, my police-issue weapon might accidentally go off. We're going for a ride."

Talltree swiveled on his stool to face Emily. He screwed up his face as recognition slowly hit him. "What the fuck, Etcitty?"

"Stand up slowly and walk out the front door. Keep your hands where I can see them and your mouth shut. I'll be right behind you."

"You can't arrest me, bitch. You don't have anything on me. Fuck off."

"Solicitation of a minor and use of an illegal substance to start with. How old is that little girl you're pimping?"

Shorty stopped working on the glass he was rubbing with a dirty rag and watched the pair with squinted eyes. He started to walk over, but after Emily pulled out her badge, he backed off evidently deciding it wasn't worth getting involved with the law. He returned to polishing glasses and attending to his heedless customers. The girl had taken notice, but Martinez leaned close and whispered something. Her eyes rounded in fear, but she remained seated and quiet.

"Let's add questioning in a murder investigation to that list," said Emily.

For the first time, Talltree's eyes showed a flicker of fear. "That's bullshit. I didn't have nothin' to do with any murder."

"Stand up. Put your hands on the back of your head."

Emily nudged Talltree toward the exit. They were about to step outside when she heard the scream. The girl had tossed her drink in Martinez's face and was struggling with him, trying to run away. He grabbed her by the wrist, but she continued to yell, and the diversion gave Talltree the opportunity he needed.

He must have been high on meth because his reaction was swift and calculated. In the split second that Emily turned her head, Talltree elbowed her in the throat, swung around, and wrenched the Glock from her hand. With his free arm, he grabbed her in a headlock and using her as a shield, the gun pointed at her head, he began backing out the door. Martinez pulled his weapon but looked uncertain how to respond.

"Yeah, I recognize you, you dumbass rookie," said Talltree. "Thought you could pull something over on the old veteran, did ya? You forget I was a cop? Put that piece down on the counter nice and easy and let the girl go, or Shorty's gonna have to mop up little Miss Etcitty's shit for brains, and I know he don't want to do that."

The bartender and patrons froze in place, afraid to make any false move that might set off Talltree. Shorty still grasped the glass and towel he had been using, another man froze with his beer bottle suspended halfway to his mouth, but no one moved. Martinez set his revolver on the countertop and let go of the girl's wrist.

"LuAnn. Grab that gun and get over here."

The young woman hesitated, shaking visibly, and Talltree fired a warning shot shattering a bottle on a shelf behind her. Splinters of glass flew in every direction. "Now, bitch!"

# 38

For Abe, sunk low in the passenger seat, waiting, the sound of gunfire was earth-shattering. He knew Emily would never fire her weapon indiscriminately. He bolted upright, his heart pounding, and started to jump out of the car. But before he could move, the barroom door opened, and Talltree backed out, his arm fastened around Emily's neck, and the barrel of her police weapon jammed into the back of her head. A thin wraith of a young woman, her eyes like a trapped animal, followed. A gun dangled limply from her hand. Martinez stood immobilized behind her. Abe wished he had never told Emily about this place and hoped to god she wouldn't get killed because of him. Talltree approached the space between the car and a battered pickup and took the gun away from Emily's head, aiming it at Martinez. Abe slid back down, afraid to even breathe, clicked the door handle open, thinking, *if this doesn't work, it's all over.* When he sensed Talltree was close enough, he kicked the door open, pushing it with all his strength. A vision of Raven's smiling face flashed through his mind. He would not make his little girl an orphan.

The impact caught Talltree off guard, knocking him off his feet with Emily tumbling on top. The gun fired wildly in the air, and Emily struggled with Talltree over possession. Abe rolled out of the car and landed on his knees near Talltree's face. He pulled back his fist and landed a punch on the ex-cop's jaw. The blow snapped the man's head sideways, the second punch knocked him unconscious. Emily stood, picked up her Glock, and pulled out her handcuffs. Only when Talltree was cuffed and lying face down did she look at Abe. His right hand bled from fresh wounds.

"Thanks," was all she said. Her voice sounded hoarse and scratchy as she struggled for breath, but her eyes spoke volumes—love, gratitude, and maybe a little newly found awe.

"Anytime," Abe said, a slight smile turning the edges of his mouth.

In the meantime, the young prostitute had dropped the gun she was holding and was running as fast as her broken heels would allow toward Talltree's truck. Martinez quickly overtook her, put her in cuffs, picked up his weapon, and brought her to where Abe and Emily stood.

"Well," Emily gasped. "We're not all going to fit in that little car of yours. Call in for assistance, Martinez."

At the station, after Talltree and the young woman had been booked on numerous charges, Emily left Martinez to write up the report and returned to the police cruiser to drive Abe home.

"You saved my neck again, Abe. I might not have been able to get out of that jam without your help."

"We're a team. I had to do whatever I could. I kept thinking about our little girl and how she needed both of us."

Emily placed a hand on Abe's knee. "Me too, but I should have called in my 1020 and requested backup. Not following procedure's going to get me killed someday. I'll probably get slapped with a disciplinary warning over this."

"Well, we got the job done. You've got plenty to hold Talltree on. What about the girl?"

"LuAnne Hoskie, seventeen years old, has been transported to juvie. A social worker is trying to locate her parents or caretaker. I can't help but feel sorry for her. At one time, I was close to going down that road myself. At least she'll get into a counseling program now."

"Did you explain why you were after Talltree to the captain?"

"I haven't said anything yet. When I get back to headquarters, I'll tell Littleben everything I know. I can't cover for Todechine any longer. It's time to get it all out in the open."

"How do you think he'll take it?"

"Shock, disbelief, sadness. But, he won't sit on it. I think he'll get a warrant for Gomez's arrest, and maybe one for the chief as well."

"Todechine had a breakdown, Em, and he lost his wife. Save some sympathy for him."

Emily swallowed hard. Her chest felt heavy like she couldn't get enough oxygen, and she took a deep breath. "He stepped over a line, Abe. That makes him complicit in the death of two men and the attempted murder of Bobby Grayfeather. We all have to face that reality."

The police unit crunched to a stop in front of Abe's house. "You should see a doctor about that hand. You could have some broken bones."

Abe wiggled the fingers on his right hand. "I connected a good one, that's for damn sure. It hurts like hell, but I don't think anything's broken. I'll soak it and wrap it up. Don't worry sweetheart."

Abe cupped Emily's chin with his left hand, turned her face toward him, then leaned over and kissed her. "You are everything to me. I don't think I could live without you. After we get back, I'm heading out to Will's place to spend some time with my other best girl and wait for you to come home."

Emily held Abe's face with both hands and returned the kiss. "See you after work, Rambo."

Captain Littleben sat behind the desk with the newly typed three-page report submitted by Martinez scattered in front of him. The captain remained stone-faced and silent while Emily presented her case against Gomez, Talltree, and Todechine, laying out a theory that tied all the pieces into a coherent picture. When she had finished, Littleben gazed impassively out the window for several moments. His eyes appeared distant as if he were lost in another time and place, his mouth remained set in a stern line.

"When Ben Todechine and I were both rookies, our first assignment was here at Huerfano. That piñon tree outside the window was only about three feet tall. Look at it now."

After a long minute of silence, he turned his attention to Emily. "You got any proof these men are involved in a conspiracy with Strathmore Minerals?"

"The security guard that the chief hired is in the FBI's custody. Basically, he confessed to my partner, Abe Freeman, that he had taken Raven and hid her in a shed as a warning to me to back off the investigation. I think EPA agent Sanford wanted out, and his body was found at the bottom of a cliff. Gomez's truck tracks were near the scene. Councilman Chee's death was no accident, and I believe Talltree and Gomez were involved in the attempted murder of a Strathmore Minerals employee, Bobby Grayfeather. Grayfeather may have overheard incriminating evidence against Whittington, the manager at Strathmore Minerals."

"That's not proof, Emily. What is the chief's connection to any of this?"

"He needed money, Captain, a lot of it to cover Daisy's medical expenses. Whittington paid him to keep his mouth shut and to obstruct the investigation of Strathmore Minerals."

"That's pure supposition."

Emily pulled the mini-recorder out of her jacket and pushed the play button.

Littleben propped his elbows on the desk and held his head with both hands. When the tape ended, he rubbed his neck. "There's not enough here to make a case stick. But, I'm going to have Gomez brought in for questioning, and I'll personally interrogate Talltree. Considering the charges against him, he might opt for a plea bargain."

"And the chief?"

"I'll give him a day to deal with Daisy's death. If he doesn't turn himself in, I'll put out an APB on Friday. Where's Whittington?"

"We know he flew in a private plane to Colorado, and as far as I know, he hasn't returned yet. I expect he'll be in Window Rock on Friday. He's probably confident the tribal council will approve his request for mining uranium on the reservation."

"That's what it's all about, isn't it? Greed."

"Isn't that usually the case, Captain?"

Littleben sighed. He glanced at his watch. "Four o'clock. It's been a long day, and you've been busy. Go home, Emily, and I'm ordering you to take tomorrow off. Report for duty Friday morning in Window Rock. I understand there's going to be some kind of demonstration."

"Yes, sir."

"Be careful, and don't let things get out of hand. Go on, now. I'll take care of Gomez and Talltree."

Emily stood and turned to leave but was stopped midway to the door by the Captain's words.

"One more thing. Do you think you're the Lone Ranger and your boyfriend is your trusty sidekick, Tonto? You didn't follow procedure and your actions endangered everyone, including yourself and that young rookie you're supposed to be training. Don't be pulling any more of your rogue bullshit. I should write you up, put you on probation. You know that don't you?"

"Yes, Captain."

"I won't, this time, but if you ever try to pull a go-it-alone Wonder Woman stunt again, I'll recommend a demotion."

As much as Abe wanted to be curled up under a warm blanket with Emily, he was resigned to sleeping on a pallet in Will's trailer along with the other men while the women and Raven shared sleeping quarters in the extended addition. He awoke early Thursday morning to the smell of coffee and a flaming fuschia sky tinged with purple streaks. New Mexico sunrises never failed to instill in him a sense of awe. After pouring himself a cup, he stepped outside to witness dawn's full glory and was surprised to see Will leaning against a fence post.

"Look how the sun glints off the snow patches on top of the mesa," Will said. "The holy ones really know how to create a beautiful picture."

It was like looking through rose-colored glasses. Even the snow was tinted pink. Abe sipped his coffee and watched the colors lighten from deep mauve to golden orange. "They do for sure, Will. Think it's going to be a nice day? Since Emily's off, I'd like to go on a long horseback ride with the girls, see some of those places Em's always talking about."

"You'll be okay today. See those cirrus clouds streaking the sky like horses tails? I figure there'll be one or two days of good weather before a new storm rolls in. Rain's a good thing. The land needs moisture."

Abe knew that for a fact. Water was always in demand in the high desert country. There was hardly enough vegetation for the sheep and goats to graze on in the years when the rain gods were generous. He looked across the rocky sage and cholla-dotted land. When he had first arrived in New Mexico, he had barely noticed the different vegetation, but now he could differentiate the golden heads of Indian ricegrass from delicate clumps of New Mexico feather grass. The changing season had turned green patches of feathery bluestem to showy red. It was a beautiful vista capped off with a now cobalt sky.

A cacophony of caws caught Abe's attention, and he looked west to the source. The sky was dotted with hundreds of black birds. Crows converged from all directions. Unlike ravens, who do not flock but remain with a mated pair, crows assembled each winter to form large congregations. No one knew quite why, but it was probably due to reasons of safety when they found a place to roost for the night. Strangely, to Abe's thinking, a flock of crows was called "a murder." The thought caused a shudder to run down his spine.

"Hi, daddy," said a small sleepy voice behind him. "What are you looking at?"

I'm looking at a murder didn't seem like the correct response to a six-year-old. "It's a flock of crows, sweetie. Come here and see." Abe brushed rumpled black curls away from eyes the color of lapis lazuli, picked up his daughter, and placed her on his shoulders.

They watched the birds in silence until they became tiny black spots in the east. "How would you like to saddle up Red after breakfast and go riding with mom and me?"

"Yes," She bounced on his shoulders. "I'll wake up mom."

"Let her sleep a while. Your mom needs to rest. We have all day." Although Emily had tried to hide the marks of Talltree's elbow and hands with a scarf, Abe had felt a rush of anger when he saw the ugly bruises surrounding her throat like a beaded necklace of coal. She had talked little last night, in an attempt, Abe felt sure, to keep from using her raspy voice and the pain caused by speaking. For that reason, he had not questioned her concerning the meeting with Captain Littleben. She had briefly told him that the Captain would take Gomez into custody along with Talltree which gave him cause for relief. And although Emily said she would be returning to work on Friday, he secretly wished she would never go back.


Later that morning, Manuel flipped blue corncakes in a cast iron comal on the wood stove while Will tended to a sizzling pan of bacon and Bertha gave advice on proper cooking techniques.

"You need to turn them over as soon as the bubbles form on top," she chided.

Manuel nodded, winked at Raven, and delivered a hot cake to her waiting plate. Abe was content to sit back and enjoy the enticing aromas of bacon and fresh coffee, relishing the peaceful moment of having his family together.

"Save some of that for the rest of us," he said to Raven as he watched her smother her corncake in a pool of chokecherry syrup. She giggled, and it felt so good to see her usual cheerful self that Abe grinned.

When Emily joined them, she was dressed in blue jeans and flannel shirt with a bright blue scarf tied around her neck. Her hair was held back in a loose ponytail giving her a girlish look.

"Good morning." She kissed the top of Raven's head and planted a peck on Abe's cheek. Her voice sounded hoarse but less scratchy than the day before. "Why did you let me sleep so late? I should have been up long ago."

"There will be another dawn tomorrow," Bertha said wrangling the spatula from Manuel. "You can get up early and greet that one. The holy ones won't hold it against you." She told Manuel and Will to sit down and let her finish fixing breakfast.

Even Manuel knew there was no arguing with Bertha.

The morning meal proceeded in a cheerful, relaxed manner with talk about trails to take on the ride and no reference made to the events of the previous day or the one forthcoming.

# 39

The following morning Emily crept out of bed before dawn's light. She dressed quickly and silently taking extra care not to wake her sleeping daughter. Bertha rolled onto her side and started to speak, but Emily shushed her with a finger to her lips. She strapped on her duty belt and hat and was out the door by five a.m. Martinez would be waiting for her at the station. Afterward, they had a two-hour drive to Window Rock.

Abe had returned to his house the night before, and she knew, as much as she had tried to dissuade him, he would be somewhere in the crowd of protesters in Window Rock. *Stubborn man*, Emily thought as she maneuvered the police SUV over the dirt road leading out of Huerfano Canyon. Still, she had to smile as she recalled the events of the day before— a day infused with the sun's warmth, breathtaking vistas, and love. They had let the horses take the lead down a twisting path to a small stream at the base of the canyon. Emily rode in front astride Will's pinto, Chico, followed by Raven with Abe bringing up the rear. Flat sandstone boulders with bowl-like indentations where water collected lined the stream. Emily had folded a blanket to make a soft pallet and placed it on one of

336

the smooth surfaces. Within minutes, Raven had lain down, curled her small body into a question mark, and fallen asleep.

After the horses had quenched their thirst, they grazed on the patches of grass that lined the stream. Emily spread another blanket on a nearby flat boulder. She cuddled in Abe's arms, relating the details of her conversation with Captain Littleben.

Abe had seemed relieved. He brushed back the strand of hair that had escaped her ponytail. "I'm glad he's there, taking over. Now maybe we can have some peace of mind."

They stretched out on their backs, Emily's head resting in the crook of Abe's shoulder, and watched the clouds, like fat white sheep, scamper across a field of blue.

"We still don't have Whittington," Emily had said.

Abe kissed her, a long sweet kiss. "You will."

If they weren't afraid of waking Raven, it would have been the perfect place to make love. They stayed entwined together until the puffy whites gathered into dove gray columns.

It was still dark when she turned into the station early the next morning. The Blazer's headlights picked up Martinez leaning against his car.

He ambled over to the SUV carrying a pair of travel mugs. "Morning, Sarge. Am I in the driver's seat?"

"If you can drive and talk at the same time," Emily said. I want you to fill me in on what I missed yesterday." She accepted the insulated mug he handed her, grateful for the kid's foresight.

"I can do that." Martinez slipped his lanky frame behind the steering wheel and found the lever to slide the seat back. When they were both buckled in, he pulled onto the highway.

"The captain brought me into his office. He had my report in front of him, and he took his time grilling me with questions."

"How'd you do?"

"I told the truth like you advised me. When we were finished, Captain Littleben sent me out with Begaye. Gillmore took another cruiser, and we went after Gomez with a search warrant."

The coffee must have come from Martinez's house because it didn't taste like the usual sludge found in the break room. Emily closed her eyes and savored a sip. "What happened when you got to Gomez's place?

Martinez's face lit up with what looked to Emily like self-satisfied smugness. "His truck was there, so we knew he was home. Begaye and Gillmore went to the front door to deliver the warrant, and I covered the back."

"What about the dog?"

"I remembered what Abe did with the dog treats, so I brought along a few pepperoni sticks. Brutus didn't even bark when I waved one in front of him."

"Brutus?"

"Yeah. I decided to call him that after the big brute jumped into the back seat. He's at the station now. Might be our new mascot."

"Hmm. What about Gomez?"

There was that grin again. "Old Gordie Gomez didn't know I was waiting for him and took off running out the back door. I ran after him and brought him down with a flying tackle."

Emily laughed. "I'd like to have seen that. The fat man couldn't have run very fast."

"Well, I was a high school sprinter," Martinez said. "Don't take that away from me."

The sun was trying to break through a layer of clouds when they turned onto Indian Service Route 5 outside of Farmington. Martinez glanced at Emily. "What's our mission today, Sergeant Etcitty?"

"Keep the peace." She drained her cup. "Thanks for the coffee, Martinez, and for bringing Gomez in."

"The captain's gonna tighten the screws on both him and Talltree today. I figure he's going to play one against the other."

"Smart man, the captain. Betcha one of those dickheads rats on the other to try to save his neck. Anything new on Whittington?"

"He still hadn't arrived at the airport when I checked last night."

Several miles outside of Window Rock, they encountered a caravan of pickup trucks and crowds of people, some on horseback, others on foot, all headed toward the seat of the Navajo Nation. Men, women, and children marched down the middle of the road carrying signs and chanting anti-uranium mining messages

"What do I do now?" Martinez said.

"Beep the siren and turn on the flashers. We've got to get around these people. Officers from all over the rez are scheduled to be on crowd control duty today."

Martinez frowned. "I don't think I like this assignment—going against my own kind."

"Like I said, our job is to keep the peace and prevent anyone from getting hurt. We're not going against our people."

When they heard the siren, the crowd parted like a curtain being drawn. Martinez slowly made his way through the opening in the road then passed the line of trucks. But as they entered the town and neared the Council Chambers, the crowds grew even more substantial. Nearly every person held up a sign or banner. *Radioactive Pollution Kills; Stop Uranium Assault on Children; No Uranium Mining!* A large group has assembled near the front of the Chambers. All of them wore red headbands and chanted in unison, "Now's the time. Clean up the Mines, Respect the ban on Navajo land." Emily thought she saw Keetso standing in front leading the protesters. A man with a black wool cap pulled down close to his eyes stood behind the demonstration organizer. *What the hell? Is that Abe?*

Yellow tape stretched along the sidewalk made a flimsy barricade between the protestors and the seat of tribal government. Navajo officers stood on one side of the tape, but over twenty heavily armed Anglo men carrying riot shields and wearing flak jackets and riot helmets loomed in front of the Council Chambers. When a group of protestors surged onto the street, the guards moved forward with batons and pushed them back behind the yellow tape to a park on the opposite side of the roadway.

"Who do you think hired those private security guards?" Martinez asked.

"One guess," said Emily.

An officer waved the SUV through a roadblock, and Martinez found a parking space with other Navajo Nation vehicles behind the Chamber building. Their own riot gear lacked chest guards and shields, but they put on the helmets they had been ordered to wear.

"I just have one question," said Martinez. "Who are we supposed to be protecting?"

The answer to Martinez's question roiled up from her gut leaving a bitter taste of bile in her mouth. Emily spit the word out. "Whittington." After blowing out an exasperated woosh of air, she added, "Let's take up position in that park. Remember, we're here to do no harm. Try to keep everyone else from doing something crazy."

A podium and speaker system had been set up on a bandstand in the park. Men and women lined up and waited patiently for their turn to speak against the uranium mine.

An elderly woman dressed in a long black skirt, purple velveteen blouse, and turquoise jewelry held the microphone and spoke in Navajo to the crowd. "I come from the Red Rock Chapter," she said in a quavery voice, "where a lot of the women became widows because of uranium mining. No amount of money can bring back the husbands, fathers, and sons we have lost."

A man told the people that several of his brothers had died from the effects of uranium and that their animals had been affected. "I watched two of my brothers die," he said. "Sores were all over their bodies."

A married couple from Two Gray Hills talked about how uranium waste was dumped into the washes, and how low-grade uranium was piled near their cabin. "The children played on the mounds," she said. "They swam in the pools."

Emily listened to the stories while she let her eyes roam over the crowd. Many of the men were wearing red headbands, and the women had covered their hair with red scarves. Keetso had indeed done an excellent job of organizing. *Where's Keetso now*, she wondered, and *what happened to Abe?*

Her attention became diverted by a "whup whup whup" sound overhead. As the blade slapping of a helicopter's rotors drew nearer, the demonstrators also turned their eyes skyward. The realization of who would be arriving in a helicopter caused the crowd to not only raise their eyes, but to lift and shake their fists as well, and a chorus of chants erupted.

"*Doodá leetso!* No to uranium mining! *Doodá leetso!* No to uranium mining!"

The helicopter made two circles then dropped to a landing pad in the back of the chamber's building. The *Dinetah* voices grew louder, and the people began to push their way forward toward the adobe walls of the Navajo Council Chambers. Their advances were met with pepper spray from the white civilian guards. Emily and other Navajo officers were attempting to calm the protesters, urging them to stay back behind the police lines when someone launched a tear gas canister at the crowd.

Emily felt a burning sensation on her skin and in her eyes. Her throat tightened, and she gasped for breath. Martinez fell to his knees, coughing and vomiting. Temporarily blinded, she could not immediately see the speaker who had advanced to the platform.

"My people. Remain calm. Do not react with violence against the aggression of those who wish to provoke you. We shall win this battle with dignity and prayers. The legacy of uranium mining on the Navajo Reservation is known by all of you. Your loved ones have suffered, your crops and animals have been poisoned. There are five hundred and twenty abandoned uranium mines on the rez, and only five of those have been decontaminated. We are here to insist that no other mines are opened, and that cleanup at all sites will be implemented."

Emily covered her mouth with a handkerchief and wiped her tearing eyes. As her vision cleared, she saw others gasping from the effects of tear gas, angry men shook their fists at the security guards, as women tried to comfort crying children. The Navajo policemen interspersed with the crowd passing out water bottles to those affected by pepper spray and tear gas. Blinking through burning eyes, Emily caught a blurry glimpse of the speaker, Malcolm Keetso. A man in a black wool cap stood on one side, and her brother, Will, flanked the other.

Emily shook her head in disbelief, but she didn't have time to deal with Abe.

"Martinez, are you all right?"

"Yeah," he gasped, "or I will be." He rubbed his red-rimmed eyes and stood.

"I've got to notify the officer in charge of Window Rock police to get his men between those shithole guards and the demonstrators before a full-scale riot breaks out."

Emily retrieved the portable radio from her utility belt, but the Navajo officers had already begun to assemble in the street and form a defensive line between the security guards and the protesters. Within minutes, a human barrier of over fifty men and women stood shoulder to shoulder facing the security guards.

Behind her, a familiar baritone voice boomed over the microphone. She recognized the Protection Song Will sang in Navajo. A drummer joined in, and others picked up the chant.

*Now, Slayer of the Alien Gods, among men am I.*
*Now among the alien gods with weapons of magic am I.*
*Rubbed with the summits of the mountains,*
*Now among the alien gods with weapons of magic am I.*
*Now upon the beautiful trail of old age,*
*Now among the alien gods with weapons of magic am I.*
*nagée nagée alíli kat bïtása*

The combined voices of the *Diné* appealing to the gods for protection against the evils of uranium permeated every corner of the surrounding area, reverberating against the red rock pillars of the Chamber building. The people continued to sing and chant until the massive double oak doors of the Chamber flew open, and Ernest Whittington, flanked on one side by Tribal Chairman, David Tso, and on the other by Councilman, Charley Redhorse, stepped onto the terrace. A hush fell over the crowd as they awaited the final results of the vote. Charley Redhorse raised Whittington's arm in a sign of victory. But, before he could make an announcement, a single gunshot shattered the silence.

Grabbing her portable radio, Emily sent a distress call, "10-32! Need immediate assistance. Shot fired. Victim down. Send an ambulance to Navajo Council Chambers," she shouted, then turned to face the crowd. When Whittington crumpled to the pavement, a simultaneous gasp erupted from the protestors, and for a fleeting two seconds, they seemed too shocked to move. Then, pandemonium broke out as people scrambled for cover. Some dropped to the ground while others grabbed their children and scattered in all directions.

Several of the security guards bent over the body of Ernest Whittington. Others pulled out their assault rifles and ran toward the park. Navajo officers joined them.

Emily jerked her head in the direction of where the sound of the shot had come from and saw a man with a black wool cap racing in the same direction. *No, Abe. Please!* She pulled out her service revolver and took off at a dead run, pushing her way through the panicked crowd, trying to follow Abe and stop him. When she heard the second shot, then a third, the blood seemed to freeze in her thudding heart.

# 40

"Clear the way!" Emily shouted, but couldn't avoid running into those who were trying to flee. She hadn't realized Martinez was at her side until she stumbled and he reached a hand down to help her up. The shots had come from an area near the grandstand. Emily could hear Will's voice over the speaker, but his words landed on her ears in a nonsensical jumble. Something about remaining calm. How could she be calm?

She spotted an open space with a native man and a woman with bloody hands kneeling beside a body. Chipeta Longtooth? Reality didn't register. Were there two bodies on the ground?

"Move aside, let me in," Emily said, pushing Chipeta away. Oblivious to anyone else, she dropped to her knees, saw Abe lying in a pool of blood, a blood-soaked red handkerchief tied around his head. She dropped her head to his chest and cried, "Oh, Abe. No, no, no."

"He's alive," said Chipeta. "I was able to stop the bleeding. You've got an ambulance on the way, right?"

In response to Emily's silence, Chipeta added, "Couldn't do anything for the other one."

She didn't recognize him at first. Not until she saw the turquoise ring he always wore. Chief Todechine still grasped the gun that had delivered the killing bullet to his own head. Sirens screamed in the background.

Emily ran alongside the EMT's as they carried Abe into a waiting ambulance. She scrambled aboard and grasped his hand while the blood-soaked kerchief was removed, the bullet wound cleaned, and a pressure bandage applied. The EMT's words came to her through a fog.

"You'll have to move back, ma'am. We need to get in there." He gave her a quick once-over. "You say this is your husband?"

"Yes," she said without hesitation. "Is Abe going to be all right?"

"He got lucky. A little to the left or right and the bullet would have entered his brain."

The other technician hooked Abe to a portable oxygen tank and blood pressure monitor. "What's the victim's name?"

"His name is Abe Freeman. Tell me, is he going to make it?" She tightened her grip on Abe's hand. It felt cold. She had tried to talk to him, but Abe had remained unresponsive.

"Lost a lot of blood. Do you know his blood type, Mrs. Freeman? Uh, Mrs. Freeman?"

It took her a while to register someone was talking to her, asking a question about blood types. She shook her head, felt ashamed. Why hadn't they ever spoken about this possibility?

"Hurry, please. Can't you go faster?"

"Don't worry," said one of the EMT's. "We're only twelve minutes away from

*Tsehootsooi* Medical Center. We'll be there in a couple minutes." He glanced at her again. The EMTs were Navajo. "You look familiar, Officer. Aren't you Emily Etcitty? I think we had some classes together at Community College."

Emily wasn't in the mood to indulge in small talk. Everybody on the reservation had a connection one way or another, but she couldn't think of anything except Abe. Luckily, she didn't have to respond because the ambulance had reached the hospital and was backing up to the emergency doors.

The swinging doors to surgery closed behind the gurney carrying Abe, shutting Emily out. The doctor had told her she would have to wait in the stuffy room with straight-backed chairs, stale coffee, and stressed-out strangers. First, she found the receptionist and dealt with the paperwork, explaining that she knew this was a Navajo facility, that Abe was not Native American, but he was her husband. It was the second time she had used that term. Emily returned to the waiting room and paced, wishing she had taken up smoking so she would have something to do with her hands besides chewing her nails. A call came in on her portable, and she picked it up.

"Martinez here, Sergeant Etcitty. How's Abe?"

Emily had forgotten about Martinez. She had left a rookie in charge to deal with the other body, the chief, without any instructions. Taking a deep breath so her voice wouldn't break,

"He has a bullet lodged in his skull. He's in surgery now, still hasn't regained consciousness."

"He'll be all right. They've got great doctors there."

He was trying to comfort her, she knew. "Tell me what's happened, Martinez."

"Witnesses said Abe was standing on the podium near Will and spotted the chief. He saw him point his service revolver toward the front of the chambers and ran over to try and stop him. He didn't make it before Todechine fired the shot that killed Whittington, but when the chief raised the Glock to his mouth, Abe tried to wrestle it away. They scuffled, and the gun fired, hitting Abe. May have been accidental. Then, Todechine finished the job on himself."

"I, I should be there," Emily stammered.

"Don't worry. You need to be where you are, with Abe. We've got plenty of law enforcement here. FBI agents are thicker than deer flies in summer."

"What about the vote?"

"The councilmen returned to the chambers for a revote. Charley Redhorse was banned from voting. In fact, the Feds took him into custody for suspicion of taking bribes. Guess they've been doing their homework. I updated the captain on the way it came down. Everything's under control."

Her temples pulsated like a metronome set a high speed, but she acknowledged the kid had passed the test. "What about the demonstrators? Was anyone else hurt?"

"No. The crowd dispersed peacefully and headed for home. Keetso was brought in as a witness, but the woman who came to Abe's aid disappeared."

Being a wanted felon, Chipeta Longtooth would not want to be questioned by the police. For a brief instant, she and Chipeta's eyes had locked in recognition. Emily felt regret she didn't have a chance to talk to her, and to thank her for possibly saving Abe's life. "Thanks, Martinez."

"It's just police work, Sarge. You've got the tough job, but your brother should be here any time to help you out."

Just then, Will lunged through the waiting room doors and wrapped his sister in a big brother bear hug.

"I should have been the one to stop Todechine, not Abe," she said through tears.

"No, *shilah*, don't do that self-blaming thing. Remember, Abe was up on the podium where he could see over everyone's head, and he is always looking around, like an eagle, always looking out for you."

"I can't lose him, Will. I just can't."

Will led her to a chair and sat next to her. "Abe's hard-headed like you, little sister. He'll come through. We'll wait and pray for the holy ones to give him strength." After a moment, he added, "I should call mom and let her know what happened."

"No, I don't want her to get upset in front of Raven."

"She's going to hear about it on the radio or TV. Better she hears from me."

Emily knew he was right and nodded slowly in acquiescence. "You talk to her Will, I can't. But, tell her to promise not to tell Raven. She's gone through so much, and if she knows her dad is hurt, it will crush her."

Will placed the call to his mother. After telling her not to come to the hospital, to stay there with Raven, that he would call as soon as they learned anything, they waited, pacing, sitting, praying, and staring at the closed double doors. Four hours later, the doctor, a young Iranian, still wearing blood-stained scrubs, appeared in the open doorway.

"Officer, will you step in here, please. Are you related to the patient?"

"Yes. Abe Freeman is my husband. Can my brother come with me?"

"Of course."

Will followed her and the doctor into a small consultation room furnished with two well-worn stuffed chairs and a small cigarette-burned coffee table with an overflowing ashtray. Emily remained standing beside Will, waiting for the doctor's words.

"My name is Doctor Ahmad, and I am a surgeon. Your husband suffered a penetrating wound to the upper cranium. That means the bullet was lodged in the skull and did not exit. The patient was comatose when we initially examined him, but shortly afterward showed signs of regaining consciousness. A CT scan was performed and revealed no damage to the brain."

Will closed his eyes and rocking on his heels, softly sung a prayer of thanks.

Emily made a teepee with her hands, covering her face and her tears of gratitude, oblivious of her undone hair and blood-stained uniform where she had cradled Abe's head. "Is he going to be okay, then? When can I see him?"

"I'm sorry, not at this time. The patient is under sedation and will not revive for several hours. He will remain in ICU under close observation for twenty-four hours or until my team decides it is safe to have visitors. We had to perform a craniotomy to prevent chances of a hematoma putting pressure on the brain."

"A what?" asked Emily.

"I had to temporarily cut away a portion of the skull, and after successfully extracting the bullet, I replaced the bone tissue. It will eventually grow back together such as any broken bone, but will leave a scar in the upper-center of your husband's forehead."

"Can't I just look in on him, see for myself how he's doing?"

The doctor looked at her with dark sympathetic eyes. "Sorry, come back tomorrow, Mrs. Freeman. I assure you he is stable, and we will call you if there is any change." He stood, erect and somber-faced.

"Come on, sis, there's nothing we can do here. Abe's in good hands. I'll take you home."

"No, take me to headquarters, Will. I'll go crazy waiting around the house, and I need to see the captain."

Emily rapped on the door and was beckoned inside. Captain Littleben looked like he'd aged ten years in the last two days—dark circles under his eyes deepened with the lines in his drawn face. Todechine's death must have hit him hard. She figured she didn't look much better, and unconsciously, smoothing her uniform and touching her hair unconsciously.

Littleben was not alone. Two FBI agents sat facing him. They were the same team that had interviewed Abe a couple days ago. When Emily entered, they both stood and met her.

"Sorry about your boyfriend," said Jack Monroe.

"He's going to pull through," Emily stared past the agents and looked directly at the captain. "It'll take some time," she said in a breathless tone.

"Tried to be a hero, didn't he?" the one called Monroe said.

Emily ignored the comment. She dropped into the chair Harrison offered.

Littleben rubbed the back of his neck, something Emily noticed he did when he was under pressure.

"It's been a tough day for all of us. I'm relieved to hear your boyfriend is going to be all right."

"Thank you, sir. I want to present a full account of the findings of my investigation into Ernest Whittington and Strathmore Minerals and what led up to today's events. I'd like to add, I couldn't have carried this investigation out without Officer Raymond Martinez's assistance."

"Start from the beginning, Emily. We're listening."

*Let the Feds take it from here. I'm tired.* Emily took a deep breath. "It all began on Saturday, October tenth when Steve

Sanford was discovered near a poisoned waterhole with a bullet in his shoulder."

# Epilogue

Abe ran his fingers over the keys, a warm-up drill before launching into Chopin's *Nocturne in E-flat Major*. It had been nearly six months since the shooting, and except for a dime-sized scar in his forehead, there was no indication of his previous wound.

He had set the scene for the evening dinner, candles and a chilled bottle of champagne, and Raven had gathered a handful of early spring flowers from the lowlands near the river. A Mason jar containing Blue Flags, pink wild plum blossoms, and desert dandelions held center-place on the table.

Raven would soon be finishing first grade. Having excelled in all her subjects, especially reading, her teacher had suggested that she should skip second grade and be promoted to third. He had beamed with pride for his only child, but, Abe had felt especially pleased when he found his daughter picking out the notes to *Clair de Lune* on the piano.

And, Emily? Well, he'd soon find out when newly appointed Chief Etcitty came home from work, and he asked her to marry him.

Abe played flawlessly, letting the music build until his fingers danced playfully over his favorite part—the dramatic trill-filled finale.

# Acknowledgments

First and foremost, I would like to give thanks to my beautiful family for their continued support and encouragement. Thank you, Karen Hawes, for all your efforts in promoting my work and pushing me to excel. As with my previous novels, I am deeply indebted to the terrific group of fellow writers I meet with on a regular basis. Many thanks, Pat Walsh, Steve Anderson, John Johnson, Richard Fox, and Annie Lord for all your critiques and editing, but especially for your continued friendship. Without your diligence, my manuscript would be missing those ubiquitous quotation marks and contain a slew of redundant errors.

I would also like to give recognition and appreciation to Rita Gilmore and Aretta Begay for sharing their knowledge of Navajo ceremonies and traditions. Their input has been invaluable in providing insight into the Navajo culture.

Much thanks to Carita Tanner for her edits and beautiful cover design. You have been a life-saver, Carita.

Finally, *Blood and Thunder,* by Hampton Sides proved to be an enlightening read in providing historical background for the westward expansion and the ultimate conquest of the Navajo. And, I learned a great deal about the lasting effects of uranium mining on the Navajo Reservation from *Memories Come to Us in the Rain and Wind, Oral Histories and Photographs of Navajo Uranium Miners and Their Families,* compiled by The Navajo Uranium Miner Oral History and Photography Project, Director Doug Brugge.

# About the Author

Sandra Bolton's novels are based on her real-life experiences with diverse settings and cultures, as well as a desire to right racial inequality. Her first novel, *A Cipher in the Sand*, was inspired by her work in the Peace Corps in Honduras: while *Key Witness*, *Abducted Innocence*, and *Raven's Cry*, were inspired by her years spent teaching on the Navajo Reservation.

With twenty-five years of teaching experience and a master's degree in guidance counseling, Sandra is no stranger to compelling stories, but her love of writing truly began with a passion for reading. Then, her skills were honed under the tutelage of southwestern mystery writer, Steven F. Havill.

Originally from California, Sandra has traveled the globe with her military husband and three children. She now resides in Raton, New Mexico where she divides her time between writing, hiking, photography, and gourmet cooking. Sandra is currently working on a memoir with the help of her coauthor, her dog, Sam.

For more on the author and her work, visit her website, www.sandrabolton.com, or find her at her Sandra Bolton author page at amazon.com and at her Sandra Bolton Author page on Facebook.

www.ingramcontent.com/pod-product-compliance
Lightning Source LLC
Chambersburg PA
CBHW030549180626
46816CB00005B/1467